Moon Craving

continued . . .

Moon Awakening

Berkley Sensation titles by Lucy Monroe

TOUCH ME
TEMPT ME
TAKE ME
MOON AWAKENING
MOON CRAVING
MOON BURNING

Moon Burning

A CHILDREN OF THE MOON NOVEL

Lucy Monroe

BERKLEY SENSATION, NEW YORK

THE BERKLEY PUBLISHING GROUP
Published by the Penguin Group
Penguin Group (USA) Inc.
375 Hudson Street, New York, New York 10014, USA
Penguin Group (Canada), 90 Eglinton Avenue East, Suite 700, Toronto, Ontario M4P 2Y3, Canada
(a division of Pearson Penguin Canada Inc.)
Penguin Books Ltd., 80 Strand, London WC2R 0RL, England
Penguin Group Ireland, 25 St. Stephen's Green, Dublin 2, Ireland (a division of Penguin Books Ltd.)
Penguin Group (Australia), 250 Camberwell Road, Camberwell, Victoria 3124, Australia
(a division of Pearson Australia Group Pty. Ltd.)
Penguin Books India Pvt. Ltd., 11 Community Centre, Panchsheel Park, New Delhi—110 017, India
Penguin Group (NZ), 67 Apollo Drive, Rosedale, North Shore 0632, New Zealand
(a division of Pearson New Zealand Ltd.)
Penguin Books (South Africa) (Pty.) Ltd., 24 Sturdee Avenue, Rosebank, Johannesburg 2196,
South Africa

Penguin Books Ltd., Registered Offices: 80 Strand, London WC2R 0RL, England

This is a work of fiction. Names, characters, places, and incidents either are the product of the author's imagination or are used fictitiously, and any resemblance to actual persons, living or dead, business establishments, events, or locales is entirely coincidental. The publisher does not have any control over and does not assume any responsibility for author or third-party websites or their content.

MOON BURNING

A Berkley Sensation Book / published by arrangement with the author

PRINTING HISTORY
Berkley Sensation mass-market edition / February 2011

Copyright © 2011 by Lucy Monroe.
Cover art by Tony Mauro.
Cover design by George Long.
Cover hand lettering by Ron Zinn.
Interior text design by Laura K. Corless.

ISBN: 978-0-425-23980-3

BERKLEY® SENSATION
Berkley Sensation Books are published by The Berkley Publishing Group,
a division of Penguin Group (USA) Inc.,
375 Hudson Street, New York, New York 10014.
BERKLEY® SENSATION and the "B" design are trademarks of Penguin Group (USA) Inc.

PRINTED IN THE UNITED STATES OF AMERICA

10 9 8 7 6 5 4 3 2 1

For my son Zach. Your brilliance delights me, your insistence on marching to your own techno tune challenges me, your enjoyment of the paranormal connects to me and your heart touches me! You are a wonderful son and a young man any mom would be proud to call hers. May your dreams be realized, may your heart be blessed with joy and may your life be one of purpose and celebration. You have certainly brought both to mine!

Thank you! Much love, Mom

Prologue

THE BEGINNING

Millennia ago God created a race of people so fierce even their women were feared in battle. These people were warlike in every way, refusing to submit to the rule of any but their own . . . no matter how large the forces sent to subdue them. Their enemies said they fought like animals. Their vanquished foes said nothing, for they were dead.

They were considered a primitive and barbaric people because they marred their skin with tattoos of blue ink. The designs were usually simple. A single beast was depicted in unadorned outline, though some clan members had more markings that rivaled the Celts for artistic intricacy. These were the leaders of the clan and their enemies were never able to discover the meanings of any of the blue tinted tattoos.

Some surmised they were symbols of their warlike nature and in that they would be partially right. For the beasts represented a part of themselves these fierce and independent people kept secret at the pain of death. It was a secret they had kept for the centuries of their existence while most migrated across the European landscape to settle in the inhospitable north of Scotland.

Their Roman enemies called them Picts, a name accepted by the other peoples of their land and lands south . . . they called themselves the Chrechte.

Their animallike affinity for fighting and conquest came from a part of their nature their fully human counterparts did not enjoy. For these fierce people were shape-changers and the bluish tattoos on their skin were markings given as a right of passage. When their first change took place, they were marked with the kind of animal they could change into. Some had control of that change. Some did not. And while the majority were wolves, there were large hunting cats and birds of prey as well.

The one thing they all shared in common was that they did not reproduce as quickly or prolifically as their fully human brothers and sisters. Although they were a fearsome race and their cunning was enhanced by an understanding of nature most humans do not possess, they were not foolhardy and were not ruled by their animal natures.

One warrior could kill a hundred of his foe, but should she or he die before having offspring, the death would lead to an inevitable shrinking of the clan. Some Pictish clans and those recognized by other names in other parts of the world had already died out rather than submit to the inferior but multitudinous humans around them.

Most of the shape-changers of the Scots Highlands were too smart to face the end of their race rather than blend. They saw the way of the future. In the ninth century AD, Keneth MacAlpin ascended to the Scottish throne. Of Chrechte descent through his mother, nevertheless, his human nature had dominated. He was not capable of "the change," but that did not stop him from laying claim to the Pictish throne (as it was called then) as well. In order to guarantee his kingship, he betrayed his Chrechte brethren at a dinner, killing all of the remaining royals of their people—and forever entrenched a distrust of humans by their Chrechte counterparts.

Despite this distrust but bitterly aware of the cost of MacAlpin's betrayal, the Chrechte realized that they could die out fighting an ever-increasing and encroaching race of humanity, or they could join the Celtic clans.

They joined.

As far as the rest of the world knew, though much existed to attest to their former existence, what had been considered the Pictish people were no more.

Because it was not in their nature to be ruled by any but their own, within two generations, the Celtic clans that had assimilated the Chrechte were ruled by shape-changing clan chiefs, though the fully human among them did not know it. A sparse few were trusted with the secrets of their kinsmen. Those that did know were aware that to betray the code of silence meant certain and immediate death.

That code of silence was rarely broken.

Stories of other shifter races were told around the campfire, or to the little ones before bed, but as most of the wolves had seen no shifters but themselves in generations, they began to believe the other races only a myth. A few knew the truth, but it was a truth they were determined to eradicate from shifter memory.

But myths did not take to the sky on black wings glinting an iridescent blue under the sun. Myths did not live as ghosts in the forest but breathed air just as any other man or animal. The Éan were no myth; they were ravens with abilities beyond that of merely changing their shape.

And they trusted the Faol of the Chrechte (the wolves) less than the wolves ever trusted humans.

Chapter 1

Come, the croaking raven doth bellow for revenge.
—WILLIAM SHAKESPEARE

Donegal Lands, Scottish Highlands
Twelfth Century AD

The raven flew high above the earth, her keen vision spying five Donegal hunters in the forest below.

The red and black of their plaids peeked through the trees, leaving no doubt to the true number, but she could only *hear* three of them. Two were silent as they stalked their prey. Even her raven hearing, honed sharper than her talons, could not detect the sound of their movements.

They had masked their scents as well, showing they had better control of their Chrechte nature than the others. These two Faol of the Chrechte were dangerous.

No wolf could be trusted, but one who mastered his beast was one who must be watched most carefully. He would not be easily taken in by the tricks of the Éan. It was good her raven family had set her to this task. Another, less seasoned fighter could fail too easily with wolves such as these.

Sabrine had been protecting her people since her fifteenth summer, a long seven years past.

She circled lower, preparing for her landing. This had to look natural, but she did not relish taking human form merely to fall through a few tree branches. She was still a good distance from the men, though closer to the earth, when an agonizing pain pierced her left wing.

Her first instinct was to pull her wing to her body, but she forced herself to keep it extended so she could coast lower rather than spinning out of control. She would not die before saving her people from the wolves' treachery.

As she neared the earth, she let her raven fall away, taking on her fully human form, just as she had planned to before the foul arrow had pierced her wing. Tree branches scratched at her body as she tumbled toward the ground.

She ignored the minor pain for the larger purpose. She would use the wolves' thirst for blood against them. Their own actions would make way for her to find welcome in their clan.

As a helpless human female.

Dark amusement rolled through her with the pain of her landing. She grabbed the arrow, broke off the tip, gripped the other side, and yanked it from her arm.

As her world turned black around the edges, she threw the offending weapon as far from her as possible.

Barr's big body spun silently at the sound of an arrow leaving its bow. Rage rode him harder than an Englishman's seat on his horse. No visible sign of the wild boar, there was no damn excuse for using the weapon.

Muin's attention was focused on the sky, not the forest where it was supposed to be, the youngest in their party standing with his bow still lifted as if prepared to shoot again.

It would be easier to train the English, Barr thought

with a snarl he made no attempt to suppress. He'd known Chrechte cubs with better hunting instincts.

"What the hell was that, boy?" Barr demanded in quiet tones meant to get his anger across but not to carry.

"I saw a raven," Muin whispered fervently. "My gran-da says they're bad luck and to kill them on sight."

"Oh? And did your gran-da also teach you how to hunt?" Barr demanded with barely restrained wrath. "Did *he* teach you to warn our prey of our approach?"

"The boar would not have heard the arrow." Muin's attempt at defense carried no weight with Barr.

He moved so he towered over the beardless boy. "What happens when you kill a bird in the sky?"

Muin swallowed, his face twitching despite the fact he so obviously tried to hide his nerves. "It falls to the earth."

"That is right. Do you suppose the bird will show us the courtesy of landing without sound?"

"Nay, laird."

"Nay."

Not for the first time since coming to the Donegal clan as acting laird and Chrechte pack leader, Barr wondered if he had the patience for the task. He'd liked his position as second-in-command for the Sinclair just fine, but the king had requested this favor. Barr wasn't swayed. However, his former laird, Talorc, had seconded the request, adding to it his own that Barr train the Chrechte among the Donegal clan. Naturally, Barr had agreed.

He knew Talorc had developed a soft spot for Circin, the young warrior who had challenged him and ended up being trained in the way of their people for his trouble. Since Circin was to lead the Donegal clan one day, both by the king's edict and the reality that he would one day be the strongest Chrechte amidst the Donegals, it was imperative he learn to control and utilize his wolf's nature.

The task was not an easy one though, not with poorly

taught Chrechte who seemed oblivious to their instincts and blind to their surroundings . . . on a good day.

Muin wasn't usually one of the idiotic ones though. That was the only thing saving him from a hard knock to the ground.

The young clansman's face took on a hue as ruddy as his plaid. "I, uh . . ."

"Acted without thought. I would agree."

"I'm sorry, laird." Muin ducked his head, the shame he felt a palpable taste in the air around them.

"Do it again and I'll toss you like a caber."

"Yes, laird."

"And, Muin?"

The youth raised his face to meet Barr's gaze. Barr had to respect the courage it took to do that. He didn't usually frighten grown men like his twin brother, Niall, did, mostly because he knew how to smile and his brother didn't. Not that Barr had had reason to do so lately. However, his size alone intimidated many among the Donegal clan, Chrechte and human alike.

"Yes, laird?" Muin asked.

"We are Chrechte. We respect all life. We hunt for food, not for sport."

"But the birds, they're bad luck."

"They're birds. Only old men who remember their yesterdays better than today and *cubs* believe a bird brings or takes luck. You are a warrior. Act like it."

Muin straightened, pulling his shoulders back. "Aye, laird."

Barr shook his head and turned to continue their pursuit of the wild boar, for all the good it would do them. If their hunting party returned with a kill, he'd revise his opinion of these young Donegal Chrechte.

Earc would still have the boar's scent at least. The other Sinclair warrior who had come with Barr to train the Donegal soldiers and the Chrechte among them never gave up on a hunt.

And he had not on this one, but he looked puzzled by the path the boar took through the forest. "It's running from us," Earc said in a voice no human would have been able to hear.

"You think it smells our younger Chrechte?" They had not yet mastered the ability to mask their scents for long periods of time.

"I dinna *ken*. Something has it spooked. 'Tis running without thought for direction, I'm thinking."

"Circin and I will get ahead of it and chase it back to the rest of you."

Earc nodded.

Shifting into his wolf form, Barr followed the boar's scent, determined to bring down their prey. Circin, the other Chrechte who had control of his change, followed suit. The others, who did not, followed at a faster run than most humans could manage.

The scent of something besides boar teased at Barr's wolf's senses, demanding his attention with subtle power. Something tantalizing and different. Something his wolf could not ignore. Even more imperative than prey, it insistently drew his wolf's attention from the hunt.

The boar all but forgotten, the wolf strained to follow the new scent, causing his canine body to twist with preternatural grace. Never breaking the pace of his running, and not waiting for approval from his conscious mind for the change in course, the wolf followed where the inner beast demandingly led.

Barr's human mind tried to decipher what his senses were telling him, but he had never encountered a scent quite like this one. Nor had he ever reacted to smell alone with this impossible-to-deny need.

A need so basic, it found acceptance in his beast, while his human mind remained mystified.

Was the smell that of a human? He raised his snout to sniff the air more fully. Pine. Loamy earth. Sunshine. A rabbit. A squirrel. Dead leaves and dried pine needles. And the scent. Undeniably human, undeniably *more*.

And female. Not in heat, but with the subtle fragrance of her sex. Though no wolf's musk mixed with the other smells.

If not a wolf, she must be human. His sense of other had to come from her unique scent.

For, if not wolf, what else was there?

Mothers told their cubs tales of other shifter tribes, but those were just fairy stories told to entertain little ones. Wolves were the only Chrechte he or anyone in the Sinclair clan had ever known. If other shifter races existed, the wolves would be aware of them. They were too territorial not to be.

He broke through the trees and came skidding to a halt, his claws scrabbling at the ground for purchase. *He had been running too fast*. Not since he was a cub had he approached an unknown situation with such lack of restraint. More than troubling, if his brother or his former laird could see him now, they would fall on their asses laughing.

Even that assurance of humiliation barely found purchase in his mind; his attention was too focused on the source of the scent.

She lay on the ground, her raven black hair covering one breast, but the other one completely exposed to his gaze. Though not overly generous, it was perfectly formed and tipped with a rose pink nipple that begged for his lips and tongue to wake it. From the shape of her delicate feet, to the feminine slope of her hip, to the gentle curve of her shoulder, and all bits in between, she was perfectly formed to engender carnal hunger in Barr and his beast.

The black curls gracing the juncture of her thighs glinted with a blue sheen under the sunlight just like the long tresses covering her head. 'Twas truly like the ravens of the air. Carrion birds they might be, but they had an elegance of color and form not to be ignored.

Barr spared a quick but sincere hope Muin had missed with his ill-timed arrow. The thought of loveliness such as this, even in the mere form of a bird, destroyed for mere superstition sickened him.

Barr's naked woman continued to lie unconscious on the forest floor. Her fragile beauty called to his protective instincts, touching a part of his wolf that had never before come to the surface. Though tall for a female, she would still be puny beside his human body. He wanted to put himself between her and any potential threat.

'Twas not a feeling he usually experienced for any but those he called clan, and never had he felt it to this depth.

Her current state only made the need to protect grow, until his wolf snarled with it. Her lovely, pale skin was marred by numerous small scratches, as if she'd been running through the bushes. Perhaps another wild boar had found her bathing and she had been forced to flee?

He loped forward, sniffing at her with his enhanced senses. Perplexed in both mind and instinctual memory, the elusive sense of *otherness* continued to tease at him. But something else was there, too. Blood. In greater amounts than the scratches would account for. He had not perceived it before because that *other* scent had so confused him. But blood it was.

Her blood.

A killing rage hazed the usually sharp gray and white images his wolf's eyes saw. The wee one was wounded, her perfect, milk pale skin obscenely marred by a hole in her upper arm, still oozing sluggish rivulets of red.

He quickly examined the area around them, but saw no sign of what had made the injury. However, it did not appear to be from a stray tree branch. The wound did not have the jagged edges of an injury inflicted while running, by something as innocent as a tree branch in the wrong place. He nudged her arm with his snout so he could see the other side.

Whatever had pierced her had gone all the way through, leaving a matching tear in the skin opposite.

Had she fled from attack, not by a wild animal but something much more dangerous? A human.

There were no clans to the north of them from this side of the Donegal holding. It was all wilderness and Barr could not decide where she, much less her attacker, had come from.

A soft moan slipped from between her small, bow-shaped lips, the hand of her uninjured arm moving restlessly as if reaching for him. He had transformed back to human by the time a set of alluring brown eyes flickered open.

Dark pools of confusion stared up at him as she blinked slowly once and then twice. A small furrow forming between her brows, she went to move, but then fell back with a gasp, pain marring her beautiful features.

"What happened?" The words came out in a whisper as if speaking was difficult.

The sense of otherness disappeared as if it had never been. He was so startled by it and by her asking him the question he burned to have *her* answer, he took a moment to speak. "I do not know."

"Who are you?" Her voice was a little stronger, but not by much.

He could not dismiss the feeling she was used to having her queries answered quickly and completely though. Unless she was a queen, which he very much doubted, 'twas odd for human woman in their world. Whether man's or beast's instincts, he did not know, but he was certain he was right, however.

"I am Barr, laird of the Donegal clan, on whose land you now find yourself."

"Barr?" Shock dilated the pupils of her dark brown eyes,

making them look almost all black, like those of an adult raven. *"Laird?"*

He had birds on the brain. "That is right." Though why the news should shock her, he could not imagine. 'Twas not as if he did not look like a laird.

No man in the Donegal clan even came close to being as intimidating, but then she could not know that.

"I . . ." Her mouth stayed parted, as if words trembled to come out, but none did.

The sound of running footsteps nearby drew Barr's attention, making him realize how intent on the woman he had been. He should have heard the approaching Donegal clansman much sooner.

Muin ran right up to them, stopping only when he was barely a foot from the human female. The youth's eyes went wide and his face turned red for the second time that afternoon, but he did not look away from Barr's mysteriously naked woman

"Earc and the others are still hunting the boar. He sent me to join you in case you needed assistance. Do you need assistance, laird?"

Barr's wolf growled at the other man's obvious interest in the wounded woman's nudity. He covered the blatantly possessive action with a barked out, "Look at your laird when you address him, Muin."

The Donegal soldier jumped back at the sound too low for human ears, his gaze immediately moving away from the raven-tressed female.

The woman paled and flinched, filling Barr with immediate concern. She must be in pain.

"Laird, who is this?" Muin asked, with a furtive glance at the woman.

"Look away," Barr's voice rolled across the air with fury, causing a physical flinch and further stepping back of the young hunter. "Retrieve my plaid and dinna get your scent all over it."

"Where—"

"Follow my scent if you can," Barr instructed from between clenched teeth.

"Yes, laird." The man ran.

In a belated show at modesty, the woman pulled her hair forward over her shoulder, so both breasts were covered, one leg coming up to block his view of her tantalizing triangle of black curls. "You *must* be laird; he obeyed you without argument."

"Did you think I'd lie to you?" Humans could be odd, and though he'd known this one for mere minutes, he suspected he would find her even more incomprehensible than most.

"Maybe."

"Why?"

Disgust flickered over her face, but it went so quickly, it could have been a trick of the afternoon light. "The Faol of the Chrechte sometimes do."

Shock gripped him and would not let go. *She knew he was a wolf?* And why had she used the ancient name so few remembered even in their spoken histories?

"You are surprised." Her head canted, birdlike, to one side. "Why?"

A ridiculous question, and yet he answered it. "Only the Chrechte and some of the humans related to them know of our wolf natures."

"But you shifted from your wolf form in front of me."

"You were not conscious."

She muttered something that sounded like *typical wolf.* "Clearly, I was."

"So, are you mated to a wolf?" The thought made his hackles rise, though he could not say why.

The look of utter revulsion once again stayed on her face for less than a second, but this time he had no doubts it had been there.

"You hate the Chrechte," he said in a flat voice, shocked

once again—both by that truth and by how deeply it bothered him.

Turbulent fury turned her eyes into a brown lightning storm. "I do not hate the Chrechte."

Her vehemence was undeniable; so was the sense there was more she wanted to say, but her lips remained firmly closed, going bloodless she pressed them so tightly together.

He guessed, "You have Chrechte family, but you were born without the ability to shift into a wolf." It was not a rare story and for some, the situation caused bitterness.

"I cannot shift into a wolf," she said, her tone implying that was no great loss to her.

Barr would never forget how the brother of the Balmoral laird had been impacted by his inability to change. Ulf's own father had rejected him because of it and that had twisted Ulf so he lost his sense of honor and compassion. That had eventually caused untold harm to his remaining family, laird over the Balmoral, Lachlan. Lachlan's mate had suffered as well, but all had been brought to rights. Eventually.

Clearly, Barr's charge felt some sort of ambivalence toward her Chrechte family as well. Though he doubted very much it would lead her down the path Ulf had taken, if for no other reason than because she was a human woman and fragile.

"What are you doing here?" he asked, wanting the answer before Muin returned.

She looked around them. "In the forest?"

"On Donegal land." He barely restrained rolling his eyes. He had no doubt she knew exactly what he meant and had chosen to play at misunderstanding.

"I do not know."

"What?"

She did not look like she was jesting, but she had to be. "I am hurt," she said as if that should explain everything.

It did not. "Yes, you are."

"How did I get that way?"

"Shouldn't *you* tell *me*?"

"But I don't know."

Funny, there was no scent of a lie and yet, he hesitated to believe her. That had never happened to him before. "How can you not know?"

She merely looked at him.

"The wound in your arm looks like it came from a human weapon." It was too isolated to be a bite or claw mark. "Were you attacked?"

"I must have been. By a violent knave with no conscience." Her voice was filled with loathing, too much so not to know her attacker.

"Who was it?"

"I do not know him." This rang with absolute sincerity, but did not match the near hatred in her earlier tone.

'Twas a puzzle to be sure. "Little one—"

"My name is Sabrine."

That was something at least. "What clan are you from?"

"I don't know."

"How can you not know?"

She pressed her hand to her forehead, like she was trying to push thoughts inside. "I should know, but I don't."

"Did your fall addle your brains, I wonder?"

"It must have." She tried again to sit up. This time she succeeded, though the pain in her expression said it cost her dearly to do so. "I do not like the idea of my brain in a muddle."

Again there was no scent to indicate a lie, but the words did not ring with full truth all the same. It must be her confused state perplexing his wolf's senses. "I am sure you do not."

"What will I do?"

That was one answer he did have. "Until you remember where you are from, you will return to the Donegal holding with me."

The urgency his wolf had felt to be near this woman had lessened since she woke, but it was not gone completely. It was as if it was still there. Only hidden from him, which made less sense than Sabrine's inability to remember her own clan, while able to remember about the Chrechte.

He had hidden nothing from his wolf since his first change, and vice versa; they couldn't. Man or beast, they were one and the same.

Had she been Chrechte, he would have guessed she was masking her scent and distracting his wolf's senses, but even doing so could not completely mask the wolf nature. And she had none. Muin returned with Barr's plaid before he could finish pondering this oddity and determine what it meant.

Keeping his body between the young Donegal clansman and Sabrine, Barr used his plaid to cover her nakedness, careful not to jostle her arm or her clearly tender body. He then gently lifted her into his arms.

And something fundamentally both wolf and human settled inside him at the rightness of it.

Chapter 2

As he carried her through the forest, Barr's scent wrapped itself around Sabrine, demanding recognition, insisting on some sort of reaction from her raven.

He was no longer masking any of his presence, neither wolf nor human. It was a blatant warning to other predators that one more fierce than they walked in their midst. It would keep all but crazed boar from them.

More than a warning though, it also acted as a potent wine to her senses. She could smell nothing but the wolf in man's skin that carried her.

That should have disgusted her, but instead she found herself unwillingly intrigued.

For the first time since taking on the duties as guardian for her people, Sabrine's raven wanted to come out and play.

Despite the pain of her injured wing, she wanted to take to the sky in flight. And not as a patrol, looking for any potential threat. She longed to do dips and swirls she had not enjoyed as anything but tactical maneuvering since leaving her childhood behind.

Perhaps her fall from the sky truly had addled her mind. It was the only explanation. For her desire to frolic. For the desire building in a slow burn throughout her body.

For the inexplicable and totally unacceptable urge to cuddle closer to his altogether too impressive naked warrior's body.

He did not smell *evil*, but he was wolf. He could not be anything else. And yet her bird wanted to rub itself against him, taking in his scent on a primal level none of her own people had ever made her long for. He was so different from the men of the Éan.

Even for a wolf, Barr was huge. Taller than all of the men in his hunting party, he would also easily tower a half head above any of the Éan, even the golden eagles. Sabrine was of a height with most of her brethren, but this man called her *little one* and she could not gainsay him.

Not merely high in stature, his shoulders were so large he would not only have to duck, he would also have to turn sideways to enter her home. Not that she would *ever* lead him back to her people.

That way lay madness, death and destruction.

Still, she could not shake the feeling of safety being in his arms gave her. Every step he took made his bulging muscles ripple against her. And instead of strategizing ways to compensate for his superior strength in a battle between them, she had far too strong a desire to allow that strength to stand as shield between her and any that would do her harm.

Her mind was more than addled; she'd lost it completely.

Otherwise, she would never want to reach up and touch his wheat-colored hair so badly, she had to clasp her hands together lest one do it of its own accord.

She knew a golden eagle with hair the same color, but the eagle's skin was not as darkened by the sun as Barr's.

Barr's masculine allure was altogether too appealing in every way.

He knew he was magnificent among men, too; he carried her, uninhibited by his own nudity and with no regard for the curious glances cast their way by the young soldier Barr had sent back into the forest for his plaid.

As disgusted as it made her with herself, Sabrine could not help a reaction of purely feminine awe to him. None of the Éan had ever caused her to react thus. She had always been alone, a warrior among, and for, her people.

Now Sabrine fought the unfamiliar sense of connection that had been trying to form between her and the giant warrior since waking to his presence. No wolf should cause such feelings.

The Faol of the Chrechte were not to be trusted, not to be confided in and absolutely never to be mated with.

There were horrific stories of wolves using their Éan mates to lead them to the bird Chrechte only to kill the entire flock, including the grievously deceived mate. True, the stories were old ones, but that was only because the Éan had learned their lesson. They did not mate among their Faol.

For generations, the Faol had done their best to rid the earth of the Éan. She could not let herself forget that important fact. Their theft of the *Clach Gealach Gra* from the caves of the *usal* spring was only the latest in decades' worth of treacheries the wolves had perpetrated against her raven people.

The sacred stone was necessary for the coming of age ceremony in order for her people to fully realize their Chrechte gifts. Those Éan who did not come into their special gifts could not father or give birth to children, something most Éan considered as sacred a gift as their own Chrechte nature. Worse than robbing her people of this basic need was the fact that the theft of the *Clach Gealach Gra* was no doubt an insidious attempt to guarantee that the remaining bird shifters did not live beyond the current generation.

Her people lived like shades in the forest already, hiding from the wolves and humans alike, hoping the cruel Faol would believe they had succeeded in killing off the last of the Éan. Their numbers were too small to do anything else. Besides, it was not in a raven's nature to kill. They could defend alongside the hawks and eagles, but they could not go on the attack with them. Since the hawks and eagles numbered less than half of the Éan combined, defensive strengths were their only true alternative. Clearly, their defensive attempt to hide had not worked.

No matter that the last hunting party had not come seeking her kind since she was a wee child and had lost both her parents to such an attack. The wolves still must suspect the Éan continued to exist, if not thrive, and they had hatched this wicked plot to rid the world of the birds once and for all.

She would not let them succeed. She could not. She would find the Heart of the Moon and return it to her people for safekeeping, before her own younger brother had to face his coming of age without the sacred talisman.

The feeling of safety Barr's bulging arms holding her body so securely to himself gave her was nothing but a vapor, with no substance and far more dangerous. She would never truly be safe in a wolf's arms. If he discovered her real nature, he would finish the job his hunter's arrow had started.

No matter how pleasing she found the man, he was and always would be Faol of the Chrechte.

Her sworn enemy.

"What has you going tense, lass? Have you remembered something?" he asked, his deep voice rumbling through her like water rushing over rocks and leaving her insides just as disturbed.

She almost blurted out, yes, she'd remembered he was her enemy. She almost yanked herself from his arms, but she didn't. Her years hiding her fear and every other emotion while she protected her people gave her the strength to remain outwardly unaffected. She must keep her purpose at the forefront of her mind. That purpose required him to see her as a human female, *as fragile*.

"No. I was thinking about your clan," she said, twisting the truth but not breaking it.

She had to practice a deception to save her people, but she would not lie for simple expedience. She was no wolf.

"They will not harm you."

"You're sure?"

"They would not dare. You are under my protection."

Inexplicably, her heart caught and pleasure pushed out the pain of their people's shared past for a single, incredible moment. No one had ever promised her protection before. If the strongest of the Éan's warriors did, she would tell him she could protect herself and believe it.

But this man, this wolf, was more powerful than any Chrechte she had ever encountered. He *could* protect her. Were he truly her champion he could protect her people.

But no Faol ever stood guardian for the Éan and none ever would.

"You're claiming her, then?" the other Donegal wolf asked, his tone filled with the same respect bordering on awe he had used each time he addressed Barr.

The giant warrior carrying her said nothing, so Sabrine decided to answer for him. "No one is claiming me."

The one called Muin gave her a look that clearly said her words carried less weight than his laird's actions.

She frowned up at Barr. "You are not claiming me."

"Right now, I am taking you to my home to care for your wounds."

"Right. Good." Her head was bobbing and she made herself stop. "No claiming."

"For now."

She gasped, then glared, but Muin just smirked. Barr ignored them both.

"Forever," she insisted.

Barr stopped and looked down at her, his stormy gray eyes questioning. "You do not want children?"

Her heart clenched again, but this time in pain. Though every Éan was taught from birth that the bearing of children was the only way to protect their future as a race, she had decided long ago not to have bairns.

"I would not have children only to leave them orphans when I die."

"'Tis a morbid thought."

Perhaps he considered it so, but then he was a wolf, not a raven. No one hunted his people intent on total annihilation. "It is the way of the world." Her world anyway.

"Not all children grow up orphans. Not even most."

"Among my people, *enough* do."

"You remember that, but not who your clan is?" he asked cynically.

She turned her head away, the taste of any lie she would have to tell bile in her mouth.

"It isn't that you don't remember your clan, it's that you don't want to," he guessed, sounding quite proud he had worked that out. Never mind that he was wrong.

But in a way, he was right, too. She didn't want to remember the decimation her people had endured at the hands of his.

She neither confirmed nor denied.

"You'll tell me."

"Tell you what?"

"Everything."

"No." Even to her own ears, the single word swelled with enough horror to drown a small village.

His countenance did not darken; he merely shrugged, jostling her body so the plaid covering her slipped just enough that they were skin against skin on her side.

Her gasp this time was for an entirely different reason than shock. It was pure sensation. Amazing sensation. Make-her-wish-for-the-first-time-to-share-her-body-with-a-man sensation.

She had never been this close to a mate, not outside of battle. And never had another man had the effect on her this blond barbarian did.

He inhaled deeply and she realized with chagrin that he was smelling her arousal.

"Stop it," she whispered, though why she bothered when the other Chrechte with them had a wolf's hearing, she did not know.

Barr grinned down at her, his masculine pleasure heating the air around them. "No."

"You're not claiming me."

"Your body says otherwise."

"My mind controls my body."

"We'll see."

"Would you force me to go where my mind does not want to?"

"I will not force you, but as to your heart ruling your mind, that you'll have to stop."

"My heart has nothing to do with this."

"Call it what you like, but your body betrays your true thoughts on the matter."

"It betrays nothing but animal reaction."

"That is an odd thing for a human to say."

"Humans are animals, too, they simply have one nature, not two like the Chrechte."

She grabbed the plaid, trying to adjust it so her skin was not burning along his. He would not let her but continued walking, keeping her pressed close to him.

Arrogant wolf.

Curious clanspeople surrounded them as Barr carried her into the compound nearly an hour later. Each wore the red and black plaid of the Donegals.

One older woman peered at her and Barr with knowing

amusement. "So, it would appear you had a successful hunt, then, laird."

"Aye, I found the lass in the forest."

"In her all together by the look of it."

A young boy asked, "Did a wild animal attack her and steal all her clothes, do you think?"

"Aye, lad, that's just what happened," Barr lied without a second's hesitation.

"She looks a wee bit worse for the wear," the old woman said. "Best get her to the keep. Let Verica have a look at her."

The words surprised Sabrine. She knew humans could be kind, but this woman belonged to the clan that had stolen the sacred stone. In Sabrine's mind all Donegals were cruel and selfish, like the wolves that had made the clan their home.

She didn't have much time to ponder the thought before she was in the keep itself.

It was not as large as some of the clan buildings she saw on her nightly flights, but it was bigger than any dwelling among the Éan. Barr carried her into the main hall, where three long tables made a U shape at one end and a large fireplace warmed the other. No chairs sat in front of the fireplace, but that didn't stop a small group of soldiers from congregating there to sharpen their weapons.

Barr walked past the soldiers after giving them a cursory greeting. One asked who she was and Barr called her his guest. This elicited curious stares, which Muin clearly intended to satisfy as he joined the soldiers by the fire.

Barr did not seem to care as he continued across the vast room, around the tables and toward a staircase.

Stepping onto the first riser, he bellowed, "Verica!"

And then he took the stairs two at a time, managing not to jostle Sabrine despite his speed. His grace did not surprise her—wolves were not clumsy—but his care for her comfort did.

A beautiful woman, petite in stature, stepped out of a room off the landing. Presumably the Verica the old woman had referred to and Barr had called for. She had hair the same color as Sabrine's but with bits of dark red mixed in. The nearest Sabrine had seen to anything like it was a hawk and golden eagle shifter. He had dark brown hair with streaks of gold like his second shifting form's feathers. It was extremely rare for a shifter to be born with both their parents' animal forms. She'd only ever heard of three her whole life and one was long dead.

Sabrine could not imagine what had caused this small woman's coloring until she got closer and the woman's scent became clear.

She smelled like a wolf.

No other shifter had the true black hair of the raven but the raven itself. Which meant that this woman was a wolf-raven dual shifter. The only way that could happen was for one of her parents to have been each.

Horrified by the implication of that knowledge, Sabrine stared in mute shock at the other woman.

Who in turn glared at Barr. "You bellowed?"

"This woman needs a healer."

"What did you do to her?"

"Do not dare ask such a thing."

"Why not? Am I supposed to pretend Circin doesn't seek my services nightly for wounds you inflict?"

"Your brother is to be laird one day; he must be a strong warrior."

"He's still a boy." The tiny woman did not seem in the least intimidated by her oversized laird.

Either she was fearless, stupid or amazingly good at masking the scent of her emotions, a skill the Faol did not share to the same degree as the Éan.

Sabrine decided she was going to like this woman.

"He would not thank you for saying so. A Chrechte

who has reached sixteen summers without ever wielding a sword in at least mock battle is a disgrace."

"Circin is no disgrace!"

"Nay, but his trainers are."

Something moved in the woman's face, a flicker of disquiet at the mention of the trainers. "I discouraged Circin from training with the older Chrechte of the clan when he was younger."

"You will have to explain your reasons for doing so after you see to this woman."

"This woman's name is Sabrine, and well you know it, Donegal laird." Sabrine gave Barr a frown.

He smiled in return. "I wondered if you had lost your voice with your memory."

"You've lost your memory?" Verica demanded and then turned back to Barr. "Why did you not say? An addled brain can be very dangerous. She could appear normal and then simply fall asleep and not wake up."

Barr let loose another one of those bone-chilling subvocal growls. Both women flinched.

"She will not die."

Verica nodded as if by saying so, the laird made it so. "Someone must watch her through the night."

"I will do it."

"You? But you're the laird!" For the first time, the wolf-raven woman looked rattled. She'd taken her leader's nudity in stride, though that was not surprising considering men in the Highlands still battled and hunted in their natural-born state as often as not. "She's not your mate, is she?"

"I'm no wolf's mate," Sabrine said with more certainty than she felt.

Her reactions to the giant Faol were either explained by knocking her head in her fall to the earth or a connection she could never risk acknowledging.

Not only for the safety of her people but for her own

safety as well. The Éan would never accept one of their own mated to the enemy.

She could be killed for treachery, but at the very least she would be banished. And her people could not stand the cost of losing her.

Both Donegals gave her varying looks of speculation. Barr's bordered on confident assurance. Verica's was tinged with surprise, but she didn't ask the question shimmering between them.

Instead, she indicated a room across the landing. "Let's get her lying down."

Barr started moving, but he didn't stop at the room his clanswoman had pointed to. He went to the next door and shoved it open.

"You're claiming her?" Verica asked, managing to sound completely scandalized this time.

Why did people keep asking him that? And he didn't bother to answer on this occasion, either. And really. Did Verica need to make it sound like Barr could do far better? Sabrine would make a strong mate for any man, even the big laird. If she planned to ever take a mate. Which she didn't, and especially not a wolf shifter.

Instead of answering for him, like she had with Muin, Sabrine pinched Barr. Good and hard. He could give assurances himself this time.

He jolted and then stared down at her. "What was that for?"

"Answer your clanswoman. Tell her you're not claiming me." Sabrine looked at the other woman. "He said he'd watch over me tonight, naturally he'd think to do it here. It's not necessary, I'm sure."

"Are you a healer then?" he asked.

An unexpected twinge of old pain pierced her heart. "No." Had her parents lived, she would have been. Her mother had been a healer, but their deaths led Sabrine to the path of a warrior.

"Verica is and she's decent. She says you need watching, you'll be watched."

"Don't think I haven't noticed you didn't answer her as I requested."

"Oh, was that a request? Sounded like an order to me."

"Perhaps I could have worded my request more tactfully."

"You could have refrained from pinching me."

"No, really, I couldn't."

Chapter 3

"You're awfully mouthy for such a fragile little thing."

"Compared to you, a mother bear is a wee thing." She didn't deny the fragile argument because she needed him to see her as just that. Weak and not a threat to be watched while she searched the keep and surrounding huts if need be for the stolen *Clach Gealach Gra*.

If only he knew the truth about her.

Verica laughed aloud. "You two are better than the old men over the checkers table."

Instead of getting angry at the woman's mockery as Sabrine expected, Barr shook his head as he laid Sabrine on his bed. "With wisdom like those two impart, I'm surprised this clan has lasted at all."

"You're not the only one." But Verica's voice lacked the humor Barr's had had; a dark tone Sabrine had to wonder at swam just below the surface of the other woman's words.

"You'll not believe what Muin did today and told 'twas because his grandfather taught him."

"What's that?"

"He shot at a raven in the middle of our hunt for wild boar."

"Was the fact he shot at the bird what you find so appalling, or that he did it during the hunt?" Verica asked.

"Both. We're Chrechte. We respect life; we do not kill for sport."

Sabrine could not believe what she was hearing.

"What did Muin say to that?" Verica demanded.

"Nothing. What was there to say?" Barr's unconscious arrogant assurance the other man had to agree with him was as alluring as it was ridiculous.

Sabrine found it difficult to stay focused on the conversation with Barr's continued nakedness, though Verica seemed utterly unaffected.

Still, Barr's apparent naïveté astounded her. "You do not truly believe all of the Faol feel the same?"

"Any under my authority had better."

Verica flipped her uniquely colored hair back over her shoulder. "What did Muin say his reason was for shooting at the bird?"

"He said his grandfather told him ravens were unlucky." Outrage colored his tone a bright red. "The only thing unlucky about that raven today was it flying in the sky where an idiot boy could see it."

"So, your clan did not teach as much about ravens?" Verica asked in a neutral voice.

"That they are bad luck?" he asked, as if he continued to find it nearly impossible to believe someone thought such.

This was wholly unexpected and Sabrine did not know how to interpret his attitude as a Faol warrior.

"Yes."

"No. Every Sinclair knows that all animals are necessary for our world to remain in balance." He made a sound of disgust. "And Talorc, our . . . *their* laird, would have sent someone to the healer for suggesting a hunter pay closer attention to superstitions than to the hunt."

"Truly?" Verica asked.

"I do not lie."

"You told the boy outside that a wild animal had attacked me and taken my clothes," Sabrine interjected.

"We do not know that is not what happened."

"So it was not a lie?" she asked, finding the whole conversation beyond her knowledge of the wolves.

Barr shrugged. "There are lies and there is stretching the truth when it will not harm."

"You need to put a new plaid on," she blurted out.

The nearness of his naked presence was overshadowing all else.

"You do not like my naked body?"

"I think she likes it too much. I will get my basket of remedies." Verica curtsied and left the room.

The walls that seemed spacious before started to close in as Sabrine realized they were well and truly alone.

Barr sat beside her on the bed and then proceeded to start tugging his plaid from her body.

She grabbed at it. "What do you think you are doing?"

"Verica cannot clean your scratches if she cannot get to them."

"I'll remove the plaid when she returns."

"You were not so modest in the forest."

"I didn't have a choice."

"Come, I've already seen your delectable body. It's of no consequence if I see it again."

"Truly? You think to convince me with insults?" But was it an insult? He thought her body delectable. Though his scent had said he found her sexually appealing, 'twas not quite the same.

"It's not an insult."

Maybe that was not a lie. "Turn your back and I'll get under the blanket."

She expected him to refuse, but he stood and turned around so his back was to her. She made quick work of ripping away the now-bloodstained plaid and climbing between the bedding.

The blanket was the softest wool she'd ever felt and different colors than the Donegal plaid. Sabrine remembered something Verica had said. "Are you from a different clan?"

That would explain his being laird when the Éan spies had named a different man.

"Aye, I was born a Sinclair."

"But you have the armband of the Donegal laird."

Verica came into the room carrying a large steaming bowl of water. "That's because Scotland's king and our former laird, *Rowland*"—she practically spit the name—"saw fit to give my brother's rightful place to another clan's warrior." A girl followed behind her, carrying a basket that was half her size.

"I am training your brother to take his rightful place when he has reached maturity." Barr donned a plaid with deft movements.

"And when will that be?" She put her hands on her hips and stared her laird right in the eye. "When he's a grandfather?"

The girl put the basket down, her downcast gaze flitting back and forth between her mistress and her laird.

"If the boy isn't ready to lead by his twenty-fifth birthday, I'll wash my hands of him and this superstition-riddled clan."

Rather than look offended at the slur on her clan, Verica nodded as if pleased. "I have your word on that?"

"You do."

Verica opened the basket and handed the girl a packet of herbs from within. "Drop two pinches into the water and stir."

The girl did as she was told, then Verica took some of

the water and mixed it with several other ingredients in a smaller bowl. Verica wet a cloth in the large bowl of water and began thoroughly cleansing Sabrine's wound on her arm. When she was done, she and the girl made a poultice and applied it to both sides of the wound. "That should draw out any poison."

Verica wrapped the upper arm in a linen bandage before carefully washing each scratch and treating it with salve. Barr watched everything with close scrutiny. Verica showed no more concern for Sabrine's modesty than Barr had though. Which was no surprise, Sabrine supposed. They were both Chrechte after all. Humans in the Highlands were not an overly modest bunch, and the Chrechte were even less concerned with exposure. However, in her case she'd discovered a sense of modesty she'd not known she possessed.

She felt as shy as a human virgin in Barr's presence.

Barr knocked a young human male on his backside, the impact sending up a cloud of dust around the warrior in training.

He'd left Verica watching over Sabrine, with instructions not to allow anyone else in his room. There were things he was certain she had yet to reveal. Determined to be the one she told them to, he used her injury as an excuse to keep her isolated. If keeping her in his bed and away from the other males of his clan pleased the wolf more than it should, that was his secret to keep. His new clan was curious about her though. No fewer than five people had asked about the naked woman he'd found in the forest. Gossip spread faster than a pitcher of spilled ale.

Barr was too busy training soldiers to satisfy their curiosity and he left it to Muin to tell what he knew. Which was less than Barr; that was little enough.

Though the younger Chrechte still managed to make a full meal out of it.

"When your opponent is bigger than you, use his size against him. Use your speed, your agility to stay out of his reach," Barr instructed the young man he had knocked down.

The soldier's intent expression would be a welcome sight on some of the Chrechte Barr and Earc had been working with.

These human men wanted to learn.

"I try, laird, but you're faster than me despite your size."

"Keep trying." Excuses wouldn't protect the clan.

The soldier nodded, falling back into a fighting stance.

"Muin, stop your gossiping and get over here," Barr yelled to where the young male flirted with a Chrechte woman.

"Rowland didn't allow us to train with the elite soldiers," one of the other Donegals mentioned from where he and a small group of human men waited their turn to spar with their new laird.

Disbelief jarring him harder than any of these soldiers' attempts at a strike, Barr stopped and turned to face them. "He kept you separated for training?"

"Aye."

What kind of fool did not prepare his clan to battle other Chrechte? Relying on the wolves completely for protection was a weak strategy that left far too many in the clan vulnerable. It was no wonder their king had demanded the older Chrechte step down from his role as laird. Not that the king would know of Rowland's bias toward his Chrechte brethren, but even a human would see the misuse of clan resources and poor tactical stance the old man had taken.

If a human warrior did not learn how to fight his stronger counterpart by training with them, the clan was left weakened and vulnerable when their enemies might well outnumber them in Chrechte warriors.

"Who did you practice with then?"

"Each other." From the look of things that was not exactly stone sharpening stone.

"Who taught you?"

The men looked down and at each other but would not meet Barr's gaze.

"Answer me."

"Rowland said we had to earn the right to be trained by staying on our feet for one minute with an elite soldier. We never could."

Of course they couldn't. Without proper training, a human soldier had no chance against the wolf nature of even the poorly trained Donegal Chrechte. "Rowland is an idiot."

A shocked gasp sounded. But the man who had spoken looked like at least he openly agreed with Barr.

"He's our laird," Muin said in a scandalized tone as he jogged up.

Barr didn't hesitate. He knocked the Chrechte flat on his back with a blow meant to get notice. "*I* am your laird. Rowland is an old man who forgot the importance of every member of his clan. I don't make those kinds of mistakes."

"No, my laird." From what he'd seen the former laird was close friends with Muin's grandfather, but there was no hesitation in the younger warrior's agreement.

"You earn your right to be trained by giving your loyalty to your clan," Barr said to them all.

The youth he'd been sparring with drew himself up, his face set in hard lines. "We've done that."

The other men nodded.

"Aye?" Barr prodded.

He did not doubt it, but they needed to be made aware in their own minds that they spoke bone-deep truth.

"Aye." The youth's tone was vehement, his head jerking

up and down in agreement. "We build homes and repair our keep. We hunt to put food in hungry bellies, no matter our circumstances or the weather like to freeze us. We stand by our families, serving them as we do the clan as a whole. We try to learn to fight, but are left to train amongst ourselves."

The other men nodded, adding comments of their own, the frustration they knew at the hands of Rowland and his ilk evident in every tense fist and grinding jaw. Their loyalty had been met with mockery and disdain.

Barr would allow no such travesty to happen again.

"Teaching you to hold your own against superior strength, skill and speed is my responsibility. I don't fail at the tasks I take on," he warned them.

Several of the men smiled, looking pleased by his promise. They weren't smiling two hours later, but they weren't complaining, either. Though each and every one of them, including Muin, sported fresh bruises and some had been bloodied as well.

They stopped their practice when Earc returned with the Chrechte hunting party.

"Did the boar get the best of you?" The hunters looked as beat up as the soldiers Barr had been training.

"You can damn well smell the blood." Earc's nostrils flared. He was clearly in no mood to be teased. "You know we caught our prey."

But the final kill had obviously been a hell of a lot harder than it should have been with three wolves, even if only one of them could control his change.

Earc would mate soon enough and gain the ability to shift at will. That was one thing Barr and Talorc had argued over. Talorc maintained that sex constituted a mating. The wolves in his pack not born with the ability to shift at will like Barr could had to wait until mating to make that happen. To his knowledge, only the white wolf and its descendants were born with that ability. Others had to have sex after their transition to adulthood in order to control the change. It made little sense to Barr, but then there was much in his world that remained a mystery.

The inability to shift at will put Sinclair warriors at a tactical disadvantage to clans like the Balmoral, who had no such mores assigned to sex outside a mating.

He did not know what the Donegals practiced.

Circin and Fionn came forward, carrying the boar on a sturdy branch between them.

"Fionn looks like he wrestled the boar before you killed it."

"Let's just say he needs to learn a subtler way to hunt."

"You instructed him?"

"He didn't listen well the first time."

Barr doubted the pig had been the only one in the forest who Fionn had to defend himself from. Earc was a patient man, but he was not a saint.

"I got the lesson," Fionn said in a weary voice.

"That is what matters, but if you fail to listen to my second again, it won't be his wrath you face."

Fionn winced but nodded. "Understood."

Sabrine was sleeping when Barr returned to his room to check on her.

"I gave her a calming drink of steeped herbs," Verica explained. "She was restless and wanting to get up."

"Are you sure it's safe for her to slumber?"

"She's only dozing, not in a deep sleep."

"Your senses are finely honed." It was not always a simple matter to distinguish between the two.

"It helps me in my role as healer."

He found that easy to believe. "Explain to me why you held your brother back from training with the older Chrechte."

Circin was by far the most dedicated of their trainees.

He obviously hungered for the kind of mentoring he'd gotten among the Sinclairs and now received from Barr and Earc.

Circin would make a fine laird one day, but he was years behind where he should be in his training.

"I wasn't ready for him to be a man."

"Your words ring with truth, but there is something more." Like with Sabrine earlier.

Verica fussed with the blanket over the dozing woman. "Nothing you need concern yourself with."

"I am your laird. Everything about those in my clan concerns me." As much as it was not a position he would have had by choice, now that he had the responsibility, he would uphold it completely.

"That is a laudable sentiment to be sure, but some things are private."

"If you have a reason for distrusting the other Chrechte in this clan, I need to know."

"I have nothing more than a feeling. I won't make accusations without substance."

He had to respect that. "I'll admit, I wish some of the others showed your reticence to gossip."

Her lips twitched. "We're a small clan. Word travels faster than footfalls in some instances, but curiosity makes it go even faster."

"I noticed."

"Did questions about your captive keep you from training?"

"Nay." He was a warrior, not an old woman. Gossip didn't keep him from his duties. "And she is not my captive. Sabrine is a guest."

"So, I can leave the room?" Sabrine demanded from the bed, her eyes opening. "I was under the impression"—and she gave Verica a measured look—"that I was not to do so."

"For your own protection, I would prefer you not leave

this room unaccompanied." There, now that was mindful of her feminine sensibilities, wasn't it?

Talorc's wife insisted a woman preferred not to be dictated to. Barr could allow his guest to think she had a say in the matter, but the truth was he would have his way.

"I need protection among your clan?" she asked, not sounding as surprised by that as she could have been.

"You are a stranger to them. The Donegals are not overly friendly with those they do not know."

"You think I will get my feelings hurt?" The disbelief tingeing her voice was rather naïve on her part, he thought.

But then she had suffered memory loss. Perhaps she had forgotten how easily a human woman's emotions could be damaged. Even the Chrechte women of his former clan took exception to things he never saw as beyond innocuous.

"You are not yet sufficiently recovered to venture out of this room. You need healing rest." He patted her uninjured arm in what he hoped was a consoling manner. "You're fragile and must conserve your strength."

She stared at him with blatant incredulousness for three full seconds before she blinked, and then nodded. "Right. I'm weak and need my rest."

His senses had prepared him for her argument. This sudden capitulation startled him.

"Aye, that is exactly what you need," Verica replied before Barr had the chance. "Tonight at least, you'll take late meal in bed."

"You'll see to it?" Barr asked.

Verica nodded. "Brigit and I will have our meal in here as well."

He was tempted to join them, but the clan still needed his visible presence as often as possible, to solidify his role as their laird in all their minds. The healer and her young apprentice would be good company for Barr's mysterious and much too alluring guest.

* * *

Rowland joined Barr at the head table before the food
had been brought in from the kitchens. Though the older
Chrechte had showed no happiness at being forced by his
king to cede his leadership, he always ate with Barr. Earc
said it was because Rowland still considered the head table
his.

After learning what he had today, Barr wasn't sure how
long he would allow it. The man's presence only fanned the
slow-burning fury his inadequate former leadership caused
in the new Donegal laird.

"I heard you called me an idiot, boy," the old man said
in querulous tones as he sat down.

Barr was fairly certain none of the men he'd been training had said anything, but the training yard was near the
kitchens. And there had been a group of watchers during
the entire training time. Barr could easily have been overheard.

"I heard you neglected to train men eager to do their
duty by the clan." The old man opened his mouth to speak,
but Barr forestalled him. "Worse, I've seen with my own
eyes how badly you taught those you did bother to train."

"Now you listen here—"

But Barr had heard enough. He leaned down until their
faces were inches apart. "No, old man, you listen to me. I
am your laird and you will address me as such if you need
to address me at all. You lost your position through idiocy
and neglect, but if you think to challenge me for the right
to lead this clan, think hard. I *will* kill you."

Rowland's grizzled visage twisted in a scowl. "You
need to show respect for your elders."

"Respect is earned." So far, the only thing this man had
earned from Barr was a swift kick.

"I led these people since my dear friend and our rightful

laird was killed while hunting when Circin here was but a boy." He indicated the untrained heir with a gnarled finger. "That is deserving of respect."

For his part, Circin looked less than impressed by Rowland's claim. Certainly no affection toward the older man showed in the future laird's expression or manner.

Rowland may have taken Circin's father's place as leader of the clan, but he'd not fulfilled his role of mentor for the man's children.

"It would be if you hadn't done such a piss-poor job of it." He wasn't about to sugarcoat his words for the sake of the man's ego.

Rowland tried to look dignified, but it was too far a stretch to Barr's way of thinking. "We do not need to discuss this here."

"We won't be discussing anything at all. Challenge me, or shut the hell up."

"With age comes wisdom."

"For some, and some of us turn into fools," Osgard said.

The old man was the only other Sinclair who had accompanied Barr to the Donegals. It had not been by choice, but rather his only option in the face of his actions in regard to their former laird's mate. Osgard had taken his banishment from the Sinclair clan hard but accepted it. He'd earned the punishment and both knew and acknowledged it.

The confused thinking he'd shown back at the Sinclair hold that had led to his unacceptable attitudes had diminished away from the constant reminders of memories that had clearly grown too heavy to bear. Though he still had days he spent in his room, lost in a past too real for him to fully forget.

Barr nodded toward Osgard. "I could use your eye during training tomorrow."

"I'm a cantankerous old bastard. You think your trainees can stand the lash of my tongue?"

"They stood the knock of my fist today."

"Real potential as warriors then."

"Aye."

He saw the grins and ducked heads their words caused out of the corner of his eye.

"Bah!" Rowland stood up and stomped out of the hall.

"Good riddance." Osgard tugged on a beard more gray than white but getting there. "I hear your hunt was more successful and less bloody than our Earc's."

"'Twas the same hunt until our laird decided to go seeking naked women rather than game," Earc said with a knowing grin and a wink.

Osgard snorted. "Are you saying you don't prefer a nice clean-smelling woman over a sweaty boar? Only I'm thinking you would do your hunting right here."

Earc, tough warrior and staunch Chrechte, blushed like a youth in the throes of calf's love. "I'll not be hunting women *anywhere* at present, thank you."

"If you say so." Osgard sounded unconvinced.

"I do."

"All right then."

"All right."

Barr listened to the exchange with growing amusement. He did not know who Osgard believed Earc had set his eye on, but the old warrior had certainly struck on something.

"Was she nude when you found her?" Earc asked in an obvious bid to turn the topic.

"Aye. Bleeding and unconscious, too." The memory of Sabrine's state still had the power to make him growl.

Chrechte around the hall flinched, some even making barely aborted movements to bare their throats.

"What happened to her?"

"She doesn't remember."

"That's troubling," Osgard said. "I knew a soldier once. Took a blow to the head. Forgot his wife's name and where to find their cottage. 'Twas dead within the week."

"From the blow?" Circin asked.

"Nay, from his wife. She found him sleeping in a widow's bed."

The table erupted into guffaws and backslapping, but Barr did not laugh. "She will not die."

Osgard gave him a long, shrewd look. "It's like that, is it?"

Chapter 4

"He's got her in his bed and insists on being the one to watch over her through the night as Verica has said she must be," Circin said.

"He has now, has he?" Osgard asked.

"Surely you jest," one of the other old Chrechte men said from his seat at the other table. "She's a stranger we know nothing about. You cannot take her to mate."

"You dare attempt to tell me what I can and cannot do?" And who said anything about mating? To be sure, his wolf felt uncommonly possessive, but Barr was not yet certain his naked lady of the forest was the one he was intended to claim.

He did not deny the possibility to himself, if no one else though.

"You are our laird now. You owe this clan your loyalty."

"The clan has it, but when the time comes to choose my mate, I'll not suffer *your* interference, or any other."

"Who you choose to mate will affect this clan."

So would banishing the old men who whined like little

children and gossiped like old biddies, but Barr forbore mentioning that fact. Not all the old men were a pain in his ass, just two or three and as much as they might irritate him, this *was* their home.

"You'll trust your laird's choice just as you'll accept her," Osgard said at his most irascible.

Earc nodded as did several others around the tables, surprising Barr. He expected loyalty, that was a given, but he had not expected support of his decisions so quickly.

That said more bad than good about how the clan saw the former leaders among them.

Verica's patient sniffed the food warily, her small nose crinkling in her poor, scratched-up face. What had caused this delicate woman to be out in the woods alone in the first place, much less get attacked?

Sabrine's lack of memory worried Verica more than she wanted to allow her laird to know. Yet she was equally as concerned about what had brought the woman to her current state. It could not be good and might well spell trouble for their clan.

Not that Verica begrudged Barr's offer of help to the young woman, but the clanswoman could not help wondering what trouble it might bring, both from within and without the Donegal holding.

"The laird's cooks are better than most," Verica assured the other woman, certain Sabrine would smell nothing but well-prepared mutton and vegetables in her wooden bowl.

"My mum is one of them," Brigit said, pride in her voice, but then her heart-shaped face took on a wounded cast. "My da is dead."

Verica tensed, her heartbeat increasing though she kept a carefully neutral expression on her face. Discussion of the dead clansman could lead to trouble for both Verica and her apprentice healer.

Sabrine gave Verica an oddly concerned look, almost as if she could read Verica's thoughts despite her better than average attempt at controlling her expression. Growing up a double shifter in the Donegal clan had been a die-or-try training ground for learning to hide both her bird nature and her true thoughts and feelings.

"How did he die?" Sabrine gently asked the girl.

"A wild animal got him while he was hunting." Brigit recited the words as if she'd been taught to say them, but they held no conviction.

She had to learn to dissemble better. Those who had hurt her father would think nothing of harming the child. Only Verica could not blame Brigit for her lack. Her father had been gone less than a year, not long enough for her to bury her grief as deeply as it had to go.

Verica found herself saying, both for the child's sake and as a very subtle warning to Sabrine, "Just like my da."

"Your father was laird before Barr?"

"Nay, before that even, before the laird Barr replaced." Rowland, a cruel and stupid man, if cunning like the beast inside him.

Verica had always believed he was responsible for her father's death but could not prove it. Even if she had been able to, it would have done no good. Rowland had too much power with the Chrechte wolf pack and the Donegal clan they lived among.

Best she remember that before loose lips caused more pain for all of them. "That's enough talk of the past," she said. "Eat your food, Brigit. Your mother would find it amiss if your bowl was returned to the kitchen untouched."

The food was good and Verica noted that Sabrine ate hungrily, as did she and Brigit.

"How long has Barr been laird?" Sabrine asked as she set her bowl aside.

Verica picked it up and placed it with her own on a table by the door, warning herself to caution when speaking with

this woman. There was something about Sabrine that invited
confidences, but sharing such was dangerous. Deadly so.
"Less than a month."

"He is ever so much better than our old laird."

Verica's head moved in an infinitesimal nod she could
not help, though she gave her charge a chiding frown. "Do
not speak disrespectfully of Rowland."

The girl's lip protruded in a stubborn pout. "He was not
a fair leader."

"No, but he's still a powerful man in our clan. It could
go badly for you and your mother if someone heard you
say so."

"It cannot get worse for my mum." Brigit's pout turned
to a pain-filled expression that caught at Verica's heart.

"What do you mean?" Verica demanded, a sick feeling
in her stomach. She knew, but how she wished she did not.

She'd seen the way Rowland looked at the young widow
before the woman had ever lost her husband.

Brigit's face blanched and she closed her mouth so tight
her lips disappeared. The girl shook her head.

And Verica's disquiet intensified. "Tell me."

"Mum says I mustn't."

Sabrine's body went tense, and an expression Verica
had only ever seen on a warrior's set her face in feral lines.
"Does your former laird hurt your mother?"

Brigit's eyes filled with tears, but she wiped away the
moisture with a fisted hand before they could fall. "Mum
and me are strong. She says so."

"You are strong." But the girl's fear had become a rank
odor around them. Verica would not question her further.

"It is all right. You do not need to say anything you
don't want to," Sabrine said before Verica could.

Brigit nodded, her tension easing a wee bit. "You always
say the walls have ears," she said to Verica. "So does Mum,
but they don't. It is not possible." These words held no more

conviction than her recitation of her father's death. Brigit looked around, her expression filled with fear and impotent anger. "Sometimes I think they really do though."

More like Rowland had Chrechte spying for him. Not much got past a wolf's hearing. Not even when it was said behind closed doors.

"Rowland is your previous laird?" Sabrine asked, the disgust in her voice when she said his name an exact echo of what was in Verica's heart.

"Aye," Verica affirmed. "The king forced him to step aside so the Sinclairs' second could take the role."

"Barr used to be second-in-command to the laird of the Sinclair clan?" Sabrine sounded like she found that strange indeed.

They all had, no matter how much the clan silently rejoiced at the turn of events. And each and every one of them wondered how long their good fortune could last as well. How long before Barr and his second, Earc, ended up the same way her father had?

The thought of Earc dead hurt in a way Verica refused to acknowledge. The man was not for her.

She nodded as she moved around the room, tidying it. "That's right."

"And he's the most bestest warrior." The awe in Brigit's voice was refreshingly different from the reaction their former leader caused.

"He's big enough." Sabrine's praise sounded grudging.

Very different than the reaction of the other Donegal clanswomen, who did their best to garner the new laird's attention. Not that it had done any of them any good so far. He'd shown not the slightest preference, focusing entirely on improving the protection of their holding.

"But he's fast, too," Brigit said with enthusiasm. "Faster than any of our warriors."

"He's our warrior now, too."

"He lets Rowland stay though." Brigit's opinion of that state of affairs did not have to be spoken aloud; her tone and the way she held her body said it all.

Verica sighed. The new laird did not realize what a treacherous serpent shared his table every mealtime. Which only increased the chance Barr would meet the same fate as her father. Her mother had warned her da, but he had believed himself invincible.

His death had left his raven wife, as well as the rest of their clan, unprotected from Rowland's perfidy.

Just as Barr's inevitable demise would do.

"Has Barr been given a reason to banish this Rowland?" Sabrine asked.

"No."

"You have not spoken to him on the matter?"

"I have no proof of the accusations I wish to make."

They both looked at Brigit. The girl's mother probably had proof of the man's evil, but she would have to be willing to step forward. "I cannot blame another woman for not wanting to levy an accusation. Should something happen to Laird Barr, she would have no one to protect her from Rowland's wrath."

"A woman needs to be able to protect herself." Sabrine sounded quite serious.

"How?" Brigit asked, keen interest glowing in her dark eyes.

"Are the women of your clan not taught to fight?" Sabrine looked appalled.

"No. Women are too weak," Brigit recited one of Rowland's common strictures.

"Ridiculous."

"Do you know how to fight?" Brigit asked their patient.

Sabrine opened her mouth and then closed it, looking torn.

"I won't tell," Brigit promised. "Verica won't, either. She's good at keeping secrets."

Sabrine gave Verica a questioning look.

"Better than my apprentice knows." Bird shifters had to be. Verica's own double-shifter nature would get her killed if it ever became known.

Sabrine nodded then.

"Really? You can fight? Can you teach me?"

That agonized look of indecision crossed Sabrine's face again.

"Maybe when your arm is healed, we can venture into the forest one afternoon," Verica offered by way of an out for the other woman.

She knew too well how hard it was to disappoint Brigit.

"A warrior does not allow injury to hold her back from training." Sabrine was back to appearing as appalled as a nun faced with a loch full of bathing men.

"You're not a soldier, silly. You're a woman." Brigit giggled.

Sabrine's eyes narrowed, as if that truth was not particularly welcome. "Perhaps we can make time tomorrow."

"Maybe my mum could come, too."

"She must," Sabrine replied in a voice that would brook no opposition. "I will make my way to the kitchens tomorrow and invite her on our walk in the forest myself."

Brigit's smile was worth whatever effort it took to take that walk without Rowland or his cronies following. Verica started sifting through her mental list of herbs that could be added to their morning meal that might incapacitate them.

If she was caught, the consequences didn't bear dwelling on. It was terribly risky, but it had to be done.

For Brigit's sake; for all their sakes.

The sound of feminine laughter drifting from his room stopped Barr at the door. The realization that such sounds were not common here like they had been in the Sinclair holding struck him stone still.

A laird was responsible for the well-being of his people. An absence of joy among them was cause for concern, but then so was his blindness to the problem.

He had been living among the Donegals for a month, but he hadn't noticed the lack of laughter until now. It had taken bringing another stranger among them for him to become aware.

To be sure, he'd noticed other things. The separation between the Chrechte of the clan and their human counterparts. Until today, he had not realized just how deep that chasm was. The lack of male Chrechte of an age with himself was also odd. Their children were here, as were some elders, but the pack was not merely small, as Talorc and he had believed before Barr had come to the Donegal holding. It was strangely lopsided.

The wolf waited outside the door, and Sabrine wondered why he did not come in. His scent was partially masked, as if like her, he was always on his guard against detection. Nevertheless, she had become aware of his presence before he had ever reached the door. And her body was already responding in inexplicable and undeniable ways.

Her raven longed to perch in his lap and nuzzle his neck and head.

The woman in her wanted far more than mere nuzzling and the warrior she'd been trained to become was more terrified than at any other time in her life.

For the battle against her instincts might well be lost.

The heavy door swung inward and Brigit's high-pitched, childish laughter ceased abruptly, her face pinching in fear she tried to hide.

Barr came in, his shoulders nearly as wide as the door frame. He was smiling, but there was something around his eyes, a watchful expression that intrigued her. "It appears you two are keeping our guest entertained."

"She was telling a funny story, laird." Having visibly relaxed when she saw Barr, Brigit ducked her head shyly.

Barr reached out and ruffled the girl's hair while giving Sabrine a quizzical look. "Was she now?"

The young girl lifted her eyes, an expression of pure hero-worship and adoration making them shine, and nodded.

"Perhaps she'll have to tell me the story later." Again, he spoke to the child, but his gaze fixed on Sabrine.

The heat there reached out to her like fire jumping from the hearth. And she felt burned in places no man had ever touched.

Sabrine didn't think she'd be telling that particular story, ever. It had been about her knife training. Even a wooden blade hurt if you stabbed yourself hard enough. All she said though was, "Perhaps."

"Come, Brigit, it is past time I returned you to your mother." Verica picked up her basket and curtsied before scooting around Barr to reach the door.

She paused there and turned back to face him. "Wake Sabrine several times throughout the night. She is not showing any signs that need concern us, but the memory loss cannot be ignored."

His glance flicked between Verica and Sabrine, the expression in his storm-cloud eyes unreadable. "The memories must be coming back, if she can remember stories to tell."

"Our minds are not so easy to understand, laird. Sabrine remembers patches, but the blanket of her thoughts is still missing those important pieces about how she came to be in the forest. Some memories she may never regain."

Barr frowned, but nodded. "I will watch over her this night."

And much more if Sabrine was not careful. Though she

would not have believed it possible, his scent grew more potent upon increased familiarity. She had no idea what she would do when he dropped his guard and his scent hit her senses with full impact again. She rarely drank the wine her people were so good at making, but simply being in the same room with him made her feel like she'd imbibed an entire bottle on her own.

According to the heady fragrance of arousal rolling off of him, his reaction to her was every bit as powerful. And that was more than a little worrisome. Bad enough she had to fight her own desires, but standing against his could well prove her downfall.

There was a reason she did not drink wine or even ale. Sabrine did not like the vulnerability of having her senses hampered by the effects of spirits, but this was worse. So much worse. This would not go away with an hour's rest, or by taking to the air.

This reaction he elicited in her would not submit to even *her* control, hardened by her years protecting her people.

He moved further into the room and heat suffused her body, the pulse in her neck fluttering as her mouth went dry. Her hand jerked to her neck of its own volition, covering that betraying flutter.

"See that you do." Verica's bold words showed that she trusted this laird far more than she did Rowland. She trusted him enough *not* to fear him.

Barr inclined his head to her and then Brigit. "Good night then."

"Wait!" Sabrine called out before Verica could leave.

The other woman gave her a sympathetic look, as if she knew what Sabrine was going to ask and what her laird's response was going to be.

"Wouldn't it be more seemly for Verica to sit with me through the night?" She hated asking it of the other woman, particularly since it wasn't necessary because Sabrine had not actually suffered any memory loss, but the alternative was growing more untenable by the moment.

There was no sympathy in Barr's eyes, just more of that burning heat. "'Twould be more unseemly for her to remain the night in my room."

"Then allow me to go to her room." Vexation tinged her words. He was Chrechte. He knew exactly what effect he had on her and probably liked it. Darn it.

"Nay, I'll not give my bed up for the comforts of her floor."

"Are you being deliberately obtuse?"

The sparkle in his gray eyes said he was, but his squared jaw was set stubbornly as well. She was not going anywhere.

It was not in her nature to give in easily though. "Be reasonable. Would you have me branded as no better than a camp follower by your clan?"

"Sleeping in my room is paltry beside the fact you were found naked and alone in the forest."

"I do not think so." But truly? No doubt he was right.

Humans had different standards for women than men, and the Chrechte that lived among them often adopted those same attitudes.

Among her people, she wore a kilt only a couple of inches longer than the male Éan. Wearing such a garment here would be considered scandalous. It was one of the many things that confused her about the human clans.

Why were men and women considered so different? She was a warrior, but her brother never would be. Roles were determined by aptitude and desire among the Éan, but not even the Faol appeared to adhere to such standards any longer, when once their female warriors were considered some of the fiercest to meet in battle.

"I am laird."

"So?"

"So"—he drawled the word out until it was three times longer than usual—"what I think is what matters most."

For some ludicrous reason she was already furious with herself about, she had thought he was different. On the flimsiest of evidence, she had allowed herself to believe a wolf could be something besides the arrogantly cruel executioners of her people. "Of course it is."

He frowned at her. "Was it different among your clan? Or do you not remember?" he asked derisively.

For the derision, she could not blame him. She *was* using the memory loss as a convenient excuse. And he was right. Things were not so unalike among her people. The difference was that she rarely disagreed with her superior among the Éan.

Verica was not so sanguine about Barr's slight, however. She gasped. "That is hardly fair, laird. Sabrine cannot control what she remembers."

Once again, she showed a comforting lack of fear of the man who led her clan.

"I wonder," Barr replied.

"My memory is not the topic under discussion."

"No, your well-being is."

"Exactly. I prefer not to be branded a strumpet."

"Too late."

"Laird!" Verica admonished in a strangled voice.

"No one has said such, but the old biddies are already thinking it because of the circumstances in which I found you." He gave Verica an admonishing frown. "And well you know it, having lived among these people longer than me."

"What you propose will only make it worse," Sabrine insisted.

"I have already announced my intention to keep you."

Sabrine felt the air seize in her chest. Through a riotous confusion of emotions she noted the shocked fascination on both Verica's and Brigit's faces.

Chapter 5

"In my room for the night," Barr continued as if the momentous pause had not occurred. "Whether you actually stay with me or not is no longer of importance."

"That's not true."

"And you will be safer with me than with Verica to watch over you."

"She is a healer."

"Aye. I am a warrior."

"You believe I will be attacked in my bed?" What a ridiculous thought.

But he wasn't smiling, not even around the eyes, and Verica's mouth had twisted with concern.

"Your lack of family and clan affiliation puts you at risk from the less scrupulous. I have not had enough time with the Donegal clan to completely impose my viewpoint on acceptable behavior. The former laird had fewer scruples than myself."

There would be no arguments from her on that particular claim. The reports she'd had of Rowland prior to coming here had made it all too easy to believe the other man capable of stealing the *Clach Gealach Gra*.

What she had not expected was Barr.

"Had you also considered the possibility that your presence in her room could put our healer in peril?" Barr asked. "There is a reason I had her watching over you in my room today. No one would dare breach my sanctum."

Considering the things she had heard today, Sabrine had to further acknowledge the wisdom of his words. Perhaps, just maybe, she also had to revise her belief he was blind to the faults of his new clan.

Clearly he was aware and he had acted to protect not only her but Verica and Brigit as well.

The man was a mass of contradictions. He was a wolf, but he showed no signs of blatant cruelty. He wore arrogance even when he wore nothing else, but here he was explaining his decisions without a sign of rancor. The leaders of the Éan rarely gave as much. When one of the triumvirate spoke, their word was law. No questions, no argument; full obedience was expected.

Sabrine had never had moment to doubt their dictates but if she had, she did not think they would respond with the patience Barr had shown her and his own people.

"She would be safe in my room as no one would know she was there," Verica said quietly in the silence.

"Are you so certain?" Barr asked. "We are not the only Chrechte who make this keep our home."

The blanching of Verica's skin had only one meaning. She was afraid. His reminder had sparked true disquiet in the other woman. Sabrine refused to add to the clanswoman's worries.

"I will stay here. I am sorry I did not take the full import of the situation into consideration." She had only been thinking of herself, of the almost certainty that her raven instincts and feminine desires were about to storm and mayhap destroy her warrior's defenses. She could fight one, but not both. And never before had her raven's impulses been at odds with her self-protective behaviors.

Barr shrugged. "You have naught to apologize for."

"You do not know our clan. You *should* have been safe in my room." The sadness in Verica's demeanor pulled at the heart Sabrine had thought she had long since buried.

"She would be, in the future." Barr's scowl did not bode well for those who might oppose him. "I can only effect so much change at once."

"But you do wish to effect it?" Verica confirmed.

"Aye."

"When the pretty lady leaves, can my mum sleep in your room, laird?" Brigit asked.

Silence descended like darkness after a long sunset. For several beats of Sabrine's heart, no one moved, no one spoke. Brigit looked at her laird with trusting innocence, at odds with the implication of her question.

Verica watched him, too, but with a wary hope that hurt Sabrine to see. This clan had been under the power of a petty tyrant too long.

Barr's expression did not alter, but the heat coming off of him increased tenfold and the sense of impending danger surrounding him became acute. A tic started in his jaw, but he kept the rest of his features in a neutral repose as he turned to face Brigit fully. He dropped to his knee in front of the girl, his attention fixed almost entirely on her—almost because there was a tendril of connection between him and Sabrine even when he was not looking at her, even as he was so clearly furiously thinking of something else. "Is your mum in need of my protection, child?"

Again that fear hung around Brigit like dying prey as she apparently realized her question might have given her mother's secret away.

"Me and Mum are strong." Brigit's words spoken with

a quivering lip and pleading voice about broke Sabrine's rapidly waking heart. Coming among these people would carry consequences she had not anticipated and that she feared would be long lasting.

Barr nodded, his expression somber, that tic in his jaw increasing in tempo. "Aye, you are. You've managed well without your da, but you understand I am your laird?"

Tugging on a hank of her cinnamon-colored hair, Brigit nodded.

Barr made a noise of satisfaction, like the girl's acknowledgment had pleased him. "'Tis my job to protect you in his place."

Instead of looking comforted, the girl's face crumpled. "Mum says no one can help her, but she'll not let anything happen to me."

"She loves you as she should, but you love her, too."

"I do." Brigit nodded so vigorously the tears standing in her eyes spilled down her cheeks.

Barr growled so low only Sabrine's Chrechte hearing allowed her to hear it. His wolf was more than furious: the sound was one of bloodletting. But when he spoke, the laird's voice was soft, almost gentle. "I know you are worried about her, but I *will* take care of the problem now."

"You give your solemn oath?" Brigit asked, so clearly still torn.

"I do."

Verica's heart rate increased, her expression showing both fear and hope. The healer wanted her laird to protect her apprentice's mother, but she was obviously unsure he could do so.

Barr looked at the healer, measurement in his gaze. Finally, he nodded as if giving her an oath as well.

Her eyes widened and then she smiled, the expression natural and saturated with relief.

"Fetch Earc and your brother."

The woman nodded, determination and purpose setting

her face in almost harsh lines, before curtsying and leaving to do just that.

Barr laid his hand on the child's shoulder. "Come and tell me the story that had you laughing earlier."

Like Sabrine and Verica earlier, the laird apparently realized that taxing the child for answers would not be fair. Brigit had promised her mother and forcing her to break that promise would be dishonorable.

Whatever else this Faol might be, he was no bully and he clearly had honor.

"Did you really train Cathal and Lais alongside Muin today?" the child asked, showing she knew well how to keep all her secrets.

Where she'd learned the need for such subterfuge hurt Sabrine to consider.

"Aye, lass, I did. They acquitted themselves well, too."

"They're my cousins," Brigit said with pride. "Rowland would not train them but they both want to know how to defend their family."

Sabrine got the idea the girl was not talking about the greater clan. The expression on Barr's face said he'd caught the distinction, too, and didn't like it. Though he did not upbraid the child, nor did he let so much as a frown find its way toward her.

"They made a good start on it today." Barr's voice was laced with approval.

The child smiled, the expression reaching her soft brown eyes and making them sparkle. "Are you going to keep training them?"

"I am, though some days it will be Earc working with them."

Brigit seemed to think this over for a moment and then she gave a tiny approving jerk of her head. "He's almost as strong as you."

"You think so?" Sabrine teased Brigit. "It is hard to believe anyone is as big as your laird."

"Oh, he's not, just *almost*," Brigit said solemnly.

But Barr's eyes were now fixed on Sabrine. "You find me overlarge?" Seductive and rich, his tone touched her in her very core.

For the first time in memory, she found herself unable to utter a word as images of his full nakedness flashed in her mind's eye.

"Certainly, I would not call you small," she managed to force out with some semblance of calm.

"Our laird is bigger than any other warrior in the Highlands." Brigit's absolute delight in that fact shone through her face and voice.

"Except my twin brother."

"You have a twin?" Brigit asked with awe.

There were two of them? The thought made Sabrine light-headed.

"Aye, Niall replaced me as second to the Sinclair when I left."

"Is he as handsome as you?" Brigit asked and then blushed.

"Though he has a fierce scar from battle, the one he loves thinks he is more handsome than me and that is all that matters."

Brigit's wide-eyed stare declared her fascination.

"When we were much younger, our clan was betrayed by one who should have protected us with her life."

"So you think women can be warriors, too?" Brigit asked with awe.

"Nay, but they should know how to fight for their clan if necessary and protect themselves."

While Sabrine did not agree with the first part of his statement, Barr's thinking was more forward than the man who had led this clan before him.

"Will you be teaching the women?" Brigit asked in a hope-filled tone.

Before Barr could answer a knock sounded at the door.

"Come."

The door swung open and Verica entered, followed closely by a dark-haired warrior who looked near to an age of Barr. He was almost as big as the laird, and his countenance was nearly as fierce as well. They were not men she would willingly go up against; perhaps Rowland would be as wise.

Another, much younger man was behind him. This youth's resemblance to Verica was unmistakable. Right down to his black hair with almost burgundy streaks. He was a raven and a double shifter as well.

Sabrine's thoughts whirled as this near impossibility settled in her knowledge. What strange clan were these Donegals? Certainly, they were far different from anything she had expected, from their new laird to their dual shifters.

She had not known any ravens survived among the Faol. Learning of their existence brought many assumptions her people made into question.

While the boy who must be Circin's wolf scent surrounded him like a blanket on a cold day, there was no hint of his raven nature in the air around them. Which confirmed one supposition she was almost certain of: the wolves were unaware of the presence of the Éan among them. She scrutinized Circin, looking for some sign of what his special Chrechte gift might be.

Sabrine's ability to alter the perception of others was not readily apparent to even other ravens. She used it to "hide" her clan markings in the forest with Barr, her blue raven on her back and the dagger under it that represented her role as a protector of her people.

If she *were* to take a mate, a blooming vine would be added to symbolize the hope for their future. She had no plans for that marking to ever be inked into her skin.

Circin was looking at her just as closely, while the man that must be Earc had his attention fixed on Verica.

The healer was doing her best to pretend she did not

notice, but the connection between the two of them may as well have been a bright red ribbon, it was so obvious.

"You wished to see us, laird?" Circin asked, his voice still showing signs of his youth.

"I did." Barr's gaze dropped to Brigit. "I have a concern regarding Sorcha. You, Earc and Verica will spend the night in her cottage. Tomorrow, I will have answers to my questions."

"Am I right in assuming there are to be no other visitors this night?" Earc asked, his voice deep and tinged with curiosity.

"Aye."

Brigit was staring at her laird in wide-eyed shock. "*The healer* is to sleep in *our* home this night?" Obviously, the girl's hero-worship was not limited to her new laird.

"That is right."

"But what if *he* gets angry?" It was the closest Brigit had come to naming her mother's tormentor or firmly acknowledging his existence.

"Who are you frightened of?" Verica asked and then looked like she wished she'd kept her mouth closed.

Brigit's agitation spiked in the air around them and Sabrine simply could not stand it any longer. "Come here, young one."

Without hesitating, the girl came and climbed to sit beside Sabrine on the bed.

Sabrine took her hand, projecting a warm light around them the others would not see. Brigit's eyes rounded.

"Is there any warrior in this clan who could defeat Earc, do you think?"

"Only our laird."

"But he is not the one who causes your distress?"

Brigit shook her head vehemently.

"Then you have naught to fear this night."

"But what about tomorrow?"

"You must trust your laird to have considered the

morrow." Sabrine sincerely hoped her confidence in the giant man was not misplaced.

And then Barr was there, laying his big hand on the small girl's back. "I willna allow any to hurt your dam."

"She didna want me to tell anyone." Tears were close to the surface in the girl's voice and the trembling of her lip.

"Aye, and you've told us naught, but your innocent question. Your dam will not blame you."

"I promised."

"You've broken no promise." Barr's gentle demeanor with the child touched Sabrine's soul.

How could this man be the alpha of the pack that had stolen the ravens' sacred talisman?

"You will still go for a walk in the forest with us tomorrow?" Brigit asked Sabrine anxiously.

"I will."

"You'll not be leaving this bed." Barr's tone carried the weight of his position as laird and pack leader.

She ignored it. "I will."

"No."

"Yes."

"You are wounded." He sounded like he was trying to be reasonable and could not understand her recalcitrance.

"It is not so great I must languish in bed." Allowing him to believe she was a helpless human was one thing, but having him believe she needed to be bedridden defeated her purpose of searching for the Heart of the Moon stone.

Instead of arguing with her as she expected, Barr gave her a calculated look laced with a good deal of heat.

Just when she realized it might have been a tad precipitous to argue her relative good health just before spending the night under his watch, Earc said, "I believe it is time we took our leave."

No doubt the other wolf could smell Barr's increasing level of arousal just like she could. How embarrassing. She'd never been in such a situation before. Other males had wanted her, but not with the level of desire clouding the air around them so thickly she was surprised they could not see it. But the worst part was not how his wolf was reacting to her. It was how *she* was responding to him.

Her arousal drifted in the air around them as well, defying even the sick feeling she had about Brigit's mother's apparent predicament.

Earc's lips twitched and Sabrine knew he could scent her arousal as well as his laird's. She glared at him.

Barr's second gave her a startled look.

"You need not rush off," she insisted.

"Oh, I think there is every need."

Circin seemed vaguely embarrassed while his sister gave Sabrine a commiserating look. "If we do not return Brigit to her mother soon, Sorcha will worry."

Knowing when defeat loomed, Sabrine inclined her head in acknowledgment. "Then you must go."

"There is no need to sound like they are leaving you to a horrific fate. My care may not have the skill of the healer, but you will be safe from others this night."

She noted he did not promise she would be safe from him. The man might be a scoundrel, planning things she had never done but could guess at all too easily. However, he was no liar.

Sabrine turned her attention to the child. "All will be well. You must trust in this."

"I will try."

Sabrine nodded and reached for the child with an instinct that superseded even her Chrechte nature. Brigit accepted a tight hug, returning it fiercely before climbing off the bed to join Verica, Earc and Circin at the door.

They left with quiet assurances of Sorcha's welfare this night and last-minute instructions from Verica to Barr regarding Sabrine's care.

Sabrine knew the other woman had tried, but she doubted those final words would protect her from Barr's passion. Not when hers simmered right at the surface, waiting to boil over and join his.

Barr had never been so sorely tempted by a woman before.

While he had not always agreed with Talorc's strict stance on physical mating, neither did he see it as something to be indulged in for the sake of nothing more than a few hours of temporary pleasure. Joining his body with another carried the weight of possibly true bonding, and that was not a risk to be dismissed lightly. He had been more than lucky his first foray into sexual intimacy had not led to the tie forming; bad enough it had cost him two dear friends.

His fellow warrior's possessiveness of his true bond mate had made continued friendship impossible between him and Barr once he learned she had surrendered her virginity to the other man. As for the woman, neither she nor Barr had been comfortable in one another's presence again after the debacle of that one coupling.

Once a Chrechte developed a sacred or true bond with his mate, he would become incapable of performing sexually with anyone else while his mate lived. Barr didn't understand it any better than he did the miracle of his animal form and nature. He knew the truth of it, however, and had been sexually circumspect because of it.

Only a fool would not realize the strong reaction he had to Sabrine could well lead to a sacred mate bond. And Barr was far from being a fool. His wolf was drawn to the mysterious raven-haired woman in a way it had never been to another person.

In the usual way of things, he would take time to get to know the woman his wolf was so intent upon having. He would carefully consider whether she would make a suitable mate before acting on his baser urges. But this was no ordinary reaction.

His wolf was demanding instant action and his body's cravings were making that demand near impossible to ignore.

The wolf howled for release, Barr's libido ached with need and his mind fought them both. Still looking for an explanation of the sense of *other* he could not dismiss from his memory, his brain worried at this problem as well. How could she lie to him and he not smell it? For lie to him he was certain she had.

His beautiful, alluring Sabrine had no more lost her memory than he had. What her game was, he couldna fathom, but it was clear she'd been genuinely distressed about whatever was going on with Brigit's mother, Sorcha.

Sabrine's obvious compassion only made Barr desire her more, but her equally apparent deception prevented him from trusting her completely.

Could he bed a woman he did not trust? His wolf howled, "Yes." His cock jerked in response and he was no closer to resolution of his inner conflict than before.

"You look like you are contemplating invading England, but you smell like you want to invade me." Naught in her tone revealed what she felt about that, but the words themselves revealed much.

And he knew. He did not understand, but he knew it must be true. "You are Chrechte, but you hide your wolf nature so well, even I could not sense it."

"I am no part of the Faol." The loathing with which she spoke the word *Faol* left no room for doubt.

Yet . . . "You must be. You are no mere human."

"Humans have their own strength."

"Yes, they do, but *you* are Chrechte."

She did not deny it, but her mouth set in a stubborn line that told him without words she would not answer.

"And you haven't forgotten anything, except perhaps how to tell the truth."

That should be all he needed to rein in his libido, but her

stubbornness and equally undeniable strength laid waste to the last of his defenses. This woman was his match.

Eyes the color of warm earth rich with sustenance narrowed dangerously. "You call me a liar?"

"Nay." He'd learned from Talorc's mistakes with his wife and Barr would not make such an accusation without understanding the entirety of a situation.

He would not soon forget the result of Talorc's idiocy with his own wife. His friend had expressed deep sorrow and regret to Barr since then, but naught could undo the memory for any of them.

"I do not call you a liar, but I do believe you hide the truth from me."

Her frown turned lethal, but she remained mute and unmoving.

"You do not lie by nature, do you?"

"No." The word held an entire hour's discourse of meaning.

"You find it beyond you to heap one lie on top of another to protect the first," he further postulated.

"If I was lying, you should be able to tell, being the superior Chrechte warrior that you are."

"My senses say one thing, but my instincts another." And how was that possible, he wondered.

"You trust your instincts over your wolf's senses?"

"In this instance? I do." For, while his wolf could not smell the lie, it paced restlessly inside him, sure not all was as it seemed. Those same instincts told him to claim her, too. And he would not deny them.

He approached the bed, his mind settled about one thing at least. He would have her this night.

Chapter 6

Barr came toward the bed like a cat on the prowl, not the wolf that he was, sending a shiver of anticipation touched by nerves through Sabrine's raven nature. His storm-cloud eyes watched her with the power of the ancient priests that once served their combined peoples. Before the Faol decided the Éan did not deserve to be Chrechte.

The oral histories spoke of those times; they spoke of priests and healers and leaders, but they did not tell the tale of a wolf who could capture a raven with nothing but his gaze.

Nothing to prepare her for meeting Barr of the Donegal clan. No story that might help her know what to do with feelings so powerful they decimated the stronghold of her control and forged desires that would not be denied. No matter that she was absolutely certain that to mate with a wolf would be terrifyingly dangerous.

Her mind screamed warnings as her body prepared itself for the inevitable joining with his wolf. Her mind insisted she not submit, but her body had gone deaf.

For the first time in her life, Sabrine's mind was not in charge, her vaunted control buried under the burning coals of her desire. Her raven instincts demanded resolution for the need clenching her womb and drawing moisture from her core. Nipples that had never known the pleasure of a lover's touch beaded into tight buds of near-painful longing.

Muscles that usually tensed in preparation for battle relaxed, allowing her legs to fall open slightly beneath the blanket.

Barr's nostrils flared as the scent of her arousal permeated the air around them. He pulled the blanket back when he reached the bed. And she let him, making no move to hide her waiting nakedness from his gaze. Her body's yearning overshadowed any hope she had to pull away from this joining.

He inhaled deeply, his eyes going heavy-lidded. "You want me."

"Yes." There was no point denying it to him or herself.

Not when the spicy scent of her need was all around them.

"I'll have you this night." The statement was arrogance itself, but something in his tone alerted her to the fact it was meant as a question.

He was seeking her agreement, showing he had more self-control than she. He would stop if she demanded it. She did not think *she* could.

But she was no meek maiden to suffer his domination. "We will have each other."

He smiled, the expression feral. "You would have had me believe you a fragile woman, in need of protection."

"I am." Not fragile, perhaps, but definitely in need of protection. So were her people, but no Faol, not even this one who showed such concern for a human female's safety, would offer such.

"Perhaps, but you are Chrechte and strong, though you deny it."

She'd never denied being Chrechte, not once. Though

she'd denied being wolf. She could not make her lips utter a falsehood of such personal affront.

Explaining such would give away secrets she could not allow into the light.

He did not wait for a reply, nor did he seem to expect one. He simply rid himself of his plaid and weapons with short, efficient movements, revealing his magnificent warrior's body. He might not share his twin's facial scar, but Barr was by no means unmarked. Along with his Chrechte markings on his bicep and back, he had several small scars obviously obtained in battle. Each one made him that much more alluring to her. A man who fought and received wounds in the effort to protect those he called clan was a man she could admire on every level.

Even if he was a wolf.

Regardless of the sexual need coming off him, he took the time to put his daggers where they could easily be reached if he had a need.

Her own trained warrior instincts could not help noting what it would require for her to reach them, too.

He laughed as he put one knee on the bed, the sound low and seductive, sending quakes of longing through her.

"What amuses you?" She'd never been further from joviality.

"You calculated the distance to my daggers as I put them away." The knowing smile on his face was reflected in his voice.

"And you find that worthy of laughter?"

"I find your attempt to play the maiden in distress more than worthy."

His assurance of her deception did not seem to have made him angry.

"I am what I am." He could take that how he liked. She was beyond dissembling.

"And I am eager to discover exactly what that means."

It wouldn't happen, but telling him so would probably

make the daft laird laugh again. "I do not want to desire you." That was one piece of honesty she could share.

"Why?"

"You are a dangerous man for me to mate."

"So you feel it, too?"

"I thought it was obvious."

"I wonder what your voice will sound like in my mind," he said as he lowered his head to capture her lips for her first kiss.

And it was only as the words repeated in her conscious mind that she realized they'd been talking about two very different aspects of mating. She'd meant sexual intimacy.

He thought they were *true mates*.

God would not be so cruel.

No matter how appealing his person, or how intriguing his character, she could not be true mates with a wolf. Heaven would not play such a vicious trick on her.

Her disturbed thoughts splintered as his lips moved with possessiveness against hers. The taste was incredible, like spices and fresh water from the spring. Intoxicated by his nearness, she was glad to be lying down. Were she standing, she did not think she would remain upright.

She'd never known such sensations.

In her whole life, she had never considered her mouth such a bastion of sexual temptation, but the feel of his lips against hers went clear to the depths of her soul and back again.

His tongue flicked along the seam of her lips in a silent demand her body instinctively knew how to respond to. She let her lips part, giving him access to the inner recess beyond. His tongue took instant advantage, intensifying the amazing flavor scoring her senses.

He ravaged her with a warrior's power and she returned the kiss with her own feminine need to meet him strength to strength, desire to desire, softness to hardness. Neither superior to the other, and yet no question that his body was bigger, his muscles more powerful. He should frighten her, but he did not. She found his size and strength unbearably exciting, especially so close to her unencumbered nudity.

He was all she could have ever wanted in a mate and yet was the one man she could not invite into her true life. Nevertheless, she would enjoy this moment of pleasure while she had it. She had known little enough joy in her life; she would not reject this moment her raven insisted was hers. She would never know such pleasure again, of that she was irrevocably convinced—she hadn't thought to know it now. But while she dwelt among his people she would indulge in the carnally feminine side of her raven and human natures both.

He reared back, his huge body shimmering in the torchlight. "You taste like the food of the gods."

She smiled at his exaggeration. "I taste like a woman."

"*My* woman."

"For tonight."

"Forever."

She could not make her mouth utter a denial, but nor would she allow it to speak agreement.

He flexed his big muscles, making them bulge in ways that had her raven trilling with desire. He was not Éan, but he understood the need to display his strength and prowess for her, to draw her raven closer to the surface than Sabrine had allowed it since making the change in the air as she fell to the earth. She reached up and nuzzled into his neck with her nose in instinctive response, her raven seeking connection to his wolf.

A look of satisfaction came over his features as he inhaled deeply. "I can smell you now. Not your wolf, but your otherness is there for me. Only for me."

"Only for you." She could not risk allowing it to be exposed amongst the rest of his clan.

There was a reason Verica kept her raven nature subdued,

and her brother did as well. Sabrine could guess what it was, too.

The rest of the Faol did not have Barr's tolerance for *other*.

She reached up and caressed his face, the stubble of his blond day's growth scratching against her palm. "You are a special man, Barr, unlike others of your kind."

"I am glad you think so." His voice resounded with confidence.

Shaking her head, she grinned. "You are also too arrogant for your own good."

"So you say."

"I do."

"Maybe I should prevent more accusations from coming out of that lovely mouth." His gray gaze caressed her lips, making them tingle and part as if the look was a kiss in itself.

"Perhaps you should." If it meant more of that most pleasurable kissing, she was all for it.

He bent down and once again claimed her lips with passion she had no difficulty matching. In fact, it was so easy, it frightened her.

What would she do when she had to leave this man behind? For leave she must. Her life and the future of her people depended on it.

Calloused fingers brushed up her side until one giant hand cupped the small curve of her breast. He teased her nipple with his thumb until she thought she would come off the bed. Each swipe of his thumb against the tender bud sent a matching spear of pleasure through her womb, making the flesh between her legs contract as well.

Heated sexual approval radiated between them. "You are so responsive."

"You have many to compare me to?" she asked, making no effort to hide the irritation such a thought caused her.

His light brown brows rose as his lips twitched. "Not so many."

"How many?" she demanded, her hands clenching against the stonelike contours of his chest.

No man should be this strong. Nor this irresistible.

"One, maybe two."

"Which is it? One or two?" she demanded, her agitation growing.

"My laird discouraged sex for anything but a committed mating."

She recognized the distraction for what it was, but she could not help observing, "Doesn't that prevent some of the Faol from controlling their change?"

"Until they have had sex? Yes." Subtle tension drained from the set of his shoulders.

"That does not sound strategically sound."

"He believes some things are more important than strategy."

"Like love?"

Barr laughed, the warmth of it going through her in a wholly different kind of pleasure. "Maybe now he's found love with his wife, but not before. No, he considered the possibility of creating a sacred bond in a casual or badly conceived pairing something to be avoided at all costs."

There was something more there, she could hear it in her beautiful warrior's voice. "Why?"

"His father true mated an Englishwoman who betrayed our clan, causing our laird's death and that of many of our best warriors."

The woman who had caused his brother's scarring had been their laird's sacred mate. The pain that had caused the pack was in every line of his rugged features. "She was human?"

"Aye."

"It is too easy to underestimate their strength."

"That is what the Balmoral's wife says."

The Balmoral lived on an island and the Éan knew little about them. "Does she?"

"Aye, being human herself and having brought the Balmoral to his knees, I think she might well be right."

"It is the Faol my people watch most closely," she admitted.

He gave her a strange look but did not demand she explain further and for that she was grateful. She could not do so without betraying the Éan and she would die before doing that.

"So, one or two?" she asked again, when it became clear he thought he had sidestepped her last question so neatly.

He sighed, his big body pressing against hers. "Two."

"That does not make me happy," she said, not really understanding her own reaction but uninterested in pretense.

"I can tell that it does not." His eyes devoured her with their concern. "Neither woman was a lover."

"What does that mean?" He'd had sex with them. He'd just said so.

"One was a widow grieving the loss of her husband."

"So, you were just comforting her?" Sabrine asked, the sarcasm dripping like vinegar from her voice.

He looked relieved. "Yes, that was it exactly."

"How lovely for her."

This time he didn't miss her undertone and his wince gave her some measure of satisfaction.

"And the other?" she asked.

"I did not wish to live without control of the change."

"So?"

"So, I found a willing partner and had sex the night of a hunt."

The burnished lines of his cheeks said this had neither been particularly pleasant nor a moment he was proud of.

"Was she Faol?"

"Aye. We were both much too young. She was one of the rare female wolves not born with control of her change. It humiliated her."

"So, you agreed to take care of each other's problem."

"Aye. I lost two of my closest friends because of it."

"Why?" Sabrine did not understand the terrible outcome if the female had been willing. Unless . . . "Did she develop feelings for you that you did not return?"

That Sabrine could understand far too well for her own liking.

He made a sound of bitter amusement. "Not at all. She found my company embarrassing afterward. If I am honest, I will admit I found hers equally so. Though it made no sense to me."

His perplexity was almost amusing. He gave himself no quarter to experience weak emotion, but then neither did she. "You said two friends? Was the other her brother?" Or maybe her father?

"One of my closest friends turned out to be her true mate. He challenged me after realizing I had had her innocence."

"You did not kill him."

"Nay, but our friendship was buried that day."

"I'm sorry." That he had lost a friend, but Sabrine was still bothered he'd had sex with these other women. And she could not pretend to be sorry Barr was no longer friends with the female.

"I'm sorry I cannot come to you as untouched as you come to me." The sincerity in his tone assuaged some of the negative feelings plaguing her.

"It should not matter," she admitted.

"But it does."

"Yes."

"I can only promise you my fidelity from this point forward."

"Don't." *Please*. She pleaded with him with her eyes though she did not say the word aloud.

His narrowed. "Neither of us will have a choice."

"You truly believe that?" she asked, half afraid of his answer.

"Aye. You do not?"

"No." If she did, she'd be out of his bed and out of his

room faster than he could blink. *Her* true mate did not exist, and if he did, he wasn't a wolf.

"One of us is wrong."

"Yes."

"You are confident it is me."

"I am." And part of her, a really stupid part, was even saddened by that fact.

He grinned. "Let's find out, shall we?"

For a single moment, terror unlike anything she had ever known paralyzed her. What if he was right? What if he was the mate she was so certain did not exist for her?

But he couldn't be. Faol and Éan matings were rare. Of those that had happened, too many ended in betrayal and death for the Éan.

Her raven insisted sharing intimacy with this man would not hurt her; Sabrine had to believe her bird. The raven had never led her astray, not even once.

"Let's." She reached around his body, pulling him down onto her to resume those amazing kisses.

This time, he moved against her as his tongue pressed between her lips. He dwarfed her, filling her senses until nothing but him existed for her. The hardness against her body was every bit as big as the rest of him. She had no idea how they were supposed to fit together, but that was one problem she would gladly leave in his hands. She was busy coming to terms with the fire running through her veins as their bodies rubbed together in an imitation of the act to come.

She might never have experienced sex, but the Éan did not have taboos about sexual intimacy as found among the clans.

His hand moved between her legs, touching her in a spot that had her screaming into his mouth. The joy was so intense, the pleasure so immense, she could not hold it inside.

One big finger slid inside her, not deep, but just far enough that she could not ignore its foreign presence.

She whimpered and could not even work up a smidgen of embarrassment for it. He was inside her even if his member was not and the moment was so intimate, she had no other standard by which to compare it.

Other than her younger brother, she allowed no one to get close to her and this was beyond close. This was *joining*. For this moment in time, they were not Faol and Éan. They were two in the making of one flesh. He male. She female. Together one, both and neither wholly.

The finger pressed further inside and pain pulsed in her core. It was so unexpected, she could not help reacting to it.

Her sound of distress had him lifting his mouth, his breathing harsh. "I will try not to hurt you, but your body's barrier must give way."

And there would be tearing and blood. She had heard of what was to come, but to experience it was beyond anything she could have imagined.

She would not let something that women, no matter their kind, be they human or Chrechte, had been prey to for millennia hold her from this moment. "The pain is part of it."

"It can be a very small part." He kissed her softly, on the corner of her mouth.

"How do you know?"

"My widow told me, when I confessed the dismal failure of my first time."

"I do not want to hear about the widow. She is not yours, is she? You did not claim her." Her raven's feathers ruffled; Sabrine did not like him speaking of the other woman in that possessive way. Not at all.

"Nay, I did not." He caressed her face, brushing the hair back from Sabrine's face. "She has remarried."

"Then do not call her yours," Sabrine instructed testily even as she melted under his affectionate ministrations.

"As you wish, little spitfire."

"I am only little beside you." Even a wild boar would be little beside the giant warrior.

He shrugged, his finger shifting inside her, brushing back and forth with tiny movements. She could not decide if she wanted to press down, gaining more of the sensation, or pull away from the small sting of pain. His thumb slid over that place of intense pleasure again and deciding, she arched up, pressing herself further onto his finger. The connection was so small and yet so big. Overwhelming.

Forcing her to become fully aware of herself as a Chrechte female for the first time.

Chapter 7

———————

In this bed her role as warrior was far away. Her commitment to protecting her people did not dominate her thoughts. Instead, carnal yearning had her seized in its voracious grip.

"You are so beautiful." He growled the words, his voice deep with a sincerity she could not question.

She had never considered herself such and told him so.

His growl this time was subvocal and pure masculine displeasure. "You are everything I dreamed of in a mate and never thought to have."

"We are not mates." They could not be. She refused to entertain the possibility.

He gave her a secretive smile that made mockery of her willful self-declarations. "We shall see."

"Your wolf is wrong," she insisted. "I am not your mate." Her raven would never lead her into such an untenable situation.

She could think of nothing worse than to discover her sacred mate and have to leave him. Except leading the Faol to the last of her people so they could be destroyed.

"My wolf is never wrong."

"He is this time . . . ahhh . . ." His thumb flicked against her pleasure spot, sending her into a haze of desire-filled bliss in which there was no room for arguments or protestations.

Then he lowered his mouth, not to press against her lips, but to suck up a mark on her neck. The prospect of carrying his claim on her body, even for the short while it would take for the bruise to heal, sent a cataclysm of emotion pouring through her.

Her perception grew disjointed after that as his mouth and hands learned her body in a way she had never expected to experience. He caressed her breasts and the undersides of her legs. He nibbled on her shoulder, nuzzling her in a way that sent her raven into ecstasy. He tasted her, brushing his body along hers, combining their scents until she thought hers would never be entirely her own again.

He allowed her the same liberty with his big, scarred body, his muscles rippling beneath her fingertips with every caress. He tasted like the untamed wind, his wolf close to the surface just as her raven was. And instead of fearing the beast she longed to meet it.

After long agonizing minutes of building pleasure, he put his mouth on her there, between her legs . . . on that most intimate flesh, his tongue taking over for his thumb, drawing forth excitations unimaginable.

The sensations spiraled up and up and up until she felt her perceptions shatter and her body convulse in an agony of pleasure she was sure no other woman could have ever known. It was so much, so intense, she thought she might die of it, that her heart might stop, but it continued to beat a frantic tattoo in her breast. And his finger pressed forward and the sting of full penetration past her maidenhead mixed with the pleasure, adding an edge that both enhanced and detracted.

She cried out, the sound coming from her throat that of woman beyond her endurance and yet exultant at the same time.

He touched her, causing mini quakes throughout her body until she lost all tension in her limbs and melted into the ticking under her.

He reared up, his magnificent body on display for her once again, and her raven could not help preening inside her.

"Are you ready for the joining?"

She did not tell him they were already joined, for she wasn't about to admit such a weak sentiment. Nor did she say she was ready, because she wasn't sure that she was. What she did do was smile, allowing the full extent of the pleasure he'd given her show in her satiated gaze.

His eyes turned smoky black and he lifted her hips, pressing forward with that magnificent male sex against her open flesh. The bulbous tip pressed inside, bringing both intense pleasure and the sensation of being stretched and stretched and stretched some more.

"Good?" he asked, his brow beaded with sweat.

"Yes."

He rocked forward, slipping further inside. She closed her eyes, concentrating on exactly what she was feeling. There was more than a physical connection. Far more. He was mystical and spiritual and utterly terrifying. The shimmer of magic she felt at the change tingled between them, though neither was calling on their Chrechte nature. His sex filled her, but it felt like it was going beyond her own warm depths. He filled her with his very essence and her soul reached forth into his.

As the blunt head of his member hit the depth of her channel, her body clenched in another shattering climax. Her raven cawed the Chrechte word for mate in her mind, filling the silent cavern inside her, the place that had been empty since the death of her parents.

Her eyes snapped open and she met his, their smoky depths awash with a tenderness she could not understand. He was wolf. She was raven.

This moment in time might well destroy her.

But perhaps it was worth it. For the first time in years, the loneliness that was her constant companion dissipated under the heat of his presence, both inside and around her.

Her younger brother had been raised by their aunt and uncle while she started training at an early age to be a protector of her people. While she called the others family, the truth of her life since her parents' death and Sabrine was named warrior had been a searing aloneness never once breached, much less decimated as Barr had done with his touch.

She ached with the knowledge that were Barr not wolf, she would adore him. As it was, they could never mate. Sabrine and Barr could not make the family all Chrechte longed for.

Tears slid down her cheeks as the pleasure rolled through her in wave after wave, finally drawing forth his rapture, his seed exploding from his sex to warm her very depths, his body going rigid in the richness of pleasure so devastating, it verged on the edge of death.

"Mine," he shouted in ancient Chrechte.

And her raven unstoppably answered in the affirmative.

He kissed away the tears and then just kissed, her temples, her face, finally her lips.

They were still connected intimately when she slipped into sleep.

Tarc let Verica explain to Sorcha why they were there. He'd thought Barr's edict might come better from another woman, but Sorcha's upset and confusion were plain. She did her best to ignore his and Circin's presence while arguing with Verica.

Brigit stood to the side, her small face creased in worry, her gaze jumping between her mother and the healer and back again.

Earc thought one of the women should see the girl's need for comfort and deal with it.

When neither did, he reached out and patted Brigit's back, careful to rein in his strength. "All will be well."

Her head jerked around and she looked at him with wide eyes. He tried to give her a reassuring smile.

She flinched.

He caught Verica's gaze and gave her a glare meant to let her know she needed to fix this.

A smile twitched at the corner of her lips and she smoothed her hand down Brigit's hair. "Don't be scared. He's not as frightening as he looks."

Earc released a growl to let her know he was not amused. He'd wanted her to comfort the child over her mother's clear upset; there was no need to reassure her about Earc.

He was not the problem here.

Though the way Sorcha looked at him said otherwise.

"But I've no need for a guard." The lie was a rancid thing in the air around them, mixing with her desperation, making his hackles rise.

Verica put her hand on the lovely widow's arm, the healer's expression compassionate but firm. "We both know that's not true, I think."

Sorcha's gaze slid to her daughter as she hugged herself. "What has Brigit been saying?" Her tone held no accusation, nor any anger; instead it was laced with fear and sadness.

"I didn't say anything, Mum. I didn't."

Sorcha pulled her daughter to her, hugging her tight. "It's all right, sweeting. I am not angry."

"But I didn't break my promise."

"Indeed, she did not," Verica affirmed. "But the fact something is very wrong has become apparent."

Sorcha's gaze darted to the door of the cottage, her agitation showing in the shallowness of her breathing. "Her da is dead, that is problem enough."

"Aye, it is, and how he came to die is no doubt part of it."

Sorcha released her daughter and gave Earc a worried look. "He was ravaged by a wild beast when he was hunting."

Her attempt at lying was so poor, Earc winced. Clearly, the woman believed her husband had died in some other fashion.

She frowned at him. "You doubt my word?"

"Yes."

Sorcha gasped, her face draining of color.

Verica pulled the other woman into a comforting embrace. "Do not worry yourself so. You are safe and will remain so." The scowl she sent Earc would be worthy of any soldier. "Earc did not mean to say he thinks you are lying."

"Yes, I did." And the female wolf knew it. Why was she dissembling to the human?

Verica let go of Sorcha and marched over to Earc. "Be so kind as to step outside with me." The words barely made it past her clenched teeth.

Damned if she was not twice as appealing angry.

"Barr said we were to stay with the woman," he reminded Verica.

"The woman has a name. *Sorcha*."

Did she think he'd forgotten? "I know."

Verica's fists landed on her hips and her ire increased until it made Earc's blood pound—though with an entirely different emotion.

"Then do her the courtesy of using it when you refer to her," Verica snapped.

He bowed his head toward Sorcha. "It was not my intention to offend."

She stared between him and Verica with wide eyes very much like her daughter's. "I'm not offended."

He nodded and gave Verica his most patient look. "You see? I did not offend Sorcha."

"You offended me."

"I won't win this argument, will I?"

"No."

"Are you going to remain angry?" He'd hoped his laird's assignment would give Earc an opportunity to talk with her.

With her multicolored hair unlike any he had seen on a woman, Chrechte or otherwise, and her curious mixture of compassion and fiery temper, the healer had fascinated him since his arrival to the Donegal holding.

"Are you going to continue acting like an arrogant warrior with no sense of tact?"

"Is that how I've been acting?" Were warriors supposed to be polite weaklings in her mind?

"Yes."

"Then, probably."

Circin barked out a laugh and Earc turned to him. The youth quickly clamped his jaw shut, but humor lurked in his eyes.

"I will remember your laughter tomorrow during training."

Circin blanched with satisfying speed, but his beautiful sister made the sound of a pot boiling over. "You dare to threaten my brother? Do you forget that one day he will be your laird?"

"He'll never be my laird," Earc informed her with absolute certainty.

"Barr promised he would relinquish the clan leadership on or before Circin's twenty-fifth year. Do you say he lied?" She was determined to make him angry.

But he would not be drawn. "My leader would never lie, even to get a harping female over her unjustified upset."

"Did you just call me a harpy?"

The air around them simmered with her fury. It was a welcome change over Sorcha's fear. Even the cook seemed more intent on the exchange between them than her own predicament at the moment.

"I believe the point here is that Earc does not intend to stay with the Donegal clan after his friend steps down from his role as laird," Circin inserted before Earc could answer.

Verica stiffened and turned an unreadable expression on him. "Is that what you meant?"

"Aye. Mostly. Once Barr moves Circin into second-in-command, it is likely I will return to my place with the Sinclairs."

"What place is that?"

"A Sinclair warrior." It was all he had ever wanted to be.

"You will not consider staying?" Circin asked with a sidelong glance at his sister.

Earc shrugged. No one knew what the future might bring. A year ago, he would have sworn he would never leave his clan. "It's at least a few years off and not worthy of proper consideration right now."

Verica nodded as if he'd been speaking to her. "I agree. The important consideration right now is convincing Sorcha she should accept the guard her laird has assigned."

"You will not defy your laird's orders," Earc told Sorcha.

That settled, he turned to Circin. "You and I will sleep near the door. Verica can share the bed with Sorcha and Brigit."

Verica made that sound again, the one that indicated she was not pleased. But Earc did not make the mistake of asking her what was wrong. He'd always found women difficult to understand and she was worse than all the others.

Too bad she made him burn. His time among the Donegals was turning into a torturous test of his self-control.

"I have my own bed; my da made it," Brigit said.

Earc smiled down at her. "Did he now?"

"It's there." She pointed to a small alcove off the wall beside the fire.

The love she had for her dead father shone in the girl's eyes. Earc didn't know how the man had died, but from Sorcha's dissembling he could guess. The wild beast had been a not-so-wild wolf. One of his brethren.

Rage boiled in his veins at the prospect of a Chrechte behaving so.

"I will not impose on Sorcha at your say so," Verica declared. "I can make a pallet on the floor."

"I won't hear of it," Sorcha replied, her clan hospitality coming to the forefront. "If you are all intent on staying, my daughter will share my sleeping area and the healer will take Brigit's bed." Though she was responding to Verica's comments, she directed her words to Earc.

Earc could see by the tightening of her features that this annoyed the tantalizing healer.

"I will freshen the bedding with lavender," Brigit declared before rushing from the cottage.

"Accompany her," Earc instructed Circin, who was already headed for the door.

Sorcha gave a fond shake of her head. "She's that enamored of you," she said to Verica.

"She's a wonderful apprentice."

"I wanted her to wait a couple of years, at least until she was thirteen summers before she began her training, but after her da . . ." Sorcha sighed, her voice trailing off. "She needed something to overcome the grief."

"I began my training when I was tall enough to stir the herb pot, but then my mother was the one who taught me." Verica's voice resonated with an old but still acute grief.

It seemed like too many Donegals had grief of one sort or another and Earc had to wonder how much of it could be laid at Rowland's feet. As laird he was responsible for the actions of his people, even if he was not directly involved.

Barr had a lot more to do among this clan than just train soldiers and a young man for his role as future laird.

"Your dam had such a gentle way about her." Sorcha bustled about the cottage, moving this, rearranging that, her gaze straying from the door to the windows and back again.

"But she was not weak."

"Yes. She looked like a strong wind could pick her up and fly her away, but even Rowland hesitated to make her angry." The loathing and fear in Sorcha's tone when she spoke her former laird's name revealed much.

"Few opposed him after her death." There was a further message in Verica's words and Earc was an experienced-enough warrior to get it.

"Those that did died." Sorcha clamped a hand over her mouth. "I didn't mean . . ."

"Aye, you did and you'll repeat the same tomorrow when you speak to your laird."

"She'll say what she feels safe saying and not one word more." Verica's hands landed on her hips again, having what he was sure was the wholly unintentional result of pushing her rounded breasts into prominence.

Her blue eyes shot sparks of defiance. He could not help his mind wandering down a path where those same blue orbs burned bright, but with lust rather than resistance.

No matter, on this topic he would not compromise. "She'll tell her laird what he needs to know to lead and protect this clan."

"And who will protect us when he's gone? Not you; you're leaving." She made it sound like an accusation.

And he did not understand why. Earc had no intention of leaving the clan while his warrior's strength and skills were still needed.

"By the time Barr returns to the Sinclairs, your brother and his soldiers will be up to the task."

"And if he leaves before then?" She was clearly in earnest.

However, what she proposed was foolishness. "He'll not abandon this clan."

"He might not have a choice."

Sorcha nodded, but did not say anything.

"What do you mean?" Earc demanded.

Pain showed for a moment before Verica's features set in determined lines. "Do you think my father wanted to leave this clan in Rowland's hands?"

"Barr is not going to die while out hunting." In truth, Earc found it odd that Verica's father had done so. Few animals could best a Chrechte wolf and only then when it was injured or exhausted. Perhaps Verica's father had been both. "There is no beast powerful or cunning enough to get the better of Barr."

"My father believed the same, even after my mother warned him. Treachery does not need superior strength, or even cunning . . . it just needs trust." Terrible grief showed for a moment before Verica's features set in determined lines.

"Barr trusts no one in this place but me."

If he thought that truth would offend her, he was wrong. Contrary woman. She looked relieved.

Sorcha just stared at them both, eyes rounded, her nerves scenting the air around them.

Brigit came bustling back into the cottage just then, her arms filled with lavender. She rushed to the small alcove without a word to anyone.

Circin smiled indulgently in her direction before turning to face Earc. "Rowland was headed toward the cottage when he saw Brigit and I. He turned and headed the other direction." Circin scowled. "Brigit told me thank you."

He turned a searching look on Sorcha and her face crumpled. Tears welled and she fled the room, escaping to the area behind a partial wall. He assumed it was where she slept as there was no sign of a bed anywhere else. After a frustrated glance at both men, Verica followed, wringing her hands as she hurried after the other woman.

Circin looked at Earc. "What did I say?"

Earc shrugged. He thought maybe the young warrior had forced Sorcha to acknowledge something she would rather pretend had not been happening. He could not be sure without verification, but he thought he could guess what had been going on. Rowland had taken advantage of his role as laird and Sorcha's widowhood, had maybe even caused it.

The thought of another Chrechte warrior preying on those weaker than him made the bile rise in Earc's throat. He wanted to kill Rowland. The former laird was a blight on the Chrechte heritage.

"Should I apologize?" Circin asked.

"For what?"

"Hurting her feelings."

"You are not the one hurting her."

"But—"

"If you are to be laird one day and don't want your position denied you by Scotland's *Sassenach*-loving king, you will learn to accept the consequences of truth."

Circin shot a glance to the dividing wall and then to where Brigit was busy in her small alcove, the scent of lavender wafting through the cottage. "I made her dam cry."

The boy had sixteen summers, but he was so young. "You did not make the woman weep; 'tis the situation in which she finds herself."

"What exactly *is* going on?"

"She'll tell her laird tomorrow." Until then, Earc would keep his speculation to himself. They were harsh accusations to make, the kind that ended in someone's death.

Circin nodded. "If she'd done that when Barr first took over our clan, I think we'd have had a month's less time of Rowland's insufferable presence."

"She didna trust him. She had no way of knowing Barr

is a different sort of man." And damn Rowland for making the woman have to wonder. "Though she has had a month to figure that out."

"It's not that simple," Verica said quietly as she joined them in front of the fire. "She and Brigit have gone to bed, though I'll wager Sorcha will not sleep this night."

"'Tis not seemly for a woman to wager," Circin teased.

And received a cuff to his head for his efforts. "I'll show you seemly."

"You'll show him more respect than that if you want this clan to accept him as laird one day," Earc said dryly.

Showing she knew a tease when she heard one, Verica gave him a wry smile. "Aye, when we're around others, but in private, he's still my little brother."

"What am I then? Of no account in your eyes?" The humor drained away as fast as it had come. He did not like that prospect one bit.

She opened her mouth to speak, but nothing came out as a strange expression dawned on her features.

Circin laughed, the sound startling in the now-tension-filled cottage. "She sees you like family, or as near as. She never knocks me around in front of anyone else."

"I don't knock you around at all." Verica smacked his arm, belying her outraged claim.

Circin and Earc both laughed while Verica blushed a sweet pink.

"We should go to sleep." She did her best to sound bossy, but the way she worried her pleats both revealed her true inner feelings and charmed him.

"So, you think of me as a close friend?" He knew what kind of closeness he wanted to have with her and it had nothing to do with friendship.

The slight flaring of her delicate nostrils indicated she recognized his desire as well. Circin had to be able to smell Earc's growing hunger for the man's sister. Rather than looking alarmed by it, as she did, or offended, as Earc might about his *own* sister (rational reaction or not), Circin appeared contemplative. Earc wasn't sure he liked that any better.

He knew what *he'd* be contemplating if the situation were reversed. Marriage. Mating. Permanence. Whether the other warrior was ready or not.

Verica looked between them, a frown marring her beautiful features. "You two may do what you like, but I'm going to bed."

"You dinna answer my question." He caught her arm as she would have swept by him.

Time seemed to slow down and then stop as an unseen force arced between them, making his cock hard and the breath seize in his chest. Her body jerked, but she swayed toward him rather than pulling away.

Her lips parted invitingly, the scent of her desire teasing his sexual hunger to a sharp pang. And the scent of something beyond her wolf washed over him in an intoxicating rush.

"Verica!" Circin's near panic cut through the growing haze of lust between them. "What are you doing?"

She jerked back, her face going ashen. She stared at Earc as if he'd grown another head—or suddenly changed into Rowland before her eyes. "I . . ."

"You need to go to bed." For the first time, Circin sounded like a man who would one day be laird.

She nodded, her eyes filled with an anguish Earc could not understand. No matter how far gone to passion they were, he would never have taken her with her brother in the room.

Her reaction was far beyond what the situation warranted.

Was she that bothered by the thought of being with him?

The leftover fear in Circin's eyes was all out of proportion as well.

"She will take a mate one day."

Circin nodded, his expression going grim. "I merely hope he is worthy of all her trust and affection."

Since it was a sentiment any brother should feel, Earc didn't reply. Instead he banked the fire for sleeping, which he and Circin did, rolled in their plaids near the door.

Chapter 8

Barr woke wrapped around his new mate.

The scent of *other* was strong, having become a fragrance he did not think he could do without. She fit him so perfectly. Though slender and fine boned, she was a wee bit taller than most females, making her just right for him. She curled into his body as if she'd slept there all their lives.

He did not think she was a great deal younger than him, which put her past the age when most women married. Which did not mean she was unpromised. He went rigid at the thought of her being committed to someone else. She had been untouched, but that did not mean no claim had been made on her.

"What is the matter?" she asked sleepily as she turned onto her back so their eyes could meet.

Even this proof she was so closely connected to him that she felt his agitation in her sleep did not assuage his need for an immediate answer. "Does someone else think they have a claim on you?"

Shadows filled her brown eyes, but she shook her head. "You are certain."

"It is not a thing I would forget."

"You mean like your clan?"

She grimaced and then frowned at him as if he were responsible for the bit of fiction that was her memory loss. "I am promised to no man."

"You are promised to me now."

"No."

"You spoke your Chrechte vow last night. It cannot be unsaid." She looked away. He would not allow her to avoid this, however. 'Twas too important. "Do not deny me."

Suddenly she rolled toward him, wrapping her arms around his neck and holding tight. She trembled against him, her heart beating fast, a sense of sadness he did not understand surrounding her.

"Sabrine? Tell me what ails you," he demanded.

She tilted her head back and met his gaze with deeply troubled eyes, his sweet Chrechte mate not one to hide from difficulty. "No other man has claim on me as you do."

"No other ever will."

"No other," she agreed.

"You are mine."

"While I am here."

He shook his hair in fierce denial. "Always."

She swallowed as if trying to hold back a deep well of emotion. "I will never give another what I give you now."

She would learn she did not have to try to hide her emotions from him. Everything she was was safe with him.

"Nay, you will not." Satisfaction surged through him.

Even knowing that as his almost certain true mate, she was not capable of physically betraying him, he liked hearing her promise.

She laughed softly. "You're an arrogant man, laird."

"And you are a woman of rare beauty." He had never met a woman with such delicate features, put together so finely.

"No other thinks so."

That he did not believe. "The males of your former home must have impaired vision."

She tensed, but said nothing.

"When I found no mate among the Sinclairs, I gave up hope of finding one. Then Talorc asked me to come here and lead this clan until Circin was ready to take over and I hoped again. Never did I think I would find you naked in the forest."

"I never thought to find one such as you at all, especially among the Faol."

"No other man could be right for you."

"I would never allow another this close." The fierceness in her expression allowed no room for doubt.

"I am glad you waited for me."

She shook her head, once again trying to hide emotion from him.

"Do not hide from me."

"I do not hide," she said harshly. Then her gaze softened, no mask covering the sorrow that should not be there. "I cannot promise you a lifetime."

"No one knows what tomorrow may bring."

Her body relaxed in obvious relief, giving him his first moment of real worry about their future. She did not believe they were true mates. That was all. Once she realized the truth, she would settle into her life with him.

Until then, he would reinforce his claim on her through the connection of their bodies.

He cupped the gentle swell of her buttocks, kneading them as he rubbed their bodies together.

"Mmmm . . . that feels nice." She moved with him, her body arching like a cat. "You're so warm."

"It is my wolf."

"I like it."

A thought niggled at the back of his mind—why wasn't she just as warm-blooded as he? But it was lost in the heat between them.

Their spent passion lay heavily in the air around them, now mixed with the perfume of their renewed mutual desire.

He leaned down and took her mouth in a devouring kiss. The need for her to know she was his drove his passion as surely as the consuming hunger between them. To taste her mouth was to want . . . nay, need another sip, and another, and another until their flavors were so mixed there was no distinguishing between them. Not even for his Chrechte nature.

She was every bit as involved, her hunger just as wild, her response unfettered by her recent innocence. It sent lightning arcing through him, the storm of craving growing until thunder pounded in his veins instead of blood.

The connection between them was unlike anything he'd experienced with his previous partners. He'd found release in sex. He'd even found a certain level of physical pleasure he thought worth returning to for more. He had not known what it meant to really join with another, to feel the connection of their bodies in that place where his soul must reside. This thing between them gave credence to the ancient legends about true mates forming a mystical bond that went beyond mindspeak.

No one had had such in his lifetime, but his gran-da used to tell stories of such things along with the tall tales about other tribes of Chrechte besides the wolves.

But he could feel her emotions, as if they were his own. However, he knew they were not. The underlying sorrow, determination and fear did not begin in his heart. They came from hers. As did the exultation, delight and shock as he sensed she realized the fierce possessiveness and masculine satisfaction were coming from him.

She reared back from him, her eyes wide with fear. "Is this the normal way of things?" She sucked in air, but her breathing remained erratic. "I cannot believe it is. No one has ever spoken of anything like this . . . this mind joining in my hearing."

"'Tis not our minds that are joined, it's our souls."

"Does it always happen this way for you?" Her voice echoed with both hope and abhorrence at the thought that it did.

It was the hope that prompted him to provoke her a wee bit. "I thought you dinna want to hear about my previous experiences with sex."

The fear washed away in pure feminine annoyance, the hope completely eclipsed by the abhorrence. Giving a fair imitation of a growl, she demanded. "Tell me."

"No, 'tis special, just between us."

"We're *not* true mates."

He didn't bother to answer; his mind was otherwise occupied, and not by her delectable curves or the rolling emotions flowing between them. A wolf did not have to make a sound *like* a growl. Wolves just growled. She was not wolf, but she *was* Chrechte.

The ancient tales were not mere entertainment. *They were true.* There were other tribes of Chrechte, but how had they hidden themselves?

Fear spiked over the bond between them and then another wash of almost desperate determination, its source feeling slightly different than when he'd first encountered it via this unusual bond.

"Stop thinking," she instructed in a sultry voice.

Even though part of him knew she was using their intimacy to distract his thoughts, her tone and the carnal yearning coming from her made any thought not directly related to his now-weeping cock impossible.

She kissed *him* this time, her hot, sweet mouth making a claim his wolf howled absolute approval for.

She touched him, exploring his body with her small, delicate hands. That enhanced connection pulsed in the air between them, once again combining their emotions, ravishing his senses with her unabashed wanting.

Every caress went to that place inside him he swore was his very soul.

In her primal passion, she had an otherworldly beauty that defied words or expectations. She was no mere woman, definitely not human. She was a Chrechte warrior princess of old.

Sabrine pressed against his shoulder and he rolled onto his back without protest. With all the strength he sensed inside her, she could not force him to submit to her lead, but as her mate he could give his beautiful lover this gift. And give it he would.

She would see that she did not have to hide her true nature from him, that he was strong enough to both protect her and meet her as an equal as the Chrechte had done amongst themselves for millennia.

She straddled him, a wild smile tilting her bow-shaped lips. "It is my turn to take you."

The pleased satisfaction that came over her features showed she had felt his desire for her to do just that. This was the way of the ancient Chrechte mating. Living among the human clans had led to some of the Chrechte taking on many of the restrictions men and women felt they needed to live by. He was glad she was not so encumbered by human mores.

She positioned her sex against his erection and they both moaned at the delight of it.

"You are certain you are up to this?" he found himself asking, though he had not intended to do so.

But they had made vigorous love the night before, and she had been a virgin. Even a Chrechte might not be fully healed from the rending of her maidenhead.

Her look turned tender and she leaned down to kiss him. "I am certain I want you," she said softly against his lips.

"Then have me."

She did, pressing her wet and slick flesh over his hard member, encasing him in the volcanic heat of her passion.

She began to rock against him, conversely languid and fierce in her hunger. The eroticism of her actions tore through him, making it near impossible to hold back from taking over. Against expectation, his wolf actually helped him, calling on ancient instincts he did not understand but could submit to. He was warrior. He was alpha.

She was his princess though. She could lead and he would allow it. She could take and in his strength, he could give. He cared not if it made sense. It was the ways of things from old.

The caress of her flesh around him drew forth his pleasure, inexorably driving him toward completion until it erupted in a series of violent ejaculations from his cock. The sound that came from her then was like nothing he had ever heard, a high-pitched trilling that ended on a throaty wail as she spasmed around him, bringing forth another wave of ecstasy from him.

He shouted, reared up and flipped them so that she was under him while he was still inside her. His sex should be softening, but it wasn't, making her feel like a wet, silken fist wrapped tight around him.

Her eyes had gone almost black in their passion, her hair shimmering blue-black in the early dawn light streaming through the east-facing windows high in the wall.

He felt her Chrechte nature right under the surface, beating at his consciousness like bird wings against a door.

His wolf reared up to meet it, howling and prancing in victory inside him. He'd found his mate and he would never let her go.

Unable to do anything else, hoping she was still as hungry as he, he began thrusting inside her, building their pleasure again with impossible speed.

This time when they climaxed, their shouts mingled,

making a sound he could easily grow to need with an even fiercer compulsion than that to protect his people.

This was the risk of true bonds, that you would put your mate above the clan, above the pack. When your mate was worthy, that was not a problem, but if not, it led to the kind of pain the Sinclair clan had known.

His mind told him that, but his heart said something else. It said this woman, his Sabrine, his princess, she was worthy.

Earc woke to the sound of quiet movement. He was alert instantly, rising from his place on the floor to find Sorcha in front of the fire.

She smiled tentatively at him, the dark half-moons under her eyes attesting to how little sleep she had gotten the previous night. "I thought to make our porridge. The laird would not want me to return to my duties in the kitchen without his say so."

Though she said it as a statement, worried eyes made it a question.

"My instructions are to not allow anyone to speak to you until Barr has the opportunity to do so."

Her body deflated like a pricked pig's bladder and the tension roiling around them dissipated enough that his hackles, which had started to rise, settled. "That is good to know."

"You are really afraid of him, aren't you?" And they both knew Earc wasn't referring to Barr.

"Terrified." Her hands clenched, released, clenched, released several times as she watched the fire catch in silence.

"We will protect you."

"We?" she asked, sounding dazed.

"Barr, me, Circin."

"Circin is a boy."

"Aye, he could not do it alone, but he will one day be your laird. He feels the weight of that responsibility for your well-being already."

"Rowland felt no such weight."

"Rowland is a pig." That was Circin, adjusting his plaid with one hand while rubbing a hand over his face with the other.

She laughed, the sound soft and a little frightened, but amused all the same. She dared to nod. "Aye."

She quietly went about preparing their breakfast while he and Circin took turns going outside for their morning ablutions. Earc quickly took care of business while keeping his senses alert to potential danger, smoke from the kitchen fires in the keep the only sign the rest of the clan was stirring.

When he went back into the cottage, neither Verica nor Brigit had stirred yet.

He was surprised Sorcha had not woken her daughter, but he kept his own council, puzzling again over Verica's reaction to him the night before.

A quiet tap sounded on the door, but it may as well have been a clap of summer thunder for the way Sorcha responded. She gasped, fell back and then scrambled away from the fire, away from the door, her expression that of pure terror.

Earc stood and moved between her and the perceived threat even as the door pushed open, the small cottage having no bar to drop in place as many that surrounded the keep did not. Circin joined Earc, creating a wall between the frightened woman and the Chrechte, who was a disgrace to the name, coming through the door.

Rowland stopped short and glared at Earc and Circin when he saw them. "What the devil are you two doing here? Is she selling her favors all over the clan now?"

The sound that came from behind them would make any wolf proud and it did not emanate from Sorcha. Though

Earc could hear the shuffling movements of her rising to her feet and backing against the wall.

Verica's voice cracked across the cottage like a whip. "You dare make such accusations, you miserable, murdering knave!"

"I'm your laird, missy, and you'd best not forget it." Rowland's eyes narrowed in affront, his scent going rank with bitterness.

"The hell you are!" Earc stepped forward, forcing the man to back up a step though they were not yet in touching distance. "But I will make sure Barr hears you've challenged him for the right to lead this clan."

Rowland didn't have the intelligence to look cowed by that promise. "I didn't challenge that fool boy for anything. But this clan belongs to me and one day it will be mine again."

The sheer blind arrogance of the bastard robbed Earc of the breath to speak for a moment.

"You'll be dead long before I leave these people to be led by another, and it would never have been you." Barr's voice, laced with a power that Earc had never heard there before, filled the cottage.

Rowland spun to face the other man. His lips moved, but no word issued forth, his gaze darting around the small dwelling, as if looking for an escape. "I meant no offense," he finally spluttered, "'Tis merely my shock at finding my fancy piece entertaining others in my absence."

"Sorcha is no whore and you'll shut your foul mouth if that's all it has to say." Circin's tone once again carried the seeds of his future leadership.

"She's got two warriors in her cottage before breakfast. What do you call it?" Rowland sneered, sounding much more confident in his foul assumptions than his attempts at apology to Barr.

The air around Barr fairly shimmered with his fury. "My protection."

The confusion on Rowland's face made Earc want to retch. The man did not understand why Sorcha needed protection, or more likely, he did not understand why Barr felt the need to give it.

Calling him pig was an insult to swine.

"My sister was here all night and the woman's daughter. What kind of evil does a man have to be to see what you see in that?" Circin demanded in disgust.

"For all I know your sister was helping entertain you two," Rowland spat out, proving once again he lacked the intelligence of a flea.

Circin moved forward, no doubt intending to challenge the older Chrechte, but Earc could not allow it.

Rowland was no longer young, but he was not weak and he would fight dirty. Without-honor or-conscience dirty. Something Earc had yet to teach the Donegal soldiers to combat.

If the two men fought, Circin would die and Verica would grieve. Earc did not know why, but that thought was untenable. He also liked the brash young man who had once challenged the Sinclair laird for the right to the lands containing the sacred springs.

With the speed of his wolf, Earc stepped in front of Circin and sent a blow to Rowland's jaw in the same moment. "You'll apologize to Verica for your disgusting accusation or you will face me in challenge."

Rowland had staggered but not fallen. Scowling, he rubbed his jaw, a bruise already starting to form there. "You don't have the right to challenge me over the bitch. She's no kin to you."

"She's my sister," Circin said furiously.

There was nothing for it; he had to take drastic steps. 'Twould not be so bad. "She's my mate. Mate law supersedes all other."

Verica's shock reached him and wrapped itself around Earc, though she said not a word. Circin growled in satisfaction, his scent still holding anger, but happiness as well. And if Earc did not know it was impossible, he would have thought the youth had planned events to take just this turn.

Barr's expression did not change, his support of his second complete. He faced off to Rowland. "In the extreme unlikelihood you survive Earc's challenge, I will meet yours for leadership of the Donegal clan."

"I made no challenge."

"It doesn't matter, old man," Earc said, so disgusted he could barely stand to look at the man. "You'll not survive mine."

"You would allow a fight between a younger warrior and his elder?" Rowland demanded of Barr in whining tones. "It would not be fair."

"You sound like a child deprived of his treat. If you wanted to avoid being challenged, you should have kept your foul mouth shut." Not an ounce of sympathy sounded in Barr's tone.

"I refuse. I'll leave the clan," he said as if making a great concession. "But I won't fight two giants like yourselves."

"Your actions and attitude show you as a threat to this clan and your behavior toward Sorcha breaks pack law. Banishment is not an option."

"Pack law does not apply to humans."

"When you live among them, it does."

"That is absurd. They are as nothing compared to us."

Barr turned to face Sorcha. "Can I assume from his free use of the distinction between humans and himself that Rowland has revealed aspects of his nature unknown to the rest of the clan?" Even in his interrogation, Barr was careful not to reveal secrets of their people.

Sorcha nodded, the sour smell of her sweat attesting to her continued fear.

"What did he tell you?"

"He—"

"Keep your mouth shut, slut! You know what will happen if you don't."

Barr moved so quickly, none but Earc probably saw him reach out and backhand the grizzled Chrechte so hard, he flew backward, landing against the wall so hard the cottage shook. "Speak out of turn again and I will gag you."

Barr approached the now visibly shaking Sorcha. "You have naught to fear from him any longer."

Sorcha nodded, her eyes wide and filled with tears she valiantly blinked back. "He can become a wolf."

"He told you this?" Barr asked.

Sorcha shook her head. "He showed me. He said if I did not do what he wanted, he would rend Brigit limb from limb as he had done my husband." Each word came out labored and halting, a sob snaking past her tightly clenched lips after she was finished speaking.

Verica reached out and squeezed Sorcha's hand. "Never again."

Sorcha looked at Barr with near-hopeless despair. "You'll never win in battle against him."

"I killed my first wild boar on a hunt when I was eight; this wolf man holds no fear for me."

Since the Chrechte did not go through their first change until hair began to grow on other places than their heads, this was an impressive feat.

Earc could match it, adding one year.

He looked at Rowland with contempt. "You'll not make it past the first challenge."

"I apologize," Rowland said quickly, though the words were clearly sour in his mouth.

"Are you satisfied to withdraw your challenge?" Barr asked Earc.

Earc turned to Verica and repeated the question to her. She looked at him with too many emotions for him to name, but predominant was that old grief he had noticed the night before. "I'm not. He does not mean the words."

"What do you want? Me to debase myself before the whole clan?"

"Yes. If you apologize more politely to me before the soldiers in the hall over nooning meal, I will accept your words." There was something in her expression that said she knew without doubt the older Chrechte would never accept those terms.

Rowland shook with bitter fury, the power of a very strong wolf right under the surface. "I'll do no such thing, you worthless bitch daughter of a filthy raven."

Verica's gaze shot to Earc's, a new emotion overriding every other. *Fear.*

He did not know what caused it, but it did not matter. He smiled at her; he'd claimed her as his mate. She might not understand what that meant yet, but she would learn. He would *always* protect her. From anything.

He turned back to the bastard causing his new mate such distress. "We will meet in the forest in thirty minutes' time. If you do not come, I will hunt you down and end your miserable existence without hesitation."

Rowland finally had pulled together enough thought to be truly afraid; it showed in the panicked whites of his eyes. But it was too late.

Barr looked at Circin. "Assemble the Chrechte in the clearing near the small loch. All of them. Any who refuse to show will be considered outcasts from this day forward."

"You cannot do this. The king guaranteed me my place in the clan," Rowland tried one last time.

Barr was unmoved. "And your actions have destroyed the gift he gave you."

"You think you've won, but you'll see. No one wins over me." Spittle flew from the man's mouth as he screamed those words and then rushed from the cottage.

"You daft man," Sorcha said and then gasped and closed her mouth so tight her lips disappeared.

"You do not think I can best him in a challenge?" But

then Earc chastised himself. Of course she wouldn't. She did not know he had a wolf living inside him, too.

"She thinks you gave a deceiving wretch thirty minutes to plan your murder," Verica answered with undisguised worry.

He liked knowing she was concerned for him, though it was not clear whether she cared if Earc died as much as whether that would leave her human friend at risk until Barr disposed of the self-admitted murderer.

There had been no lie in Sorcha's voice when she claimed Rowland took responsibility for her husband's death.

Regardless of the reasons behind his alluring mate's worry, he sought to alleviate it. "I'll not let that miserable pile of horse's dung get the best of me."

"Do you not think my father believed the same?" Verica's distress had only intensified.

"Your father trusted him; no doubt he believed the other man's Chrechte nature would keep him from deeds too foul against his own kind, and particularly against the leader of his pack."

"He did."

"I am not that naïve."

"Do not die," she ordered.

"I will not."

She nodded, but said nothing more. He decided that if he was to kill the old buzzard he would do it with the taste of his mate on his tongue. He leaned down and kissed her. It was no gentle bussing of lips, but a full, claiming kiss—the woman needed to know that from this day forward, she was his.

Chapter 9

Sabrine stood outside the cottage, unnoticed as the old wolf stormed by.

Barr had told her to stay in his bed and rest. She'd waited until he'd made it down the stairs before following him.

She could not forget her purpose here among the Donegals. She had to find the *Clach Gealach Gra* and return it to her people before her brother's coming of age ceremony. It only made sense she keep apprised of what was happening in the clan.

Eavesdropping on Barr arguing with the old bastard that used to lead this poor clan was clearly a must in that regard.

Without a word to anyone in the cottage, Barr came out the door. Sabrine made no effort to hide her presence.

He leaned against the outer wall of the small building, his huge arms crossed over a chest only partially covered by his plaid. "You do not listen well."

He didn't sound particularly bothered by that fact. In

point of truth, if she could believe the evidence of her ears, he almost sounded pleased.

"I can listen." She could even obey. When she agreed with the instructions.

"I've no doubt you can."

"You will allow Earc to kill the evil one they call Rowland."

"Aye."

"Because he offended a Chrechte woman?"

"Because he admitted to killing a human male and mistreating a human female in a way no Chrechte should ever do."

It was not what she had expected him to say, but then his words raised another concern. Her heart wanted to believe Barr was different from other Faol, but her mind rejected an easy dismissal of a lifetime of teaching. "So, his offense toward Verica does not matter, because you now know she had a raven mother."

Barr's brow furrowed for a moment as he did a very good impression of a man who did not know what she was talking about. And then understanding dawned, his face clearing, and a new certainty settled over his features.

"You are a raven." Pride in his deductive reasoning rang through his voice, though he spoke quietly so even a Chrechte would have difficulty hearing. "Verica's mother was raven."

"Rowland already told you that." But she finally realized Barr had not believed the old man, had perhaps thought his words no more than a figure of speech.

Regret for revealing Verica's heritage, if not her dual-shifting nature, pricked Sabrine.

Wonder filled his gray gaze. "I thought the Éan were mere myth."

He really had. Nothing but truth and wonder came from him. How could this be?

"The Faol hate the Éan." All bird Chrechte knew this. Even Verica and Circin made obvious efforts to hide their raven natures. "Your people have done your best to destroy mine since long before the Faol joined the human clans."

"Chrechte are a warlike people. We all fought amongst ourselves until the packs were dying out. We joined the human clans, agreeing to cease hostilities amongst ourselves." He said it as if giving a child a history lesson.

She bristled. She knew the wolves' history, but their joining the humans did not change their need to kill the Éan. "The Faol never stopped murdering my people."

"But we don't even know you exist."

"Your pack may not." Though how that could be, she was uncertain. "But others do."

"I would have heard something."

She shook her head. Barr's arrogance, so different from Rowland's conceit, was such a part of him, his claim did not even surprise her. His absolute certainty that he knew all there was to know about the Chrechte both frustrated and amused her.

"Whatever ancient enmity existed no longer holds sway, just as the wolf packs no longer wage war with each other."

"You are wrong."

"Sabrine." Just that one word. Her name, but it held a wealth of meaning.

He was astonished she would so blatantly disregard his words, but then she had lived her life among the Chrechte, not the humans. The Éan were a matrilineal people, as they had been since time immemorial, just as the Faol had been before joining the human clans and MacAlpin's infamous betrayal of his royal relatives.

While respect was given to any in a position of authority over an Éan, men did not hold a position of superiority merely by the nature of their sex. It would not have taken so many years for Rowland to face an imminent death had he lived among the Chrechte of old.

"Do you really claim that the packs never war with one another?"

"Only when the clans are involved."

"And the clans of the Highlands are almost as volatile as the Chrechte that have joined them."

Barr shrugged. "That does not mean wolves continue to harbor some age-old grudge against the ravens."

"The Éan are more than raven, though we are the biggest remaining group."

"And the wolves of the Sinclair pack or those of the Balomoral would be nothing but happy to learn of your existence."

"I notice you did not mention the Donegals."

"Rowland's prejudices are clear. I would not assume he had no influence on others within his clan; he led them more than a decade."

"That prejudice is more than unpleasant. It is deadly."

"That is where I think you are wrong," Barr said, showing he still had too much honor to understand men who had none.

"My parents died at the hands of the Faol. They still hunt in the forest for us."

Barr's storm-cloud eyes widened and then narrowed. "Impossible."

"How did this happen?" She indicated her wounded arm, annoyance overcoming any other feeling in regard to his arrogance. How dare he doubt her words? "One of your Faol hunters shot me from the sky."

"Nay."

"Oh, yes." There was so much more she wanted to say, but this was not the place to do it. In a clan with Chrechte, she would far too easily be overheard.

"Laird?" Verica asked from the door, one hand on the doorjamb.

He flashed her a look. "Aye?"

The raven-wolf's gaze jumped from Barr to Sabrine and back to Barr again, her curiosity regarding what they had been discussing a spicy scent that clung to the air around her. "Rowland will try to kill Earc rather than face him in fair challenge."

"Aye, of that I am certain you are right. The man has less honor than the English." Barr pushed away from the wall of the cottage. He moved to stand right in front of Sabrine, placing his hand on her neck in a possessive as well as comforting gesture—for a wolf. "We will continue this discussion later."

She did not argue. Barr had to protect his friend, or that evil old Faol *would* kill him. And she'd almost grown fond of Earc after hearing him defend Verica so staunchly, not to mention the way he had protected the raven-wolf youth from facing Rowland in challenge.

Barr went back into the cottage and Sabrine found herself following without thought. Brigit was awake now, clinging to her mother's hand, her innocent gaze filled with worry. Who knew how much of the confrontation she had heard.

Sorcha was a beautiful woman, but lines of worry and unhappiness marred what once must have been a face that often creased in smiles. She clung to her daughter's hand just as tightly and watched the Chrechte men with a level of wariness Sabrine understood all too well.

Barr reached down and tucked a stray lock of Brigit's cinnamon-colored hair behind her ear. "You have naught to fear. I give you my word."

"I believe you." The child tried for a smile, and her attempt was passable.

Barr turned his gaze to the finely trembling mother.

"Sorcha, you and Brigit are to return to the keep with Sabrine. She will keep you safe in my room while the problem of Rowland is dealt with by those who have pledged you their protection."

The human woman did not manage quite as passable a smile as her daughter, but her attempt showed her courage. "Thank you."

"You do not thank your laird for doing his duty, Sorcha. A man of Rowland's lack of honor should never have led this clan and never will again."

She nodded.

He shifted so he faced Verica.

"Fetch Muin and Brigit's cousins, then join the other women in my room."

"I am Chrechte, I should witness the challenge."

"You are Earc's mate now. Rowland, or those loyal to him, may find a way to use you against him. That is not acceptable. He will be safer with you here, out of harm's way in the keep."

Verica opened her mouth, looking as if she was ready to argue again with her laird.

Agree, Sabrine commanded her through mindspeak.

The other woman's eyes widened and she stared at Sabrine with a mouth dropped open.

Close your mouth. Barr is unaware of the powers of the Éan. Were these clan women truly not taught anything of self-defense, not even how to hide their emotions?

Can you hear me? Verica responded via the mental link Sabrine had created between them.

If I choose to, yes.

But . . .

I will explain further later. "Do as your laird bids," Sabrine said, speaking the last sentence aloud.

With no further discussion, spoken or otherwise, Verica turned and left, her confusion following her like a cloud.

"What just happened?" Barr asked with amusement.

Sabrine's heart stopped and then resumed at a faster beat.

He frowned. "Do not get upset. I'm shocked she listened to you over me, but I am not angry." He still looked bemused. "'Tis a woman thing I suppose."

More like a raven thing, but Sabrine nodded anyway. Revealing the secrets of the Éan was not something she was willing to do, not today, or ever. Not even to this man to whom she was rapidly losing the heart she'd thought long turned to stone.

𝒱erica arrived in Barr's sleeping quarters only moments after Sabrine and the others. Verica's nose wrinkled and her brow furrowed as she looked around the room, her gaze finally setting on the bed. Stunned disbelief showed in her blue eyes as she met Sabrine's gaze.

"You mated our laird?" she blurted out.

Sabrine frowned. "That is not important right now. Barr is no doubt sending Muin and the human soldiers to guard this room."

"Yes, I think so."

We must leave before they get here then, Sabrine sent over the mind link.

But we can't leave Sorcha and Brigit unprotected. It was good to see the Chrechte woman recognize she was some measure of protection for the human and her child, even if she didn't hide the fact she was speaking with her mind any better than a child might.

Sorcha was too preoccupied with her own worries to notice, but Brigit was giving her mentor in the healing arts a strange look.

Sabrine straightened the plaid on the bed, her attention apparently on no one else in the room. *We will not leave the keep until the men arrive.*

Though Sabrine doubted Rowland would bother with the human woman right now. He would be too focused on finding a way to dispose of Earc before the challenge, and most likely Barr as well.

That Sabrine would not allow. She might not be able to stay among the Donegals, but she would not allow the man she had given her body, and part of her soul, to die. Not while she could protect him.

We can hide ourselves in the alcove between my room and Circin's. We can watch the laird's door from there.

Sabrine went to stand in front of the terrified human woman. "Listen to me, Verica and I must leave you here. You will be safe. Guards will arrive momentarily to watch over you. Do not inform them of our absence, please."

"What do you think to do?" This from Brigit, not her still-stunned mother.

"Save the laird and his second-in-command."

Sorcha jerked, proving she'd been listening, even in her shocked state. "But you are women."

Sabrine didn't give that foolish sentiment an answer. "You will hide our departure from them?"

Sorcha nodded.

Brigit grinned. "You *are* a warrior, aren't you?"

"I am a descendant of the royal line of my people. I have bested men in battle and I will again." She didn't mind bragging a little if it would put the child's mind at rest.

Sorcha stared at her as if Sabrine spoke gibberish, but Brigit's grin grew until it split her face. "And you will teach us to fight?"

"I will, but right now I must go."

Brigit nodded while her mother looked on in clear horror, but the human woman did nothing to stop them. Sabrine only hoped she would not alert the soon-to-arrive guards to the other women's departure.

They rushed toward the alcove, the unfamiliar long skirts getting in Sabrine's way. "Do you have a plaid from Circin's youth?"

"He's still a youth," Verica grumbled.

Perhaps in this clan, but among her people, a sixteen-year-old male would be well on his way to being trained as a warrior, especially one expected to lead. Sabrine had been fifteen summers when she picked up her first real sword, but she'd been in training and living among the other warriors for years by then. "His plaid would probably fit me without too many extra pleats," she mused.

Verica stopped dead. "You want to wear my brother's plaid?"

"You do not expect me to wear this long skirt in battle."

"We're going into battle?" Verica's fear was right there, though she'd made a respectable effort to mask it. However, her determination did not waver.

"*I* am going into battle. You will take to the sky and act as my eyes." Sabrine's damaged wing prevented her from doing her own search of the area. "You must be very careful, but you should be able to spot an assassin hiding amidst the trees."

"You think Rowland will have a cohort attack Earc for him?" Verica asked, not sounding like it would take any stretch of imagination for her to envision the same.

"I think he's a puling coward and that sort of man will have an ally in the trees armed with a bow. The cohort will attempt to shoot Earc from a distance and hope to escape in the ensuing confusion."

"I do not think he will escape Barr's wrath."

With that, Sabrine agreed. But Rowland was too stupid and conceited to realize it. "No doubt Rowland believes he and those loyal to him can keep Barr occupied."

Or, more likely if his cohort was human, he would not care and had no plans to try to protect the other man.

"What will we do?"

"You will find the assassin. You will tell me where he is and I will kill him."

Verica stared. "You truly are a warrior, aren't you?" Somehow she must have missed the import of the words exchanged between Sabrine and Brigit, or simply refused to acknowledge them.

Sabrine stood tall and proud, her battle mask dropping over her face. "I am."

Verica flinched and then rallied. *You said you were of the royal line of the Éan.* Showing she had some self-protective instincts, Verica had switched to their silent form of communication.

I am.

Is that why we can mindspeak?

Yes. Those of the royal line can do so with all the Éan.

You knew I was a raven, from the beginning.

I did.

But I hid my scent.

Very nicely, too. However, none but our line have hair the color of a raven's feathers. The blue sheen over black as midnight did not occur among the humans or the wolves they had accepted into their clans.

Oh. I did not know that.

They had both had their instances of ignorance. *I did not know any of the Éan lived amongst the clans.* She would never have believed they could survive among the wolves so intent on destroying them. *Our leaders are unaware of this fact.*

We have much to discuss.

Yes, but now, we must save your new mate's life.

I cannot believe he claimed me for mate just to protect Circin from having to fight Rowland.

Earc is a man of honor, even if he is a wolf.

Verica tilted her head, giving Sabrine an odd perusal. *Not all wolves hate the Éan. Surely you realize this, having mated Barr. My father loved my mother very much. Though, in the end, he was not there to protect her from those who did not.*

He died for his love, too, didn't he?

That is what I have always believed. My mother warned me to never let any of the other wolves know of my double animal nature.

She was a wise woman.

She was.

They waited for the soldiers to arrive and take up their

post outside Barr's door before Sabrine used her Éan power over what was perceived to make it possible for her and Verica to duck into the healer's room.

She rushed to a storage chest against the far wall and shoved it open.

Verica dug through the contents until she raised a plaid triumphantly. "This will fit you better than one of Circin's plaids, for though you're tall for a woman, your frame is slighter than his."

Sabrine stripped out of her current clothes quickly and donned the shorter, more familiar styled plaid.

The healer moved more things around in the trunk until she pulled out a leather-wrapped bundle.

Sabrine knew what it was before Verica pulled the leather away. A female Éan warrior's weapons: the knife and sword would be balanced for her slighter build.

"These were my grandmother's. I always thought my mother meant they had come down from my great-grandfather, or something, but now I realized my dam's mother must have been a warrior like you."

Sabrine handled the weapons with proper reverence. "Yes. These are very well made. You have taken care of them, too."

"My mother made me promise. She said I might need them one day. I didn't understand. I am a healer."

But even a healer might be required to raise a sword in self-defense if her secret nature was discovered.

"I would have been a healer if my mother had lived," Sabrine told the other woman as she finished dressing and attached the sword to the belt at her waist. She tied the knife with the leather straps found with it to her thigh.

"Do you regret not following your mother's path?"

"I regret her death that made my sacrifice necessary."

Verica nodded, her expression filled with empathy.

The two women snuck from the keep, Verica seeming

oblivious to the special Éan power that made it possible for them to do so wholly unseen.

Verica took to the sky as soon as they were a fair distance from the keep and the two women stayed in constant contact via the mind link Sabrine provided. One of the strongest of her line with this gift, she would be able to hear Verica now the link had been established even a league distant.

He is going to be hiding in a good spot with a vantage point to the clearing in which the challenge is to take place. Sabrine gave the other woman her best advice based on her years protecting her people against enemies just like Rowland.

It will be close enough he'll be able to kill Earc with his first arrow, but as far away as possible within that limitation.

It all depends on how good he is with the bow and arrow, Verica sent back.

You know Rowland and his cronies best. Who is he likely to get to do this cowardly act?

Every Chrechte has been ordered to the clearing.

Does he have human friends with the skill?

He doesn't have human friends at all.

Then one he could intimidate?

One of the men who hunts for the clan, Verica guessed. *The hunters live in great fear of Rowland, who has a way of making any who disagree with him disappear while they are out securing meat for the clan.*

Sabrine did not relish killing a human whose only guilt was fearing his former laird.

Sabrine made her way through the forest, keeping a direction toward the clearing Verica had told her would be the meeting place for the Chrechte challenge. Verica flew above, her raven's body a tiny black dot in the sky.

I see him. Verica's voice was a triumphant shout in Sabrine's head. *He did not think to remove his plaid.*

He is not expecting eyes looking down on him from the sky.

It is young Connor. Sadness sounded in Verica's mental voice, a true grief that tugged at Sabrine, even as she increased her pace to rival that of any wolf. Shifted or not. *He is related to Rowland, but his father cannot shift. He was born to a Chrechte mother and human father.*

Verica described where to find the young man and Sabrine ran on silent feet through the forest until she was only a few feet distant. She crept up to him and had her knife to his throat before he even realized she was there.

"Drop your bow and I may let you live." She spoke right into his ear, her raven so close to the surface, her voice was as harsh as a caw.

Chapter 10

The man's bow went slack in nerveless fingers. "I wasn't going to kill him."

"The evidence does not support your claim."

"I was only going to wound him, but if I don't shoot him, Rowland will hurt my father."

Just as Verica had surmised, the man had been coerced, but still—he was not entirely blameless. "Rowland will die this day. It is your choice if you join him or not."

The bow dropped to the stone perch the man had been standing on. Sabrine kept her knife to his throat and silently called Verica to them.

Verica landed on a nearby branch behind them and changed before coming forward.

Tie his hands, Sabrine instructed in mindspeak.

Verica did it without a word and Sabrine made sure the human hunter kept his head facing forward so he could not see the healer. She would not be the reason the woman's secrets became common knowledge.

"So, Rowland threatened your family if you did not kill for him?" Sabrine demanded, once the man was secure.

"I would not kill our laird's second. I meant only to wound him," the young Connor claimed again, his sincerity an even more pungent scent than his fear.

"You think that makes your treason any more palatable?"

Defeat settled over the hunter with the pall of impending death. "You don't understand. Rowland always gets what he wants."

"I repeat, Rowland, that demon pig, will die this day."

"If that happens, I will rejoice louder than anyone, but if it doesn't, who will protect my father? He has no Chrechte strength. He is gaining in years." Connor's voice shook with his grief on his father's behalf.

"I will not let anything happen to your father," Sabrine found herself promising.

"How can you protect him? You are a woman."

These clansmen. So ignorant. "I stopped you shooting Earc, didn't I?"

"I'm not good at fighting. I would be good for nothing to this clan if I could not shoot an accurate line with my bow for hunting."

"Is that what Rowland told you?" Sabrine asked, appalled by the cruel and demeaning words.

"Aye."

"Well, he lies. Barr is training human men to protect the clan, too." As any good laird should do.

"I heard it, but Rowland said it would make no difference. No human could ever best a Chrechte."

"You did. By not shooting Earc, you've bested him."

"But I would have shot him if you had not intervened."

Sabrine nodded. She believed him. No matter how much Connor disliked the idea of wounding the other Chrechte at Rowland's behest. Or his fear of the consequences. She knew what it was to sacrifice everything for family. The steady nearing of her younger brother's coming of age ceremony had prompted her to infiltrate a clan redolent with Faol.

"Barr must be told of your collusion with Rowland."

Connor's head dropped, his chin settling against his chest in defeat. "I know."

"I will speak on your behalf."

"What can you say? You found me with my bow pointed toward his second. Will you allow me to watch the challenge? If I am to die for my treason, I would do it knowing Rowland was on his way to hell first."

"You'll not die this day." She did not know how to accomplish that feat, but this boy was a result of the disease of hatred and fear Rowland had infected the Donegal clan with.

She was tempted to let the boy go after the challenge was over and simply not tell Barr about the aborted attempt to circumvent the challenge. On the other hand, doing so would feel like a betrayal of Barr. Sabrine could not make herself take that path.

"What is going on here?" Circin demanded as he arrived.

Verica jumped up, shifted into her raven and left in a swish of feathers.

Sabrine smiled. "I would not have known you were approaching, but for the sound you made through the forest."

He had far to go before he was a warrior of Barr's skill, but he had already made improvements since they met.

Circin looked at her and then looked away again, a burnished line appearing along his cheekbones. "What are you doing out here? Dressed like a male?"

Oh, for goodness sake. "You act as if you've never seen a woman's legs before."

"I haven't."

"How is that possible? I thought the Faol hunted together."

"We do, but the females make their change before joining the men."

This clan had taken on more of the human mores than

others further north in the Highlands, at least from what her distant observations had revealed. Barr had certainly not shown any modest regard for his own nakedness.

"Your laird sent you searching for the assassin?" she asked rather than continue their unnecessary discussion of her clothing. If he was so disturbed, he could look at something besides her knees.

The laird in training nodded.

"Good."

Of course, Circin would have been too late to prevent the arrow that might well have killed Earc. Still, she liked knowing the man doing such a fine job of claiming her heart was a cunning warrior.

"Connor?" Circin asked, his voice tinged with shocked unhappiness. "You were happier than any other when the king demanded Rowland step down from his place as laird."

"The bastard threatened the boy's father."

Circin cursed.

He looked toward the sky, where Verica had disappeared to, and then back to Sabrine. "You know."

She nodded but added nothing else in front of the man Connor.

Circin asked the man, "Are there any others in on this cowardly plot to kill Earc?"

"Nay. Rowland could not risk going to his Chrechte friends and being discovered when one of them did not show for the challenge."

Far too intent on the challenge happening below them, Sabrine did not comment. She already knew there were no others since Verica had continued to scan the forest while Sabrine made her way to the man with the bow.

Barr instructed the Chrechte to create a circle around the challengers, further hindering any plot the former laird had hatched in his puling brain. He hoped Circin would be able to find any cohort Rowland had convinced to help him, but Barr's wolf was on full alert all the same.

He commanded silence among the witnesses, so that should a twig break, he would hear it.

He measured the onlookers with his gaze. "You have been enjoined to come here to witness the challenge fight between Earc and Rowland."

"You would pit a younger warrior against our former laird?" one of the older men asked with anger.

"If he survives the challenge, I'll tear his throat out myself for crimes committed against those under his protection."

Everyone in the clearing went as silent as he desired at his promise.

He found it interesting to note that no one stepped forward to protest the man's innocence, but not surprising. A man did not start with murder and rape. Barr didn't doubt that Rowland had been abusing his position within the pack for as long as he'd held it.

Maybe even before it had been officially his.

Rowland, who had come into the clearing looking smug, was starting to sweat. He had spent the time since arriving in the clearing talking to some of his old cronies, sending darting glances to the north. His conceited arrogance was just starting to show wear like a plaid made of inferior weave. Rowland looked off into the distance once again and probably saw exactly what Barr did at the same moment.

Wearing a man's plaid and holding a sword, Sabrine stood in front of a rock outcropping that would make ideal cover for a bowman. The top of Circin's head could be seen behind her.

She raised her arm in a typical warrior's sign that all was well. Barr found himself biting back a laugh, though his mind told him he should be furious. Anger that she had disregarded his instructions warred with a sense of pride that the magnificent woman was his mate. What she thought she was doing dressed as a warrior and carrying a sword, he could not begin to guess, but it was enough to send fire through his loins.

The foul word that came out of Rowland's mouth at that moment tipped Barr's feelings toward the pride.

"You *will* fight my second," he promised the honorless cur.

Rowland spun away, giving his former pack something that was probably supposed to be a look of entreaty. It didn't work well on the man's contemptuous features.

"Will none of my brothers step forward to fight this challenge for your *old* laird?" His emphasis on the word *old* made Barr roll his eyes.

Some of the Chrechte winced, but not one of them looked ready to fall on his sword for the old bastard.

Earc stripped off his plaid, tossing it aside. As Chrechte law allowed for a wolf who was not yet in control of his change, he held his dagger in his dominant hand.

Rowland eyed it with disdain. "What do you plan to do with that, boy? You'll not be able to hold it once you shift."

"I only shift at the full moon," Earc said, no shame in his voice.

Rowland's grimace could hardly be called a smile, but the man was pleased at the news. No doubt. Evil satisfaction glowed in his eyes.

Fool.

Perhaps he had not trained his Chrechte warriors to fight their brethren in changed form, but Talorc had the Sinclairs. He'd made sure every soldier in his clan could hold his own against a Chrechte in battle. And the Chrechte were all drilled until they could fight another wolf in shifted form or not. Earc had never been bested, except by Talorc, Niall or Barr.

Since no other warrior had ever bested them, either, that

did not imply any kind of weakness in Earc's fighting ability.

In the blink of an eye, Rowland had shifted into wolf form and leapt toward Earc without warning. No wonder so many feared him in wolf form. Rowland was easily as big as Barr with a wild look in his canine eyes that would make most Chrechte pause before facing him in battle. Earc was not most Chrechte, nor was Barr. One day, God willing, they would train the Donegal Chrechte to be such soldiers.

Rowland's fast change and leap showed he was still as agile as many a younger canine as well. Not that it would do him any good.

The action, while impressive, was a dirty trick. Though not strictly against the rules of combat, it bordered on breaking them. Barr's jaw went rigid, but he checked his initial instinct, at the blatant show of disrespect, to shift and tear the wolf's throat out.

Earc would handle the challenge without a problem, Barr was confident. His confidence proved true when Rowland's lack of honor bought the former laird nothing.

Earc was ready for the powerful beast, deflecting him with a well-timed shove to the wolf's chest, sending the huge beast tumbling. Rowland rolled onto his feet, snarling and showing a set of sharp teeth, spit flying as he tossed his head.

Earc grinned and mocked, "Am I supposed to be impressed, you ugly son of a bitch?"

The wolf sprang again, but Earc wasn't giving the beast any openings, and this time he swiped at the wolf's flank with his dagger as he twisted out of the way.

Talorc had taught them to weaken a wolf with blood loss before moving in for the kill. To go in for the final blow too early was to risk sustaining an injury that might well lead to a soldier's lingering death after a fight was long over. Especially if the fight was far from the full moon and the Chrechte did not have control of his change. Shifting would not heal a wound, but it helped make sure the wound healed well and did not get infected.

He did not understand the why of it, but assumed it had to do with the same magic that brought the change over a wolf's body to begin with.

Earc was following their former laird's instructions with flawless follow-through in this battle. He avoided going down under Rowland's repeated attacks, wounding the wolf on each pass. Despite snapping again and again, Rowland's powerful jaws never closed on any part of Earc's body. It was clear the massive wolf was tiring, but he was growing more and more enraged as well.

That could be dangerous.

Furious fighters were sloppy, but they were also unpredictable.

Rowland managed a swipe along Earc's chest with his claws and the scent of his foe's blood seemed to send him into a frenzy. He went after Earc with renewed vigor, making sounds Barr had never heard from a wolf for all the battles he had fought in. Rowland's wolf was crazed with bloodlust and a bitter fury that stank like spoiled meat.

Once again, Earc showed his superior training because he was ready for the wolf's flurried attack, even though Barr was sure he'd never met an opponent so infected with bloodlust.

Earc used the beast's momentum to send him tumbling again, but this time he followed, landing on the self-admitted murderer and straddling the mighty wolf's body. Rowland had been weakened by blood loss, but was strengthened by battle frenzy beyond a normal wolf's strength. Even that of a Chrechte.

Earc refused to be unseated, however, keeping the wolf's strong jaws away from his more vulnerable skin.

Bringing his knife down in a powerful arc, Earc stabbed straight through to the heart, killing the wolf instantly.

Stunned silence permeated the clearing. None moved. None spoke. Disbelief was a living entity among them. Into this utter quiet a loud, triumphant raven's caw sounded over the shocked gathering. Barr realized that if Sabrine had disobeyed him, she'd no doubt done it with Verica's help. The raven was singing her mate's victory over the man she believed had killed her father.

A raven he had believed to be a wolf. Could one Chrechte pretend the scent of another as they could mask their own? Or was Verica the unthinkable? A woman with not one but two Chrechte forms.

'Twas a question he would have answers to, but later.

Right now was time for establishing his role as pack leader and Earc's unquestioned position as his second.

Barr tipped his head back and howled. It took a moment, but others joined him. Not Earc though. A Chrechte never took the death of one of his kind lightly, even if he had been forced to do the killing.

While others might make their approval known, and should, Earc would not howl his joy at defeating his foe for there was one less Chrechte in the world and their numbers were not high.

Earc's visage was grim as he retrieved Rowland's human weapons and presented them to Barr with solemn reverence.

Barr accepted the sword and dagger, though he had no desire to keep them. He looked around the clearing, his gaze taking in the varied reactions to Rowland's death. Relief, disbelief, horror, joy, anger, hope—and all of it tinged by shock—choked the clearing.

Barr lifted the weapons, looking at each member of his pack individually. Some did not meet his gaze, but all belonged to his pack, to his protection—until they proved themselves unworthy. "I am laird here. Does anyone question my right to lead?"

Several shouted firm denials and others howled, but

none put their vote forward in the affirmative. None challenged him.

"The Chrechte live among the human clans to protect our race. In return we protect those we live among. We do not abuse them because we are stronger or faster."

This time the affirmation was louder and the howls more triumphant. This pack had suffered under Rowland's leadership. Barr would give them a chance to prove they wanted the change he offered.

Waiting for the pack to fall silent, he carefully noted those who did *not* join in affirming the Chrechte law regarding their lives among the humans.

"From this point forward, every Chrechte male will train as a warrior." Some had been holding back and he had not made it mandatory, trying to get an understanding for why a people whose violent natures had almost led to their own extinction would not be in training for the protection of their people.

"Will you teach us how to defeat a Chrechte in his wolf form while still a human?" one young man called out.

"Aye."

Earc stood beside him. "We'll be teaching the human men in our clan how to fight Chrechte as well, without revealing our nature."

"Like you did with Muin and the human soldiers yesterday?" a woman asked.

"That's right."

"Rowland never allowed the elite soldiers to train with the humans. He said it would make us weak," one of Circin's friends said.

"Does Earc appear weak to you?"

"No!"

"His primary role among the Sinclairs was preparing humans to meet a Chrechte attack."

Looks of surprised respect showed over several faces.

"One day Circin will lead you; until that day I will train every man in this clan the way of a true Chrechte warrior."

Shouts of approval went up, the deafening sound growing until those not joining in were more conspicuous in their silence. Distance grew between them and the others, as their fellow clansmen pulled away from the disapproving visages.

Earc frowned as he looked around and clearly noted those withholding their support. "Too bad none of them would challenge you."

"If they share Rowland's attitudes, they probably share his propensity for sneakiness and ambush."

"You do not think his death will end the attempts to undermine your role here?"

"Cut off the head of a snake and the body still writhes after, not knowing it is dead."

Earc nodded his understanding. "Not all were pleased by my victory."

"Nay."

"We will have to remain ever vigilant."

"When are we anything else?"

"I don't know. When you are chasing the scent of a naked woman through the forest perhaps?"

Barr almost smiled at the reminder. "Did you see her on the rock ledge to the north?"

"I was pretending not to. She's dressed like a man."

"She's an uncommon woman."

"Aye, she is that."

"The raven who crowed her triumph when you won, I believe that was your mate."

Earc did not show his surprise, but his heart sped up. "Verica is a wolf."

"With a mother who was a raven."

"I thought the old bastard was just throwing insults, though I admit I didn't understand how calling her mother a raven was one."

"The Éan are not myth."

"Damn."

"'Tis no easy thing to accept."

"Are you sure that was Verica?"

"As sure as I can be without her admitting it."

"It sounds like my new mate and I have much to talk about."

"Before or after you bed her?"

"Does it matter?"

"Nay."

Barr did not allow the character of the dead Chrechte to stop him doing his duty. A funeral pyre was built, Rowland's wolf was laid on top and they all held vigil while the fire burned hot enough to singe anyone foolish enough to get too close.

All the Chrechte held vigil, though few showed any true grief at their former pack leader's passing.

Verica arrived, her expression cheerless despite the fact she had good reason to want the man dead.

Sabrine was with her, her own acute distaste for the deceased more than apparent on her beautiful features. She received several looks askance, but seemed unperturbed by them.

"You do not obey well."

"So you noted once already."

"No, I said you did not listen well before. I had given you the benefit of the doubt and assumed you had not heard me aright about staying in my room."

"My hearing is excellent."

"No doubt." He fingered her plaid. "'Tis a bit short on you, do you not think?"

"Longer skirts would have gotten in my way."

"Doing what? Flaunting my authority?"

"Saving your second. Circin would not have made it in time, though the culprit insists he did not intend to kill— only wound."

"You have weapons."

"I do."

"They are too small to be made for a man."

"For a man of your size, certainly."

He paused. That was true. There were some smaller men among the clans, and even the Chrechte were not always tall. "I believe they were made for a woman."

"I cannot help what you believe."

"And you will not answer my question."

"You have not asked one."

"Were I a less patient man, you would infuriate me."

"Were you a less patient man, Rowland would have been dead long before today."

He could not argue with that sentiment. "You and Verica have much in common."

"You think her infuriating?"

"I think you share a Chrechte nature."

Chapter 11

Barr did not mention the raven now; too many of the clan were close by and no howls sounded to mask their discussion as they had when he and Earc had spoken earlier.

Rowland had clearly taken issue with the raven among the Chrechte. His friends might well feel the same and Barr would not expose Verica to possible danger.

He had to dispose of the entire serpent first.

The quiet stillness in the woman beside him could bode shock, anger, worry . . . anything. She was not allowing even a hint of her emotions near enough to the surface for his wolf to identify.

"We will discuss it later," he told her.

She did not answer. Unlike this morning, when he'd had the distinct feeling she intended to try to avoid the conversation he wanted, he could sense right now she was eager for it.

Interesting. This woman, dressed in a man's plaid, would never bore him, of that he was sure.

"A new day has dawned for the Donegal Chrechte," Verica said as the flames shot high into the sky.

"The new dawning happened the day I arrived; you all merely didna realize it."

Earc nodded, his mien serious. "Aye."

Verica shook her head, but a spark of a smile showed in her eyes before they returned to watching the rapidly burning pyre.

Naught but ashes would be left before midday was reached.

The trip back to the keep was a silent one and Sabrine made no effort to speak herself. No doubt Barr knew he would face the man whom Rowland had convinced to help him. He was an honorable laird. He would not relish killing another clan member so close to the old laird.

And she could not let him. Though she had yet to figure out how best to stop him.

Connor was guilty of treason by almost any definition. The fact he had been coerced would carry little consequence with most leaders, the Éan Council of Three included.

Circin waited in the hall with Connor and the man's human father. His Chrechte mother had been at the challenge and had waited to watch her cousin's body burn.

She rushed to her son's side, a keening wail coming from her throat. "No . . ."

Sabrine watched as Barr met the father's gaze. Sabrine could not miss the resignation and determination there. It tugged at her just as his son's determination to protect his father had done.

She stepped forward so she stood beside Barr, not sure why she did so, but it felt right.

The human Donegal man's eyes widened, his solemn mask cracking in surprise.

Sabrine remembered then that the clan women never wore men's kilts. Perhaps she should have changed before coming into the hall, but she needed to be here to keep her promise to Connor.

Barr looked down at her. "This is the man you stopped from shooting his bow at my second?"

"He did not want to do it."

Barr checked, clearly surprised by the defense. "No?"

"You know what a despicable bitch's son that foul wolf was." She'd only been exposed briefly to the other man and she could not miss it. Barr had lived in the same clan with him for more than a month. "He threatened the boy's father."

The man in question made a sound of profound grief and Connor's mother started to sob. Neither begged Barr for their son's life, however.

Sabrine was certain that was not because they didn't want to, but having lived so long under Rowland's leadership, they did not know leaders could be merciful as well as violent and selfish.

The father came forward, dropping to his knee in front of Barr. "In accordance with clan law, I offer myself in my son's stead for punishment."

Barr frowned. "You are aware he is guilty of treason against his clan and his laird."

The older man nodded, the weight of his son's circumstances bowing his shoulders.

"You will die for your son?"

"No!" Connor shouted as he tried to break the ties binding him to the bench on which he sat.

His mother's sobs were quiet, but shook her entire body.

Sabrine laid her hand on Barr's arm. "Will you hear testimony on the boy's behalf?"

He stared down at her. "You caught him with the bow, what could you possibly add that might sway my decision?"

Oh, the sheer arrogance of men.

"I can attest to his mind-set when I found him. I can tell you how easily and quickly he dropped his bow. As a Chrechte I can tell you he told the truth when he said he did not intend to kill Earc, but was forced to try to shoot him with an arrow because of the threats against his father."

Barr did not appear moved. "Rowland's threats carried no weight. He was marked for death."

"Connor did not believe your second could defeat Rowland. None of us did," the Chrechte mother said with a valiant effort to control her tears.

Barr said nothing, his expression giving away only what he wanted it to. He'd masked his scent so effectively, even Sabrine could not tell what he was feeling.

Sabrine moved to stand in front of the human male. "I gave my word not to let anything happen to this man."

"To whom did you give your word?" Barr demanded with a scowl.

"To Connor, of course."

"Laird, Connor had no love for Rowland, but he is a good son," Verica said.

"He didn't want to kill Earc," Circin added.

"He has always kept our secret," another Chrechte who had followed them into the hall added.

"If Rowland deserved to die for his supposed sins, this *human*"—one of the older Chrechte spat the word—"must die for his."

Barr turned toward the old man, his expression no longer neutral. Rage cast his features in lines that probably should have frightened her but Sabrine found much too appealing.

The man was strong enough to match her. She had not known another warrior she felt this way about.

"Your opinion is of no consequence to me, old man, in this or any other matter." There was something under the surface of Barr's words, as if the other man should know exactly what his laird referred to.

The gray-headed Chrechte sneered at Sabrine as if she had said something foul.

Barr growled, the sound sending chills down her spine and arms. She had to suppress a shiver.

Barr snarled, "Do not think I neglected to mark your lack of support of my lairdship this morn."

The recalcitrant man flinched, his anger draining to be replaced by blatant fear.

"You may give me your pledge of allegiance, or leave the clan." Barr looked like he'd prefer the latter.

Fury arced off the older Chrechte but he inclined his head, just barely baring his throat.

Barr did not look pleased, but he nodded with a short jerk of his head. "You may move your things to a relative's home. Your quarters in the keep will be needed for my new seneschal."

"Who?"

But Barr ignored him, dismissing the older man without another word as he turned back to her and the man kneeling behind her.

"Step away from Aodh. His view of the back of your legs is unseemly."

She didn't laugh, but it was a close thing. "You're a very possessive man."

"Aye."

"Will you attempt to kill the human?"

"Attempt?"

She just glared. If he didn't think she could save the man, he would soon learn differently.

Barr shook his head. "Allow me the courtesy of your respect."

"I do respect you."

"Prove it."

She crossed her arms and gave him a look that told him not to let her regret it as she moved to the side.

"You are certain you wish to take your son's punishment?"

The man nodded, his determination not wavering even as his fear turned the air sour.

Barr considered the man in silence for several long moments. He lifted his gaze and met Connor's eyes. The young soldier had silent tears tracking his cheeks.

"In attempting to save your father's life, you may well have cost him it."

"No. Please. Do as you must to me, but let my father live."

"Your son loves you more than his own life, but by your actions, you prove he came by such sacrifice naturally."

Aodh did not reply, the fear for his son a solid wall around him.

"Neither of you will lose your lives this day. My mate pleads mercy and I will give it."

She'd never pleaded, but she wasn't about to argue and risk changing Barr's mind.

Barr spared her a glance, the amusement lurking beneath his solemn expression testimony to the fact he'd intended to tease her with the comment.

Then he settled his full attention on Aodh. "You will take the position as my seneschal. Proving your family's allegiance to my leadership, you will move into the keep and use your skills to improve the productivity of our holding."

"You want me to be your seneschal?" Aodh looked as if a puff of air might knock him on his backside, he was so shocked.

"Aye. I have lived in this clan for more than a month, sufficient time to see you are the kind of man to serve the clan best in this role. Next to my second, you will have the highest level of responsibility in this holding."

"Even after . . ." Aodh's voice trailed off, but his gaze strayed to his astonished son.

"It is done. Naught will be gained by revisiting the past."

It was a very recent past to dismiss so easily, but Sabrine was not about to say so.

"Thank you, laird."

Barr inclined his head.

"Will you give me your allegiance?"

"Yes!" The man dropped his forehead forward, pounding his left breast with a hard fist.

Barr smiled then, his expression dimming only slightly when his eyes landed on Connor. "I expect you to train with the soldiers, beginning this afternoon."

"But I'm not good for aught but hunting."

"You doubt my wisdom?"

Circin was busy untying the man as Connor shook his head with vehemence.

"In future, you will trust your laird to protect you as a member of his family—you are my clan."

Connor's eyes grew suspiciously bright once again, but the relief and joy rolling off him left no doubt any tears he blinked away were not of sorrow.

His mother hugged him hard and then came forward to stand beside her husband, who had gained his feet. "I will serve you any way possible."

"Rowland did not approve of you taking a human for a mate."

"No, he did not."

"He was an idiot."

Her eyes widened, but she gave a short nod.

"Help me change this clan to one all can be proud to call family."

"I will."

Sabrine returned to Verica's room to change back into her woman's plaid, the pleated skirts sweeping the floor. There was no doubt it was warmer, but the confinement of movement was not something she wished to grow accustomed to.

"Did Rowland live here in the keep?" Sabrine asked Verica.

She had a difficult time accepting her search could be made that simple, but she had no such difficulty hoping at least.

Verica didn't answer, acting as if she hadn't heard Sabrine's words. It didn't offend her or surprise her. The other woman had been acting preoccupied since leaving the hall.

Verica tucked the plaid in the trunk and closed the lid, leaving the weapons on the bed. The sword gleamed from the healer's care and the dagger remained tucked neatly in its scabbard. Sabrine's hands itched to take them up and rearm herself, but neither was hers. They had belonged to an Éan warrior long since dead and were part of Verica's heritage, even if she did not care to acknowledge it. A warrior's blood ran in her veins, just as a healer's did.

Another heritage the two women shared.

Life had dictated they travel different paths, but under the surface, they were much the same.

Still, Sabrine's life was that of a warrior and she felt naked without weapons. She had not intended to go without them so long, but she had not expected to be shot out of the sky with an arrow, either.

Her sword and two deadly sharp daggers were hidden high in a tree in the forest. She'd thought she could easily get to them if needed, but with her injured arm, it would be some days before she flew as a raven again.

"Hmmm?" Verica murmured, as if just now realizing Sabrine had spoken.

"Rowland. Did he make his home here?" Sabrine had assumed he lived in his own cottage. When Barr had told the other disagreeable Chrechte elder he needed to move out of the keep, she'd recognized her assumption might be false.

"Oh." Verica paused as if running the question through her mind again. "Yes. His room was off the hall, the same as Muin's grandfather's used to be. I'll need to clean it out and give Rowland's things to his sister."

"Was she at the challenge today?"

"No. She's not a shifting Chrechte. She's his half sister. Her mother was human." Verica frowned, a flicker of disgust showing on her features. "Their father did not recognize her, though the resemblance was undeniable. His Chrechte wife was not his true mate and he did not hesitate to sow his seed where he willed."

"Blackguard." A man caught in adultery among the Éan would be banished, at best. The Council of Three adhered to the ancient laws under certain circumstances and executions had taken place in her lifetime as well.

"Yes."

Rowland had learned at least some of his atrocious behavior at the feet of his father. "The acorn did not fall far from the tree then."

"You're right. His father hated raven shifters as well." Verica shivered, as if mention of the long-dead man still had the power to upset her.

It was a reaction Sabrine had no trouble understanding. She would never forget the scent of the wolf that had murdered her parents. Sometimes it came to her in her dreams and she woke shaking and sweating and glad no one shared her bed to see her so weak.

She'd thought she smelled it earlier, but the scent had been so faint, she now realized it had been the unusually tense circumstances that tricked her mind into thinking so. "There are others among your clan who despise our people."

"Yes, but others do not. However, to guess wrongly

which direction a wolf's inclinations take him or her could cost a raven shifter her life."

"As I guessed." Even if she could abandon her role as protector to her people, she could not live among the Donegal clan without risking death. She could not stay with Barr. Sabrine kept her voice neutral as she offered, "I'll help you clean out Rowland's room, if you like."

"You don't need to do that." Verica looked around, seeming lost and yet not so much disturbed as again occupied with thoughts that took her elsewhere. "We could ask Connor's mother as she will no doubt be the housekeeper of the keep now that her husband has been named seneschal."

"But to do so would not feel right, surely. Even if she was related to the old wolf. He caused her family too much grief."

He'd caused more than a fair share for Verica and Circin as well, but the other woman still nodded. "Exactly."

"So, allow me to help." It would be an ideal opportunity for Sabrine to make her search for the *Clach Gealach Gra*. She could not be certain Rowland had stolen the Éan's sacred talisman, but he did seem the most likely culprit. He would clearly have been happy to see the Éan die out as a race.

Verica asked, "If you are sure?"

"I have naught else to do while I wait for my arm to heal."

"Except train the women of this clan to defend themselves," Barr said from the doorway.

Both women jumped, Sabrine shocked she had not felt his approach. The wicked glint in his gray gaze said he'd masked his approach on purpose.

She bit back a smile. The man was a handful, that was certain. Any Éan would be proud to call him mate. She wished they had a future beyond the time it would take her to find the *Clach Gealach Gra* and heal enough to fly again.

"You heard about that?" she asked, hoping he would not attempt to deny her.

"Brigit was most forthcoming, though she did not mean to be."

And what did that mean? He was Faol, so could not have the gift of mind reading, which was so rarely bestowed on the Éan. But he was wolf, and he could read emotions and honesty. Brigit was human; she could not hide the truth behind spoken lies from a Chrechte.

"You do not object?"

"Nay. While I have never known a female warrior before you, I have long believed all members of a clan need at least rudimentary training in how to protect their homes."

"And their persons." Women, especially in this clan, she thought, needed to be able to defend themselves.

He jerked his head in acknowledgment, his jaw going hard at some internal thought. "Aye, and their persons."

The connection between them snapped into place in a way she had not experienced when creating a link for mindspeak with Verica. His emotions poured through the inexplicable bond. Fury at the way Sorcha had been treated, concern for other women who might have been misused, determination—though she could not tell about what, and underlying all of it was a sexual hunger directed solely at her. So strong, it rushed through her, leaving heated flames in its wake.

She swayed and Verica gave her an odd look. Determined not to be ruled by this wealth of feeling between them, feelings that had no future, Sabrine forced herself to ignore the desire coursing through her.

She drew herself up. "I would be pleased to train the women."

"Thank you. I won't make it mandatory as I have with the men."

"Why not?"

"Choosing my battles."

She did smile then. "Intelligence is an admirable trait."

"Aye."

"Arrogant man."

"You like me as I am."

She did. Too much. "How many of Rowland's cronies live here in the keep?"

If he hadn't stolen the Heart of the Moon stone, one of his companions probably had.

"The soldiers' barracks is behind the main hall." Barr shrugged. "I do not know how many of the younger Chrechte sided with Rowland's skewed beliefs, or how many of the elders did not, but 'tis something I can better guess after today."

"Are there any others besides Muin's grandfather who had their own quarters?" Sabrine asked.

Barr gave her a speculative look, his brows narrowing.

Verica didn't hesitate to answer. "Aye. Rowland's brother lives in a room on the other side of mine."

"He had a brother, too?"

At her continued questions, a watchful attitude settled over Barr, but he did not attempt to distract her from getting answers.

"Yes. The man is a good twenty years younger," Verica explained. "He was born to their parents late in life and their mother died giving birth."

"So, he is a full shifting Chrechte?"

"Oh, yes. Rowland would never have recognized him otherwise."

"Why aren't you giving him Rowland's things?"

"Padraig has no interest in material things and he does recognize their sister. It was one of the things he and Rowland disagreed on. Padraig would be the first to insist Rowland's possessions be given to their sister."

"It sounds like he and the former laird had little in common."

"Much to Rowland's chagrin, but you are right."

"Was Padraig at the challenge today?" Sabrine could not remember seeing anyone who resembled the older wolf.

Verica picked up the weapons and moved them to a shelf on the wall. "He was, but he drew no attention to himself, not by showing support of Rowland or refusing to affirm our laird's leadership."

Sabrine could not help giving the dagger and sword a last longing look.

"He was not overly loud in his affirmation." The lack of expression on Barr's features and the neutral tone of his voice gave no indication of how he regarded the other man's less-than-enthusiastic support.

"Is he angry you were brought in to lead?" Sabrine asked.

"He has shown no antagonism. In truth, he spends more time with the priest than the warriors. I know little about him."

Sabrine nodded, understanding the two men would not have crossed paths often under such circumstances. "He's never criticized our new laird as some of the other men have," Verica added.

"Did he expect to be laird one day?"

"Rowland always promised Circin would have his rightful place when he came of age, but I never believed he would follow through on that promise."

Thoughtful, Sabrine frowned. "But do you think he intended his brother to follow in his footsteps?"

She did not like the idea there might yet be a serpent in the Donegals' midst that could well rise up to strike at Barr.

"The fact his room was on this floor and the others lived on the lower level showed more than mere physical distance between the brothers," Verica said. "Padraig and Circin have always gotten along, but the man just isn't a warrior. Not like most Chrechte, and Rowland knew it. He complained about it enough, but Padraig spends his days studying the priest's Latin texts and filling sheets of his own writing."

"So, he does not avoid training because his brother is no longer in charge?" Barr asked.

"Oh, no. He was always forgetting to show up for Rowland's days with the soldiers."

Barr seemed content with that and unbothered that one of his Chrechte was uninterested in warfare.

"He's a learned man, then?" Sabrine asked. The Éan did not have the luxury of supporting scholars, living as wraiths in the forest the way they did. Though there were still those who cloistered themselves with what learning and study they could.

"He is. Padraig and Father Thomas are good friends, spending many an evening discussing topics that most of the warriors understand less than they do how to use a weaver's loom."

The Éan practiced more ancient rites of worship than the Faol. Few were born with the instinct to lead their people spiritually, but those who were had no place in their lives for the warrior's path. This was one immutable law among the Éan. And not even the Council Elder in charge of the warriors such as her ever questioned it.

She wondered if Rowland's brother was such a Chrechte. "Is he a priest in training then?"

She was not sure what they called such holy men among the clans.

Verica shook her head, sadness reflected in her gaze. "Rowland would not hear of a Chrechte taking the vow of celibacy."

The human priests were celibate? How odd. But still. "There are more important matters than procreation."

"Not according to Rowland."

"Rowland was destroying this clan and the pack that called it home." Disgust warred with worry in Barr's tone. "Men untrained for battle, women forced to provide what should be theirs to gift alone, scholars held back from that which they have been born to do. It is a perversion of all the Chrechte have achieved since joining the clans."

Verica's eyes filled and spilled over.

Sabrine stared at her, not sure what to do with the weeping woman as she did not see what reason the other woman had to grieve.

Surely Verica saw that Barr intended to make changes within their pack and clan for the better.

Then Verica threw her arms around her laird and hugged him hard. "Thank you."

Barr stared at Sabrine over the other woman's shoulder, his expression bordering on panic. He was clearly demanding she do something, but she was a warrior, not a nursemaid.

"What the hell are you doing holding my mate?" Earc demanded from the doorway.

Chapter 12

No real ire in his voice, in point of fact, Earc looked amused to no end by his friend's clear predicament.

Verica finally released her laird, patting his arm for good measure and giving him a watery smile. She turned to face Earc. "You and Barr have brought life back to this clan. I was merely saying thank you."

"It didn't sound to me like you were saying anything at all," Earc teased, the humor more pronounced now in his light brown gaze.

Verica frowned, seeming to come to herself. "What are you doing in my room? 'Tis unseemly."

"I am your mate, 'tis most seemly. Barr's presence, however, is open to misinterpretation."

"No, it is not." Barr's glare dared his second to disagree. Earc merely lifted one dark brow.

Verica shook her head. "For goodness sake, you two are like small boys the way you poke at each other."

"I have not been called small in more years than I remember," Barr said, somewhat bemused.

Earc just shrugged. "I have spoken to the priest. Father Thomas can perform our marriage before the evening meal."

Verica stumbled back, her eyes going wide, her heart rate suddenly the pace of a running wolf on the hunt. Or maybe the hare being hunted. "What did you say?"

Earc approached her, but Verica stepped back and to the side.

He stopped, his brows drawing together, the scent in the air going dangerous from one heartbeat to the next. "You heard me."

She shook her head in denial.

He nodded, taking another step toward her.

"No." Sabrine no more understood the other woman's panicked tone than she had the tears earlier. To this point, Verica had shown nothing but a rather rattled acceptance of Earc's claim. She'd been grateful, even, that the strong warrior had stepped in to save her brother from an unfair challenge.

All of Earc's affability disappeared. "Aye. I claimed you as my mate this morn, and I'll not have any challenge that claim because I have not followed up with human tradition."

Verica's eyes rolled like those of a horse not yet ridden when facing a rider for the first time, and she bolted from the room.

Earc swore.

"It appears you need to catch your mate before she makes a break for England."

Earc gave Barr a sour look. "No need to get insulting."

Barr shrugged, but a smile played at the corners of his mouth.

Earc shook his head and spun on his heel before taking off after Verica with a wolf's speed.

Barr's gaze on the empty doorway, he mused, "I think their mating may be a stormy one."

"Only until he realizes asking is more effective than ordering when it is between mates." Though Sabrine could not say for certain that's what had Verica running. The woman's scent had turned too much like that of prey for Sabrine to understand what had been going through her mind. Surely she knew that she was safe with Earc.

Or was she?

Verica was raven as well as wolf and Earc was fully of the Faol of the Chrechte.

"Is it now?" Barr's lazy drawl caressed Sabrine's insides, bringing forth the desire always simmering under the surface when she was near him.

"Yes."

"You sound very definite."

What were they talking about again? Oh, yes. "That is because I have no doubt."

"I see. You believe I should ask if you would like to accompany me to our bedchamber rather than pick you up and carry you there?"

Her answer was unnecessary as he'd already done just that.

The air around them filled with the spice of their attraction and rather than fight it, she allowed it to wash over her until she was light-headed with the effect.

She did not know how long she had with this amazing warrior of the Faol, but she would enjoy every moment given her. For one thing was certain: there would not be many of them.

Earc caught up with Verica by the time she was on the steps. He said nothing, content to wait to ask what the hell she was doing running from him until she had walked off most of her upset.

'Twas something his oldest brother told him worked well with women. Earc had no reason to doubt the other man's wisdom, for his mating was a happy one.

She didn't stop in the hall, but went outside, through the courtyard, across the fields and into the forest. The fragrance of summer-sun-heated earth and heather did not mask that of prey. The temptation to go hunting rose and just as quickly settled.

Catching a mate was even more pressing a need. Strange that, when he had not come to the Donegals planning to find his mate, or even hoping for it.

She skirted the area where Earc had fought his challenge; the smell of charred wood and ash hung heavy in the air. The reminder he had been forced to take the life of a fellow wolf today gave him no sense of loss. Rowland may have been Chrechte, but he had been on the verge of destroying his pack. There was nothing to grieve in the loss of a man so evil and selfish.

They did not stop walking until she reached the small brook beyond the clearing. She was silent, looking over the water and then up to the sky. He did not press her for words, content to wait until she told him what had sent her running from the keep.

'Twas not him because she'd made no effort to get away from him since leaving her room, though he had not enjoyed the feeling of her rushing out of the room after his announcement.

Her head tilted back and she gazed up at the sky for long moments of silence before saying, "I changed into a raven for the first time in this spot."

He looked around them. It seemed a good place for a first shift, but he could not connect to the concept she was both bird and wolf. "I did not know the Chrechte could have two natures."

"It is very rare, but when two who are different species

are true bonded, their children can carry both natures within them."

.It was information none among his pack was privy to, at least to his knowledge. The very existence of the Éan was more myth than reality for the Sinclair pack. "Your parents were sacred mates." According to what she had just said, it could be no other way.

"Yes." The wealth of meaning in that one word hit him with the force of a blow from Barr's fist.

"You hoped for the same."

She gave him a measured sidelong glance. "Truthfully, I thought never to mate at all."

"Why?"

"To risk discovery of my raven is to risk death."

Surely she did not fear him. "I will never harm you."

"You aren't like the men of my clan." It was not outright agreement, but it was close enough.

"Nay, I am not."

Instead of being comforted, she grew more agitated. Her breathing quickened while perspiration formed on her forehead and upper lip, the smell of her distress bringing a howl to his wolf's heart.

It was his job to protect his mate, from everything that might harm or cause her serious emotional turmoil. His father had taught him that truth, but Earc's wolf would have made itself known regardless.

She chewed on her lower lip, her hands twisting in her skirts.

"I love my brother."

"As you should."

"The clan relies on me as their healer."

"Are there no others?"

"None who apprenticed with a master healer like my mother, who taught me to treat a wide range of ailments."

"The Donegal clan is lucky to have you."

"I don't want to leave." She looked up at him with beautiful blue eyes that pleaded for understanding.

He could not deny her, but he still did not understand why she was so upset. He wasn't going to marry her and return to the Sinclair holding this very night, or even in the next year or two. "You are not going anywhere."

"As your mate, I would one day, sooner than later, be forced to leave my family."

"As I left mine behind to come here."

"Yes."

"I have parents and siblings to share with you among the Sinclairs." Could she not see the benefit?

"I am all Circin has."

"I will become his brother as well with our mating."

"What good will that do him with you leaving to return to the clan of your birth?" she asked, her tone accusing and anguished all at once.

And all at once he understood her reticence about the mating. "It will be years before I would return."

"I don't want to leave at all."

He could have reminded her that as his mate, she had no choice but to go where he went. He could have assured her that all would be well, that she would love life among the Sinclairs, but something held all those words back.

He looked down at her, at this woman who had suffered so much loss already in her life and still served her clan with her healing arts. She was not bitter or twisted by her sorrow, but she pulled back from wanting more.

How could he not be moved by such strength matched by equal vulnerability?

"There is only two days' journey between the Donegal keep and Sinclair's castle."

"Is there?"

"We can visit my family yearly."

"Visit?" A tendril of hope sounded in her voice.

"Aye."

"So, we would live here, among my clan?"

"Among *our* clan."

"We could stay with your family for a sennight, or more, each year." The eagerness in her tone made him smile.

She reached out as if to touch him but then pulled her hand back.

He grabbed her hand and brought it to his face. That strange charge like miniature lightning arced between them.

She looked up at him shyly. "I like when you smile."

"I like when you smell of joy rather than sorrow."

"You care if I am happy." Wonder and astonishment laced her voice.

"I do."

"Like my father with my mother," she said, almost in awe. "You are not sickened by my raven nature."

"No." Why would she even ask that? She had already acknowledged that she did not believe he was like the other men of her clan.

She turned away, a sense of caution surrounding her. "There is a thing you still do not know."

"Tell me."

"The ravens have gifts beyond their shifting nature."

"As do wolves."

She huffed, as if frustrated by his lack of understanding. "I can sense imminent death in a person."

"What do you mean?"

"You know how the raven seems to always be able to tell when death is coming within its territory?"

"Aye. It is uncanny, that."

"Those of the Éan share much with their bird nature, beyond that which others might accept."

"Explain."

"If I lay my hands on someone, I can feel if they are going to die." She said the words without any inflection of emotion, but he did not believe this gift came without great cost to one as compassionate as his mate.

"'Tis a useful talent for a healer to have." If not a particularly pleasant one for her tender heart.

"Perhaps. It was how I knew my parents did not die in the natural way of things."

He did not understand and was smart enough not to pretend he did. "Because you did not sense their deaths?" he tried guessing.

"I do not, when the death is caused by another person."

"Murder." The foul word left a sour taste on his tongue.

"Or challenge. Or battle."

That made a bit more sense. Like the ravens who shared a nature with her, she sensed nature's culling of its inhabitants. "So, you did not know Rowland would die in the challenge."

"I would never have gotten close enough to touch him to find out." Her abhorrence at the very thought rang in her soft voice. "If I had, I would not have known, as his death came at your hand."

"If your father had really been killed by a wild beast—"

"I would have sensed it before he left our cottage and warned him. My Chrechte gifts had just begun to show themselves. For the longest time, I thought it was my fault, that I had somehow ignored the warning in my raven senses. But later I realized the warning did not come if death was by the hand of man."

"And your mother?"

"Was definitely murdered." Everything about the way she held herself, the fierce expression in her blue gaze, the tone in her voice—it all spoke of absolute certainty.

A certainty she had been forced to live with since the tragedy, with no recourse against those she believed responsible. "By the bastard Rowland."

"I always believed so, but had no proof."

And no way to bring him to justice if she had, considering the stranglehold he'd had on the Donegal clan and Chrechte pack. "Now he has finally paid the price for his cruelties." Earc couldn't suppress a wish the man lived just a little longer so he could kill him again.

"He chose his victim poorly with his words this time."

"He *thought* he was targeting Circin." And the wily shifter would have killed the less-seasoned pup without remorse had Circin made the challenge instead of Earc.

"He meant Circin to challenge him. He was looking for a way to get rid of my brother."

"Aye." It had not been an overly clever move, but it would have been effective if Rowland had gotten away with it. Barr would never have allowed it, of course, but Earc had his own reasons for stepping in.

"I owe you so much. You saved my brother's life; you saved my clan." The approval in her voice gave him pleasure.

But he was not a man to take credit where it was not fully due. "Barr had no plan to let Rowland live after discovering his gross offense against Sorcha."

Verica nodded, once again biting her lush bottom lip, turning it red and tempting him to taste. "He is a good man to train my brother to lead one day."

"Aye, he is." But Earc's attention was not on his laird's positive qualities. He was far too occupied with thoughts of how his mate's mouth and the tender flesh behind her ear would taste on his tongue.

She looked up at him, her eyes shining with an emotion he had no name for. "But you are still the man who saved him."

"By claiming you for my mate." Simply saying the words made the craving between them grow until he could think of little else.

She looked down, hiding her expressive eyes from him, perhaps trying to hide her own desire, but the fragrance of her feminine arousal gave her away. "Yes."

"The connection between us is strong."

"It is." The words were almost a whisper.

"Why do you hide from me?"

"I am afraid of you."

The words were worse than any blow he had received in battle. He had spent the last month dreaming of this woman, growing more and more enamored of her until the move to claim her as mate this morning had seemed the most natural course to take.

And she feared him.

He stepped back, so that amazing connection no longer hummed between them. Perhaps it was more one-sided than he'd believed. Perhaps his wolf's senses deceived him. "What have I done to deserve such?"

She clasped her hands in front of her, twisting them as anxiety surrounded them thicker than the morning mist. And twice as cold.

"Answer me." He would have her words; he was no ogre to be feared by the woman destined to bear his children.

"I could love you," she said, her voice so quiet, it was not even a whisper.

Were he not wolf, he would not have heard. But he *was* wolf and he *did* hear and still it made no sense.

"How is this a bad thing? Should a woman not love her mate?"

Her head snapped up at that, fire shooting near-irresistible sparks from her pretty blue eyes. "And what of you? Will you love me, too?"

"'Tis a man's duty to care for his mate."

"Care for and love are not the same."

"Women may mark the distinction, a warrior does not."

"Sabrine is a warrior. I'm sure she notes it."

"Sabrine is a mystery Barr best solve before this clan is put in peril."

"You think she puts us at risk? She is no Rowland, looking for power at the end of a fist."

"She comes from a people who all believed were myth."

"Not all," she said, reminding him that Verica, too, was raven.

"How could your clan remain ignorant of your dual nature?"

"Éan are taught from childhood to mask their true scent."

"But the Chrechte nature does not show itself until a body begins the physical journey to adulthood."

"For the Faol. Ravens do not shift until that time, but the ability to mask emotion and scent is one we are born with."

"All ravens?" For not all Faol had the gift.

"As far as I know."

"And this other gift?"

"It is manifested after our coming of age ceremony."

"You have a ceremony for such?"

"All Chrechte used to, but the Faol stopped performing theirs once they joined the clans."

"'Twas too wrapped in violence and sexual mating." He remembered the stories but could not imagine participating in the type of ritual his ancestors had done. Especially at the age the ceremony had at one time been performed.

"The Éan's is more mystical."

They had moved from the topic of her fear and he was not ready to let it go, even to discuss the fascination that was the Éan. "You have naught to fear from me."

"I have everything to fear."

"I already promised never to harm you."

"But can you promise never to break my heart?"

"Nay."

She jerked back and frowned, clearly upset by his answer.

"If you love me as you claim you might, my death in battle would break your heart and I canna promise that willna happen."

"Oh."

"I willna ever touch another woman."

"If you are my true mate, you won't be able to."

He grinned. "If I am your true mate, you'll know my heart though I'm not fond of talking about what resides there."

The smile breaking over her features made her beauty glow from within. "You'd best watch out then, as the thing I feared most was that we were sacred mates."

"Why fear such a gift?"

"Look at what it cost my mother."

"Why do you say that?"

"My father was confident in his ability to protect her. He refused to allow her to hide her raven heritage. She did not tell him of Circin's and my dual nature. It was something we had to hide from our father as we did the rest of the clan, but Mum was so certain to reveal it would put us at risk."

How difficult that must have been, and continue to be, for Verica, a woman of rare honesty. "His belief his own warriors shared his honor destroyed them both."

"Yes."

"The decision of who to reveal your raven to will always be yours." It was more than a promise, it was a vow.

She shook her head, the expression in her eyes one of utter disbelief. "No warrior is as understanding as you show yourself to be."

He almost laughed aloud at that assessment of his character but saw she meant it, so bit back his mirth. 'Twas no understanding to choose to protect his mate with every defense at his disposal, including that of subterfuge when necessary. "I'm glad you think so."

"You don't."

"I am not always a patient man." A warrior had to have forbearance, but he was Chrechte and waiting did not come naturally to Earc.

"I gathered that." She laughed softly. "When you announced our marriage was to be this e'en."

"Are you reconciled to it then?"

She bit her lip but nodded.

"What concerns you now?" He did not mean to sound provoked, but affairs with a female Chrechte were no less complicated than if she had been human. And after seeing his former laird and lady struggle to make their mating a success, he had hoped if he ever mated, doing so with one of his own kind would make things simpler.

"You make it sound like I have a basketful of them."

She did, but he suspected saying so would not encourage her to reveal this latest one, so he merely gave her a look he hoped inspired confidences. It worked for his little brothers.

"I am untouched." She made it sound shameful, instead of the gift he considered it.

For both of them.

"So am I."

The black pupils of her eyes nearly swallowed the blue surrounding them. *"You are?"*

"Aye. Talorc discouraged wolves from sex outside of mating."

"By *discourage* you mean?"

"He is strongly opposed." What did she think? That Talorc had levied severe punishments if his advisement went ignored? Perhaps with a past laird like Rowland, such a thought was not so darkly fanciful. "Barr ignored Talorc's strictures, but I did not. He was my laird."

Barr said a laird had no right to dictate such personal matters, but Earc did not agree. So long as the laird was not a piece of filth like Rowland.

"So, you have never . . ." Verica's soft voice trailed off, but the pink of her cheeks told what she was referring to.

"Never."

"Not even kissed?" The shock in her tone would have been amusing if it did not make him wonder the same.

Not liking the possibility any other lips had ever touched hers one wee bit, he asked, "No. Have you?"

"No, of course not!" She frowned at him and then bit her lip. "So, how will you know what to do?"

"My da had a talk with all of us boys when we came of age to mate." Humans might have found his father's frank descriptions and unrestrained answers to questions embarrassing.

He was of the Faol, however. While sex was no longer part of the coming of age ritual, the discussion of it was and no details were left for the guessing.

"Is that usual? Among our kind? Wolves I mean."

Her question tugged at his heart as he was forced to face the truth she'd lost her father before she'd come of age.

"It is."

"The Éan are not so forthright, I think."

"Mayhap they are, but your mother did not have the opportunity to discuss such matters with you."

The pink on Verica's cheeks deepened and the pulse in her throat fluttered. "I could ask Sa . . . someone, I suppose."

"You were going to say Sabrine. Do not ever attempt to dissemble with me."

"I . . ."

"Barr shares with me like a brother. He told me you were the raven in the sky when I killed Rowland."

"You cannot tell anyone else about her."

"I know. To reveal her secret is to risk yours." He reached out and pulled Verica to stand in the circle of his arms. The oddly wonderful connection linked them more tightly than his hold. "You are my mate; I will never put you in danger. Besides, she is mate to my laird. It is my duty to protect her; mysterious secrets do not change that."

"I do not think she sees herself as Barr's mate, though there's no denying the physical bond has been seen to."

Earc smiled at the residual embarrassment in his mate's tone. "Aye. Barr considers it so and it will be; I only hope not to this clan's detriment."

"Sabrine will not hurt the clan."

"Why is she here then?"

Verica's sweet blue gaze filled with confusion. "Barr found her wounded in the forest and brought her to us."

"And you think Sabrine was near our hunt without purpose?"

Verica tried to break away from him, her eyes going stormier than the sky before a summer rain with lightning. "Are you impinging her honor? She is my friend."

He would not let his mate go and tugged her until her struggling body pressed against him. "You have known her one night."

"And a day."

"And a day."

"She saved your life."

He bristled. "You do not think I would have sensed the arrow?"

"You are not God."

"I am a Chrechte warrior."

Verica shook her head, but let her body relax against him. "You are very arrogant."

"You are very tempting."

Once again, her eyes widened, but the shock was tempered by the scent of her own arousal. "We can't do anything. Not here. Not now."

He did not agree about the here part, but the now was truth. He'd promised to help train soldiers with Barr.

"It will wait for tonight."

All of her angst came crashing back, surrounding them and filling her body with rigid tension. "Will we have a Chrechte mating ceremony?"

"Do you want one?" The truth was, he had not considered it since his family was not to be present for the wedding.

She looked into his eyes and then dropped her head against his chest, effectively hiding her expression from him. "We are not as free about our bodies as you Sinclairs seem to be."

"Ancient tradition dictates I can cover you with the furs of my kills." Doing so symbolized his ability to provide for his mate and his prowess on the hunt.

He did not know if the Éan had similar traditions. There was much about the bird shifters they would need to learn, including how best to protect them from those still bent on enmity.

"You would do that?" She was back to meeting his gaze and the expression in hers made him feel like the winner of all challengers.

"Aye."

"But are your furs here?"

"I sleep in them." It was an ancient Chrechte tradition many of the Sinclair pack still adhered to, even Talorc.

"Barr has a Sinclair plaid on his bed."

Earc shrugged. "He reminds himself this clan is not his. 'Tis for your brother's sake he does this."

"He's a man of rare honor."

"He is."

"So are you."

"I am pleased you think so."

"There is a cave, where Connor hid among the rocks earlier today. The few Chrechte who choose to honor their mates with the ancient ritual go there."

Ah, so she did consider the Chrechte mating ritual an honor and clearly wanted to participate in the rite. Modestly. He almost smiled, but suppressed the urge and asked, "Not to the sacred caves with the hot springs?"

"It is nearly a day's journey and Rowland discouraged our clan from making the trip."

"After the clan is more settled, we will travel there for a second ceremony with my family." It would please them and help his parents accept Earc's choice to make his life with the Donegal clan going forward.

"Thank you. I would like that very much."

"Now, can we return to the keep? I have soldiers to train." And if they stayed there much longer, he would forget responsibility in favor of a very private mating ceremony just between him and the healer.

Chapter 13

Barr shoved the door to his bedchamber shut with his heel before dropping Sabrine to her feet. The need to couple drove them both as they yanked off their plaids and other clothing, though he took a careful second to put his weapon in easy reach as always. Then he spun them around, pressing her against the door and devouring her mouth with his.

Sabrine did not attempt passivity, but returned his ardor caress for caress, clashing lips, tongue and teeth. She was his ideal complement in every way. A demure human would not have fit him so rightly. But Sabrine's soft skin felt perfect to his touch, hot and smooth and alluring beyond measure.

While his feelings for her were a mixture of tenderness and lust, right now the voracious desire was in full control. He lifted her by her buttocks until their sexes were in alignment and then he thrust against her mound with his rigid cock. The wet, silky curls felt so good, but he knew what would feel better and he ached to be encased in her willing, moisture-slicked flesh.

"Are you ready for me?" he demanded against her still-mobile lips.

She nodded desperately, her head banging the door twice.

He almost laughed, but his throat was too dry and his cock too desperate.

She spread her thighs, bringing her legs around to latch behind his thighs and opening her honeyed depths to him. He slid his hardened member up and down her slicked flesh until they were both groaning and he knew he had to be inside her. *Now.*

"You are mine!" he shouted as his head breached her inner sanctum.

"Yours." Her voice was naught but a whisper, only so filled with aching emotion it resonated inside him like the strongest war cry.

She arched toward him as he pushed slowly but inexorably inside.

She gripped his neck so fiercely she would leave marks and he reveled in that truth. "Fire this hot must burn out."

"No." He rejected her words immediately. They were true mates, no matter what she insisted on believing, and the passion between them would burn brightly until they were old and gray. Until one of them passed into the next life.

"It must. We'll die otherwise."

"We'll live!"

"You are so contrary."

"You are such a doomsayer." He thrust inside her. "You would build dungeons in the sky if I let you, but I will build ecstasy between us and your dungeons will crumble."

He would plant his seed. Their babe would be conceived, which was only possible between true mates when a Chrechte and a human mated. He assumed it was the same for an Éan and the Faol.

He would have to ask her.

Later.

Regardless, she would bear his child. One born of their combined strength would be the strongest warrior for generations. The prospect the babe could well be a girl did not deter his thoughts at all.

"I know what the future holds for us." Tears stood out in her near-black eyes.

She would learn they were not necessary. "As do I, but only one of us is right."

"Arrogant man. You think it is you."

"Grieving female, you think it is you." Even amidst the joy of their desire, her underlying grief did not dissipate.

"I do not want to grieve again!" The words were lost in her moans of pleasure and he let them slide away from them.

He would show her they did not have to be separated as she was so sure they did. She would learn she could trust him with the secrets of her people. He would not betray her.

She would marry him; she would speak her full Chrechte vows in the sacred caves. He would convince her of the rightness of it. He had no choice. He would not lose his mate, not to her fear or anyone else's folly.

$\mathcal{E}$arc reeked with satisfaction if not spent passion, when his friend joined Barr to begin their training of the human and Chrechte Donegal men in earnest.

"So, the wedding is on then?" he asked his second.

"Did you doubt it?"

"She ran from you like a rabbit from the wolf you are."

"She had some women's concerns."

"And you comforted her?" Barr asked with laughter in his voice.

Earc shoved him as he moved to stand in front of a group of human men. "'Tis my duty."

Barr held back his laughter. Barely. Earc wanted the

healer and he would have her, but she'd made it clear, 'twould not be easy.

They trained the men hard and by the time they broke for the day, each of the clansmen had marks to show for it, human or Chrechte notwithstanding.

Sabrine joined them for the evening meal, her demure demeanor at odds with the wild thing who had burned him to cinders against the bedchamber door that afternoon. He laid the lucky blow landed by one trainee this afternoon directly at her feet. Sparring partners of such limited experience did not touch Barr during a bout, but today one of Brigit's cousins had landed a blow to his thigh.

It hadn't been a serious one, but the fact the man had connected at all was cause for great rejoicing among the trainees.

And it was all Sabrine's fault. She'd damn near exhausted him.

Verica was looking nervous but not terrified. Whatever Earc had said to calm her obvious fears had prevailed.

Circin smiled and laughed with his friends as they teased him over his sister's imminent marriage. Father Thomas tried to draw Earc aside for counsel before performing the marriage rite and Padraig offered to counsel Verica on a woman's duty. His own countenance gave no doubt that the man who would have been a priest himself if not for the brother he'd been beholden to obey knew less of such matters than the stammering and blushing virginal bride to be.

'Twas more normal than he'd yet seen this clan and Barr allowed himself to enjoy the moment.

Of course, it could not last and the stench of bitterness and envy accompanied Muin's grandfather as he approached Barr's table. "You approved this match between our healer and your second?" he asked without preamble.

"I did."

"And what will this clan do for a healer when he takes her away?" the old man asked querulously.

What a killjoy. "He's not taking her anywhere."

"He will when you both leave Circin to lead the Donegals." The man spat Circin's name with a large measure of contempt.

Barr stood and addressed the now-silent dining hall. "One day Circin *will* lead this clan, but not until he is of an age to do so with both strength and wisdom."

Cheers sounded all around and several clapped. Circin grinned, looking not at all worried by his future prospects.

"Earc came here because his laird asked him to," Barr said. "If he stays, it will be because his mate asks him to."

"She already did," Earc said calmly with a nod for Verica.

She was twisting her skirt so hard in her hands, it was likely to pull her pleats right out if she didn't stop.

"And what was your answer?" Barr asked, sure he already knew.

"That I would claim the Donegal clan as my family upon our marriage."

The cheer was every bit as loud as before, with even more clapping and stomping feet. The healer was well liked among the clan and Earc was an excellent warrior.

"That's settled then." Barr dismissed the elder Chrechte with a look. "The wedding will be in the courtyard at sunset."

Verica twitched and her gaze jerked to Earc. He smiled and winked at her. Apparently he hadn't told her he'd arranged to speak their vows under the sky as Chrechte preferred to do.

He looked down at Sabrine to catch her reaction to the news and found her face set in that impassive mask he found so annoying. There was no way to read her thoughts or feelings; she had them swaddled more tightly than an English babe.

"You would not like to think of speaking your vows with me?" he asked her, causing many in the room to go silent as Chrechte hearing picked up his quietly spoken words.

She glared at him, but he was unperturbed. She was his. All should be made aware of that fact.

"We will discuss this later."

"You can't be serious, laird." It was Muin's grandfather again. The man had no sense of propriety when speaking to his laird.

Unlike Rowland, Wirp was not a direct threat to Barr's leadership and he was inclined to show some mercy. Osgard was not at dinner tonight to berate the other Chrechte one elder to another as he had done with Rowland.

Osgard had taken a turn for the worse with his health after witnessing the challenge. Memories and the present vied for supremacy in his mind and Barr's pity for the man grew daily.

"I have said it once and will repeat it this last and final time. The next remark made in this regard will be viewed as a challenge. Who I take to mate is my choice, no one else's, and certainly not yours."

The old man glared and opened his mouth, but Muin must have kicked him under the table because Wirp winced after a dull thud and did not speak.

Barr looked around the assembled. "Do any here question my right to choose my mate?"

"Nay, but laird, where does she come from?"

"Her memory is sketchy on that." Or at least her admission in that regard was.

"Did she hit her head in the forest?" another asked.

"Aye."

"Oh." A chorus of understanding went around the room.

Although they had heard the same the night before, now that they saw Sabrine, the soldiers seemed more inclined to accept her story. *He* wasn't, but he knew that for her to tell him the truth was a matter of trust.

Trust she did not yet feel, but would.

He was her mate.

And he was laird.

And a Chrechte of honor, damn it.

She simply had to open her eyes to these important facts.

Sabrine went to take a bite of her dinner as an unfamiliar and very faint scent came to Barr's nostrils. His wolf howled a warning and he'd grabbed her hand before thinking of it.

The meat fell from her fingers and she stared at him. He snatched her plate and lifted it to his nose. The unfamiliar scent was stronger. It could be a spice the Sinclair cooks did not use, but his wolf warned it was more.

"Verica, smell this." He thrust the plate at her.

She sniffed delicately and then turned pale, her worried gaze locking on Sabrine. "Did you eat any of your supper?"

"Not yet."

"Good."

"What is it?"

"Tomato leaves, dried and ground to a fine powder. They'll make a man very ill, but will kill a bird," she whispered the last bit very quietly. "There shouldn't be any in the kitchens."

"Then how did they get on her plate?" Barr demanded.

Verica did not have an answer and neither did Sorcha, or the other cooks. His and Sabrine's plates had been served up separately with the best of the cut of the lamb and set aside while the rest of the meal was prepared for carrying to the hall.

Anyone could have sprinkled the poison on Sabrine's plate, but how could they know it was to be hers? Sorcha had not even distinguished in the portion size, giving silent testament to her approval of the laird's mate, even if that mate herself wasn't willing to be named such.

There was no indication whoever had sprinkled the

plate with the dried tomato leaves had wanted to do anything other than make him or Sabrine ill. In point of fact, it
might well have been a test of his abilities as well.

Regardless, he did not like knowing the prank could
have been deadly for Sabrine because of her raven nature.

Sabrine stood rigidly beside Verica, still stunned the
other woman had asked her to stand up for her at the marriage ceremony. As a guardian, she spent little enough time
among her people. She had never attended a Chrechte mating ceremony, much less one of the rare weddings when an
Éan and human joined their lives.

She did not want to do anything to spoil the moment
for her new friend but had no idea what to expect. Or what
might be expected of her.

They stood before the priest, Earc beside Verica and
Barr on the other side of the groom. If a single person in the
clan was not standing in the crowd around them, Sabrine
would never have been able to tell. There were so many, the
small clan had to be present from the oldest grandmother
to the youngest babe.

While the sour scent of bitterness would surge now and
again, nothing could compete with the overwhelming affection the crowd felt for their clan healer. Joy was a heady fragrance around them, as pleasing as the heather in the hills.

Verica shook with nerves and Sabrine wondered what
she was supposed to do about that, if anything. Perhaps pat
the other woman's arm reassuringly?

She tried it and Verica gave her a small smile.

Some improvement.

Earc frowned and turned so his body was more toward
his bride than the priest. "I thought we dealt with your fears."

Verica gasped and looked around with an acutely embarrassed air. "Shh . . ." she hissed.

Earc shook his head, but his frown lessened as if he'd worked something out. "No need to be nervous in front of your clan. They are here to wish you well, not notice any stumble in speech you might make in your vows."

His attempt to speak quietly was of little consequence considering the fact that the Chrechte would be able to hear him quite clearly.

Verica frowned at her husband to be, but her harsh breathing decreased slightly and the set of her shoulders relaxed.

Earc's words had been the right ones.

He took her hand and when she very obviously tried to tug it away with another chagrined look around them, he tightened his grip. Humans could be funny about affection between mates, but Sabrine approved Earc's actions. Because as soon as he'd taken Verica's hand, the other woman's heart rate had become less erratic and her breathing had evened out completely.

After another unsuccessful tug on her hand, Verica settled beside Earc, her gaze set on his face as if the group of clan members that had made her so nervous had ceased to exist.

The priest opened his mouth to speak, looked at Barr, and closed it again.

Sabrine cast Barr a glance to see what had caused Father Thomas to hesitate. Barr stood, his arms crossed, muscles bulging, his stance rigid and controlled. The glare on his face was hot enough to burn stone and the man of God was looking singed.

Neither Earc nor Verica seemed to notice, too caught up in staring into one another's eyes. It was really almost sweet but not particularly helpful in the current situation.

Sabrine decided she would have to take moving things forward upon herself. Perhaps that was why Verica had asked her to stand up for her?

"Is something amiss, Barr?" she asked.

He cast her a sideways glance, his expression showing no appreciable lightening. "No."

"Can the priest begin?"

"Aye. I would prefer he would. 'Tis taking longer than it should, I'm thinking."

Father Thomas flinched.

"Perhaps if you were not scowling like an angry bear, he would believe this proceeding had the approval of this clan's laird."

Finally, Barr's scowl lessened, his brows drawing together in confusion now. "What would I be doing standing here otherwise?"

"I am certain the priest was wondering that very thing himself." She'd made no effort to keep the mockery from her tone. "I do not believe your job as laird requires you to intimidate the priest assigned to serve your people."

Barr looked at Father Thomas. "Do I intimidate you, Father?"

The gray-haired man with gentle eyes swallowed but nodded. "A wee bit, laird."

"'Tis not intentional." Barr looked at her, his expression asking if she was happy now.

She gave him a slight nod.

His lips tilted slightly at the corners.

The priest let out a small sigh, his relief apparent. "That is good to hear."

"You will proceed."

"Yes, laird."

Sabrine wasn't sure, but she suspected even a laird should not treat the humans' spiritual leader with such arrogance. She said nothing however, not wanting to hold the ceremony up further.

Father Thomas took a deep breath, let it out slowly, swallowed, cleared his throat and finally began speaking. He said a few words about marriage and the honor they should all feel to participate in the ceremony binding two lives like a braided cord. It was an odd thing to say, she thought, but strangely touching.

When the priest invited those gathered to join in a hymn, Sabrine was shocked when almost everyone present did exactly that. Children's high voices mixed with the warbling elders and deep baritones of the warriors. The women's voices wove through the others like the connecting threads of a tapestry, making the communal music both lovely and poignant. No matter the ugliness that resided among this clan, there was more. So much more than Sabrine would have believed possible before she came among them.

The wolves were not all evil murderers and the humans not dunces for allowing them among them. This group, singing so joyously, was a family, in the truest sense of the word.

While some no doubt still grieved the loss of their former laird, most were clearly content to look to the future and all were willing to celebrate the wedding of their tenderhearted healer.

Their connection was every bit as strong as that among the Éan and she had not expected that. The Faol had always been monsters in her mind and now they were people, some good, some bad—though too many not to be trusted.

When the song ended, Father Thomas smiled. "That was a thing of heavenly beauty and no one will ever convince me differently."

Verica smiled and Sabrine was glad the priest's words had pleased the other raven woman, though Sabrine wasn't certain what he'd said that was so pleasing. He bowed his head and prayed. Though she did not understand a word he said, she recognized the attitude of reverence. Sabrine spoke enough English to recognize the language, but she found not one syllable he spoke now in any way discernable.

She had not closed her eyes and bowed her head as many

around her had done, so she noticed the old man glaring at the wedding couple with such loathing. It was the same man who had been so disagreeable at the evening meal. Wirp, she had heard him called.

She met his gaze and his eyes widened when hers did not drop. She let the warrior that lived inside her show in her face and she gave him silent warning should he attempt to disrupt her friend's happiness.

His glare intensified, but this time it was fixed fully on her. She let him see his hatred did not frighten her. She had lived her whole life believing all among the Faol hated her to the point of death. Learning some did not made this man's loathing seem petty. It certainly had no power to hurt her.

The same was not true for Verica, however; Sabrine was certain of it. The healer was vulnerable to her clan's vagaries and Sabrine was not about to stand by while a bitter old man visited misery on her new friend.

For a brief second, the female warrior descendant from the Éan's royal line surrounded herself with the image of a golden dragon, ancient ancestor of her people.

Dragon changers no longer flew in the skies, but their memories had not been forgotten like the great beasts the Faol dismissed from their own histories as myth. Just as many of them had dismissed the Éan.

Not this man though.

She sensed he knew the bird shifters still existed and he despised them with his entire being. Right now, there was no room for his hatred though. He was too busy clutching at his heart and falling back several steps.

He'd gone as pale as milk with the cream skimmed off the top. She felt no guilt at causing him such fear.

The man's thoughts had been as transparent as water. He would do Verica and Earc harm if he could.

She would make sure the evil old bitch's son would have no opportunity to do so.

She dismissed him with a flick of her eyes and focused her attention on the priest, who had finished praying and was now stepping aside for Padraig to come forward and read from parchment he held with great reverence.

Again he spoke in that language that resembled neither Gaelic nor Chrechte enough for her to understand anything, though the more she heard the more she thought it sounded like a strange type of English perhaps.

It is Latin. Barr's voice in her head held an underlying growl that had to be his wolf and was not present when he spoke aloud.

For a moment, the implications of hearing him did not strike her. She was gifted among her people with the ability to speak to them all in such a way should she choose to do so, but the Faol had no such gift.

Or did they?

They must. The other prospect, that he was her true mate, was too terrifying to contemplate. Would Heaven be so cruel?

Can you speak thus to others? she asked, knowing her panic tinged the mental connection between them.

My brother, my father before he died. No others. He on the other hand sounded supremely satisfied by their ability to mindspeak. In fact, a burst of joy surged in the air around them enough that Earc and Verica both gave Barr strange and curiosity-filled looks.

Sabrine's stomach clenched, sweat broke out on her palms as her hands fisted. *I am no relation to you.*

You are my mate. My sacred bonded.

Her knees started to buckle and only by sheer will did she remain upright. *No.*

Aye. Oh, he sounded pleased by her torment.

But he was an arrogant man, a Faol who had no concept of what it meant to lose what you held dearest.

You are wrong. The wolf-tinged tone sought to soothe.

Had she spoken the words in her mind as her thoughts

whirled like leaves in a wind devil? She must have, but he did not understand.

I have lost those I hold dear. I will not lose you. Once again he spoke as if reading her thoughts, rather than hearing her mindspeak.

Chapter 14

Barr's arrogant assurance was too naïve to give her comfort.

Anguish held her in its implacable grip. *I cannot stay.*

He did not reply, but his scowl returned, fury emanating off of him like heat from the bread oven. No doubt here, the laird and pack alpha found her assertion less than pleasing, but then what did he think the knowledge did for her? Pain in the center of her chest made her gasp, trying to find air, trying to soothe a hurt that could not be touched by comfort.

It was her turn to receive the concerned gazes from the bride and groom. Sabrine did her best to bring forth the stoic façade of her warrior.

It did not work. Verica seemed more worried than before and Earc looked as if he was about to stop the proceedings to find out what was amiss.

Sabrine shot a "don't you dare" glare at him and, thankfully, he subsided, turning his attention back to the priest.

Thankfully, Father Thomas did not notice any of this. He was too busy handing another parchment to Padraig. The Faol scholar read from it as well. He then handed that parchment to the priest and began speaking, this time in Gaelic, the words sounding memorized like the oral traditions among the Chrechte.

He spoke of the Christ making wine at a wedding from water. When he finished, he stepped back, taking the parchments from Father Thomas with him.

The priest began speaking about the great joy and sacrament of marriage. His words landed like a spring rain on the parched soil of Sabrine's heart, causing both great joy and an even deeper sorrow. She'd never thought to have a mate, much less a husband.

She could no longer deny the true bond between her and Barr, but it did not change her future. It could not. No matter how much her heart might long for a different ending. Knowing this truth sliced into her soul with the destruction of a halberd.

The fact she felt such strong emotions for a wolf should astonish her. Somehow, it did not. Which was more proof, had she needed it, that he was her true mate. Only such a bond could overcome her aversion to the Faol to make her actually desire mating one for life. And no matter how she might wish it otherwise, love grew in her heart like tender shoots in the spring.

She knew, no matter what she might wish, this ceremony could never happen with her as a primary participant. Yet hearing the words of blessing and promise spoken for her friend moved Sabrine so deeply, she was near tears. And despite the pain ripping the heart she had so long denied to shreds, they were not tears of sadness.

She had given her life to the protection of her people just so others could have the families she had to deny herself. And perhaps Verica would live with greater freedom than any of the Éan hiding so deep in the forest. She would have children and, because of Barr and Earc, not worry the young ones would be hunted by the Faol that called themselves Donegal family.

Barr would weed out the evil among the clan and stop their threat to his own pack and perhaps even make life safer for the Éan who lived apart as well. Sabrine had to believe that he could at least make a difference for those he was sworn to protect and lead.

When the speaking of the vows came, it was every bit as profound as the promises spoken by the Chrechte in their ancient rite of mating. Though somewhat different. The attitudes of both bride and groom lent solemnity as well as joy to the occasion.

Whatever their differences, Earc and Verica were happy to be mating.

When Verica promised to obey Earc, Sabrine had to bite her tongue. It was not in a Chrechte's nature to submit to anyone without question, but no doubt the Faol man knew that. He would never expect Verica to be as biddable as the vow implied. Though as her mate and the pack beta, he would be no husband gifted with unending tolerance, either.

To Sabrine's mind, that made them a strong match, a good mating that would provide children for both the pack and the clan.

The priest spoke another blessing over them and then made a motion with his hand. "The peace of our Lord and Father be with you."

Suddenly the people around them were repeating the words to each other, clasping hands and smiling.

Sabrine found it odd and held back until Barr took her hand. "Peace be with you."

She stared at him. Peace was not the emotion most paramount when she was in his presence. At this moment in time, she could not imagine peace in any form attached to her feelings for him. Yet his hand covering hers brought forth an inexplicable delight she could not quite mask.

Her mind whirling once again, while her emotions chose to follow suit, she stared up at him.

A smile dawned on his rugged features and his finger caressed her palm as he pulled his hand away. "The proper response is: and also with you."

"I do wish you peace, though I fear you are far from it yet as laird of this clan." Not to mention a Chrechte male whose true mate would have no choice but to abandon him sooner than either would be happy with.

His eyes said he read her thoughts and still his smile grew. "You are a unique woman, my little warrior princess." He spoke the last words in an undertone, but she heard them.

Her father had used to call her his little princess. The emotions that welled up as Barr reminded her of those halcyon days before her parents' murders threatened to choke Sabrine.

He touched the small of her back, his action both possessive and comforting. *The future is not so bleak as you believe,* he said into her mind.

The rest of the clan settled back to their original places, but now Barr stood beside her rather than near Earc. His hand remained at the small of her back as well and she could feel the close scrutiny of many around them.

Father Thomas and Padraig offered Communion. She'd heard of it, from the humans that lived among the Éan, but had never seen it administered. The sense of connecting with the spiritual during the ritual was as strong as the communal worship the Chrechte practiced. It should not have surprised her, but it did.

After all had partaken of the bread and sipped from the chalice, the clan and the priest spoke that strange language, the Latin, in unison.

Father Thomas presented Earc and Verica as a married couple, though Sabrine was sure all present were well aware they had spoken their vows.

Everyone dispersed, though some she recognized from that morning headed toward the forest rather than to their cottages. They did not take a direct route, she noted, but their destination was clear to her.

She turned to Barr. *Will there be a Chrechte mating?*

The ability to speak to him thus and ask what she was curious about without worrying about being overheard was an amazing freedom. Even with her abilities among her people, she did not take it for granted.

Aye.

The sacred springs are a day's journey away.

There is a nearer set of caves the clan uses.

Why?

He shrugged. *Rowland led the pack to do things differently, but 'tis the intent behind those present at the ceremony, not where it is held, that holds importance.*

Perhaps for the Faol, but there is power in the caves of the sacred springs for the Éan. It was not only the *Clach Gealach Gra* that impacted the strength of the coming of age ceremony.

What do you mean?

She shook her head, unwilling to discuss the topic further.

Barr stood alone as the last howls of the Chrechte mating ceremony faded into silence. He wanted Sabrine beside him, but she'd refused to come, saying her Chrechte nature would be obvious to her enemies if she accompanied him. He thought she'd let that particular secret into the light when she'd saved Earc and stayed with Barr through the funeral pyre burning for Rowland.

However the Éan lived, one thing was certain. She was so used to her role as female warrior, she had not realized the fact that slipping into it amidst a traditional clan would give away her odd origins. Even a Highland clan was not accustomed to women dressing as men and carrying swords.

But he'd liked it. It had made him hot. And knowing she had put herself at risk to save Earc had scared the arrogance right out of Barr. This woman would be hard to protect, and while that worried him, it also intrigued him.

He'd heard the tales of warrior women among the Chrechte in times past, but never thought to meet one. Did not believe any yet remained.

His beautiful mate proved him wrong and showed her prowess while doing it. What would it be like to hunt with her in the sky and him on the ground?

He got hard just thinking about it.

No matter how different she was from the other females he had known, Sabrine was the ideal mate for him.

Not that she agreed. Damn it. Even though she could not deny their sacred bond, she refused to be recognized as his mate before his clan. Her rejection was like a splinter in his soul he did not know how to draw out. It felt like a betrayal of not only his wolf but the man who had put duty above personal desires his entire life. She, his beautiful, perfectly-matched-for-him mate, was his *reward*. As only a sacred mate could be.

Only she refused to be counted as such.

He had always believed that his prize merely waited on the other side of one more sacrifice, that elusive mate he had wanted since learning what a sacred bond could bring. He had watched his brother finally find joy with his own true mate. Their family increased by one, Barr had begun to hope, if only in the most secret recesses of his soul. A tiny voice, barely recognized had whispered that mayhap he would not die without knowing his own.

Well, he knew her, but she insisted their time together was limited.

As the power of the mating ceremony swelled around the Chrechte in the cavern his personal confusion increased.

How could she hope to deny him the future their natures destined? How could she withhold children, companionship, intimacy? Did she care nothing for the losses they would both suffer if she tried to leave him?

He would not let her do it.

No matter what she thought she had to do, he would not let his mate abandon their sacred bond.

Barr waited for the weight of the silence to grow heavy with meaning before speaking the final Chrechte blessing on the couple, as pack alpha, and leading the others out of the cave.

Earc would couple with Verica and their joining would be the final act in a mating that only death would sunder.

Barr envied his second, but did not begrudge the other man his future contentment. Earc was more than deserving of the gift Heaven had chosen to bestow on him.

Barr refused to believe he was not equally as deserving.

Instinct drove him to shift into the wolf and he raced through the forest, not toward the keep, but away from it.

It took some time and careful tracking with his wolf's senses, but he found the spot in the forest where he had first come upon his mate. He sniffed at the leaves and grass, the trace scent of his mate and her spilled blood almost gone from the spot. He snuffled at the earth and then turned in an agitated circle before dropping to curl into the earth where she had lain.

Verica felt the press of spiritual power as her Chrechte brethren exited the cave. She heard the others leave, but did not watch them go, her eyes fixed firmly on her new mate.

Earc watched her with a hunger she feared she would not be able to satiate. Her desire for him was very strong, but the voracious need emanating from him was all warrior wolf and so powerful it was a living presence between them.

"You look worried, mate," he said softly.

She nodded, her throat too dry to speak.

He cupped her face in his big hands. "What has you so concerned?"

"I don't know how to do this."

"This?" he asked, looking almost amused.

She frowned, tugging the fur farther up her body. "Yes, *this*."

He pulled on the fur; it slipped before she could grab it again. Her breasts were exposed, her nipples hardening immediately in the cool night air.

One of his hands slid down to curl over her rounded flesh and his golden brown gaze flashed with arousal, the wolf a shadow in his irises. "This . . ." He hefted her generous curve and brushed one thumb over her nipple, sending pleasure arrowing directly to her womb. *"This is beautiful."*

She could not speak past the lump in her throat. She had never thought to have a mate, but if she had ever allowed herself to fantasize about even having a *husband*, it would not have been a man so amazing. A man whose strength could be trusted, a man who protected others at cost to himself, a man who stirred her like no other.

Because she had never known one before Earc came to live with her clan.

Watching her as closely as a parent did a babe taking its first steps, he squeezed her nipple between his thumb and forefinger. *"So* beautiful."

"I am not so special."

"You are." Sincerity lent his husky tones an almost harsh edge.

He caressed her breast, his big hand so gentle, she wanted to weep. And so much more. It sent shivers of pleasure through her that she had not known she could feel.

His nostrils flared as heated wetness formed between her legs.

She nuzzled into his hand, her own wolf craving the

connection, her raven seeking that affectionate touch against her neck and head.

His eyes flared with something warm and tender and he leaned forward to rub his raspy cheek against her smooth one. The fragrance of their mingled scents surrounded them, making her feel safe in a way she had not since her da did not return from his last ill-fated hunt.

Earc's hands on her body added to more than her sensual pleasure. Each caress enhanced the sense that she was no longer alone, no longer solely responsible for her brother's welfare, no longer required to watch over her shoulder as well as what was before her.

Because this man, this wolf, who had claimed her for mate, would protect her from what might try to sneak up from behind.

An image of Earc standing before her, sword in hand, came into her mind and she knew it did not come from her. He was affirming the fact she was his to protect now, just as he was hers.

She didn't try to tell him so; she was no warrior, but there were other ways to protect someone. She'd been keeping her brother from his enemies for the years since their mother's death.

That job was now Barr and Earc's responsibility. The sense of freedom and relief that realization gave her was so great, it made her light-headed. She swayed in Earc's hold.

He pulled back, his golden brown eyes boring into hers. "What is amiss?"

"Nothing." Joy flowed over her in an unstoppable wave. "Everything is finally coming right."

A smile curved his gorgeous mouth. "Aye, it is right."

Her happiness bubbled forth in laughter. "I'm going to like being your mate, I think."

"Without doubt."

She shook her head at his arrogance. "I am glad to no longer be alone."

"You have had your brother, have you not?"

"I had to protect him, protect our birthright, *alone*."

"Now, 'tis Barr's and my responsibility."

"That is exactly what I was thinking."

"You were thinking about your brother while I kissed you?" Earc asked, sounding none too pleased by the prospect.

"It was all part of my newfound joy."

"You find happiness in my arms."

"Not as much as I plan to," she admitted boldly.

His grin fell away as a feral expression took over his features just before his lips closed over hers again. This kiss was one wolf claiming another, nothing held back and yet, he was not rough with her.

His lips demanded a response; his tongue tasted and insisted she return the tasting; his hand on her breast slid down to touch her most intimate flesh as his mouth staked the mating claim.

The scent of her feminine arousal blossomed to a strong fragrance as he brought forth more wetness from her heated depths. He touched a spot that made her body go rigid with excitement. He did it again and she cried out against his demanding lips.

A dark laugh sounded between them, but it was not coming from his mouth. She went absolutely still. The laughter sounded again, this time exultant.

And then his voice inside her head. *Aye, you are my true mate and none will ever take you from me.*

I thought we had to . . . Her mental voice failed before she could finish.

She could feel his shrug, though his body had not moved. *Chrechte magic does as it likes.*

She had no answer for that. Her mum used to say the same when her touch healed one clan member and not another.

All thoughts fled as Earc's hands on Verica's body built

her pleasure to a near-terrifying precipice. Her fear mixed with the overwhelming delight and he soothed her with mental images of her body being cradled against his in perfect safety. "It is all right, my precious one. Jump off the cliff; I will catch you."

She did, releasing the rigid control on her muscles. Her body convulsed in a cataclysm of sensation so overpowering, she could not think, could not move, could not speak; she could only feel and what she felt was the most amazing and delightful experience of her life.

Her womb convulsed, her core throbbed and bursts of light exploded behind her eyelids. Her wolf howled; her raven trilled in a way a real raven would not and her human woman simply screamed her pleasure. She was still shaking with the joy of it when he lay her back and came over the top of her, his hard member pressed against the opening to her body.

"We are one," he said in Chrechte.

"Always to be," she replied in a panting voice.

He surged inside. Pain blossomed and she bucked against him, trying to throw him off. He would not be moved, but his eyes filled with regret. "I would have avoided the pain of breaching your maidenhead if I could."

She believed him, despite the sense of utter satisfaction covering him.

He shifted and she whimpered. He went absolutely motionless, his every muscle rigid with the effort. "Tell me when I can move."

"Next year mayhap."

"I am not laughing."

"Neither am I."

"I do not want to hurt you."

"I can see that you don't."

His face was contorted with a pain easily equal to hers, though of a very different nature. But his body did not move.

"You are overlarge maybe."

"Chrechte men are not small."

"Then you might think Chrechte females would be created to accommodate them," she said in a strained voice as her body continued to fight the pain of his initial invasion.

"You are."

"How can you be so sure?"

"My da and my brothers."

"Hah. All males." What did they know?

"Do you trust me?" Earc demanded in a tone she could not ignore.

She stared up into his gaze. "Yes."

"Relax your body."

"You'll move."

"I won't."

She wanted to ask him to promise, but knew he would find such lack of trust a direct negation of what she had just said.

I will not move, he said, using their true bond connection, his voice growling with the honesty of his wolf.

She willed her body to release its tension. Unbelievably, as she relaxed the burning pain between her legs began to subside.

True to his word, even though her body no longer fought his presence, Earc did not attempt to thrust deeper.

As her tension eased, the profound reality of having him inside her struck Verica. "You are a part of me," she whispered.

"Yes." His voice was harsh with his effort not to move.

"It is wonderful."

"It hurts you."

"It did, but it is still wonderful."

"Did?"

She swallowed but nodded infinitesimally. "It is not so bad now."

"Can I move?" His own voice was barely a whisper this time.

The burning had dulled so she could once again feel the pleasure. When he had promised her he would catch her when she jumped off that terrifying precipice of pleasure, he had done exactly that, holding her while she flew for the first time out of her raven form. She could trust him to turn this pain to renewed delight.

Besides, her wolf was so close to the surface, if they didn't do something soon, she'd be howling. "Yes."

He pulled out, just a little, and then pressed forward, his rigid length filling her so completely their connection was both fully physical and uncompromisingly spiritual as well. This was the true Chrechte mating and he had been right, not being in the sacred caves did not matter. She felt the presence of their Chrechte magic all around them.

This union was blessed.

She arched upward and gasped as pleasure sparked a fire of need inside her. It blazed out of control as they moved together, building the heat of their joining so even her raven and wolf felt singed.

And then that ultimate pinnacle came into view again, her body striving toward it with mindless need.

As they climaxed together, she saw his wolf and him both. She blinked, but the image did not shift. She had no choice but to simply accept as her body surpassed even the earlier moment of completion to the point she was barely lucid.

He curled her into his body as they slipped into sleep and she heard him whisper against her hair, "Tomorrow, you will show me your raven."

Sabrine finished her search of Rowland's room and his things. The *Clach Gealach Gra* was nowhere to be found. Though she had come across a disturbing collection of raven and eagle feathers, which she took to burn in the way of her people.

She did not know of a certainty that they came from Éan, but she could not help believing the feathers were a way of counting kills. She took them to the hall and built a fire from the banked embers in the fireplace. She lay each feather on the flames, whispering the words of departing for Chrechte warriors as each one caught and was consumed by the fire.

Her heart ached as she watched evidence of the Faol's treachery against her people disappear in the flames. Éan disappeared, never to be heard from again. How many of those she had known could be accounted for in the collection of feathers she now burned with reverence and respect?

The sound of a wolf's nails clicking across the floor brought her head up.

She had been so intent on performing the final rite of passage for her Chrechte brethren, she had not sensed her mate's approach. The fact he did so as a wolf and she still had not known chilled her with a deep terror she could not shake.

The giant blond wolf came toward her, his eyes filled with intelligence, *with Barr*. But his form was that of his Chrechte nature. The Faol. A jaw that could tear a bird in half with one well-placed bite, claws that could cut through all-too-fragile skin and feathers with an ease that sent shards of atavistic fear through her.

Even knowing this wolf was in fact her newly discovered true mate, she could not hold back her flinch as revulsion washed over her.

A low whine sounded from his throat, but he did not drop his head or look away from her.

"Your former laird was a hunter of the Éan."

Chapter 15

Barr shook his majestic head, a low growl sounding.

But she would not let him dismiss the situation so lightly. "He may not have been *your* laird, but he was pack alpha of the Faol in this clan. The clan you now lead."

Barr moved closer, his regard intent, the scent of his wolf stronger than it had ever been around her.

One part of her, the woman who had been raised to protect her people from all potential threats, but particularly the wolves among the Chrechte, demanded she move away from the danger. Her raven insisted on moving nearer her mate; she needed the man who had taught her such pleasure to show himself, and her heart and mind felt torn in two.

"Shift." She meant to demand it, but the word came out more a plea.

You fear my wolf? he asked with their mental connection.

She shook her head, refusing to matespeak with a wolf.

Didn't he understand? In this form, he could not be her mate.

The air shimmered around them and then Barr was there in his human form. He straightened, towering over her, his expression grim. "You hate my wolf."

She could not deny it. "The Faol has always been my enemy."

"Not all wolves are murdering bastards like Rowland."

She looked down at the last feather in her hand; it was from a raven. "He killed many in their bird form and more as humans. It is not something I can forget." Not ever. He had not killed her parents, his scent had been wrong, but he had no doubt been cohort to the ones that had.

"He had nothing to do with me."

"He was laird here before you. You shared your table with him for more than a month."

Barr's scowl darkened, but guilt shadowed his eyes. "I did not know he was a murderer."

"You knew he was *wicked*."

"There are wicked among all people, human and Chrechte alike." He looked at her as if expecting agreement.

She was in no mood to be agreeable. "None so wicked as the Faol."

An inexplicable sense of guilt pricked her as the words fell between them and his anger spiked along with unmistakable hurt.

"Your people are so peaceful that your women train as warriors." This time his mocking tone dared her to disagree with him.

"I became a warrior after my parents were murdered by the wolves you would call friend."

"I never called Rowland friend and well you know it. None that I call friend would hunt another Chrechte without cause."

"They believe they have cause."

"Why?"

"That is not my question to answer."

"You know more than I do of this unacceptable feud. Tell me what you know."

She found she could not deny him. "They despise the raven for being a carrion bird, or so I have heard. But they kill the eagle among us as well, so who is to say why they truly wish us gone?"

He thought for a moment, as if contemplating that very thing. As if he thought she truly wanted an answer.

When in fact the why had ceased to matter a long time ago.

He shrugged his magnificent shoulders, drawing attention to the naked body he found so comfortable. Despite their argument and the way her rejection of his wolf had hurt him, his member was thickened and almost erect.

She yanked her gaze from his manhood, but not before his quirked lips told her he had noticed her interest.

She frowned.

He winked and then sobered. "Mayhap they fear you."

She remembered the look on Wirp's face at the wedding when she gave him the image of her ancestor the dragon to gaze upon and thought perhaps Barr had the right of it, but then again, maybe not. "All Chrechte have more to fear from humans, who outnumber our kind so vastly we must hide among them."

"Aye, but the special gifts the Éan have because of their Chrechte nature are a thing that might inspire envy and envy can move to hate with the blink of an eye."

"So, you *understand* these murderers who would continue the decimation of my people until we are gone?"

Barr's eyes darkened and he shifted closer until she could feel the heat of his body. "I dinna say that. I merely speculated the reason behind their hatred might well be envy and fear, no matter what they claim to the contrary."

Despite herself, she nodded. She'd long suspected that to be the case, but the claims made by the Faol that the

Éan were not *worthy* to be Chrechte had long plagued her people.

Barr's hands settled on her shoulders. "You canna hate my wolf. He is a part of me."

And the arrogant man was so sure she could not hate *him.* Of course, against all expectations in her own heart and from any who might know her, she didn't hate the wolf laird. In point of fact, she was well on her way to being irrevocably in love with him.

An emotion that could only lead to more pain for her and yet one she had no hope of denying.

"A wolf and a raven can only mate in their human forms; I think that means something."

His hands landed on her shoulders, the intent to hold her unmistakable. "It means we are magical beings with two forms and destined for a future together as life mates."

"A wolf and a raven cannot mate for life; it never ends well." He needed to understand. This connection between them could not last. It simply could not.

"Perhaps that is true of the past, but the Chrechte no longer dwell in caves and unreasonable hatreds have no place in our new life among the clans."

"Tell that to this raven." She tossed the final feather in the flames, speaking the death blessing.

Barr's voice joined hers and Chrechte power sparked in the air around them. Wind that had no origin rushed through the room, taking the smoke up through the chimney in a whoosh.

Barr spoke a final blessing on the Chrechte that had gone before pricking his finger with his knife and sprinkling a drop of his own blood on the fire in an ancient offering most humans among them would not understand. "Rowland is gone along with those he sent to an early grave."

"But his cronies still live among the Donegals." She had to make him see how impossible any future together among this clan would be. Taking him to her people was equally impossible. Barr would never be accepted among them because of his wolf. "Shifters like Verica still hide their raven natures. Warriors like your Muin are still taught to kill ravens in the sky even though they do not know the Éan exist. You are a fool to believe so much has changed."

Though she could wish it were not the case.

"I am no fool."

She simply shook her head. She could not answer.

"You are my mate," he growled as his head lowered.

"I am raven."

"Mine." His mouth slammed down on hers, the kiss filled with angry frustration as he repeated the word, *Mine,* over and over again in her head.

She replied with her own frustration at finding the perfect mate only to have him be wolf, her anger at the unfairness of life that made the Éan live as shades in the forest while their Chrechte brethren lived in their own hiding amongst the humans.

For one brief moment, she gave vent to her truest desires and the dark feelings that knowing they would never bear fruit caused in her heart.

They made love there, in front of the fire, her borrowed plaid their only cushion against the hard floor. And she did not care. The rest of the keep slept while she and Barr claimed each other in a ritual as old as time.

The next day, Sabrine began training the women to defend themselves. She took them to a clearing in the forest, far enough from the keep that the women did not need to worry about being watched by curious children and amused warriors. Looking like a woman quite pleased with her new mating, Verica joined them.

She brought along her grandmother's weapons and offered them to Sabrine to use in her teaching.

Sabrine ran a loving hand along the blades but shook

her head. "You must learn to defend yourselves without weapons other than the dirk most of you carry for eating and preparing food."

"You can teach those of us who wish to learn to use the bow and sword later, can't you?" one young Chrechte female asked.

"If I am here."

The knowing looks Sabrine got from the other women did nothing for her temper and she pushed them hard to learn basic hand-to-hand fighting techniques she had known before she was old enough to have her own dirk, much less a proper dagger.

Over the next days, Sabrine spent time each afternoon training a handful of the clanswomen in the arts of female warfare. Though they would have been greatly indignant had they realized it. They saw the lessons strictly in terms of defending themselves and their families.

The fact so many were willing to join her and Verica in the forest each afternoon said much about what had been happening in their clan over the past years.

Sabrine did want to help the clanswomen, but she also did not lose sight of her primary reason for being among them. She searched diligently for the *Clach Gealach Gra* but had found not so much as a hint to its whereabouts. Her sense of desperation grew daily as her younger brother's coming of age ceremony grew closer and she could not lay hands on the necessary sacred artifact.

Her days were not limited to the women and searching though. Barr had very definite ideas about how mates behaved and they seemed to include copious amounts of sexual intimacy.

Barr did not limit his lovemaking to the nights, but would spirit her off to his bedchamber in the middle of the day without compunction. Sabrine found it all too easy to justify acquiescence. Her continued freedom to move within the keep and beyond was made easier by her obvious relationship with Barr.

Some of the clanswomen gave her askance looks, muttering about strange women found in the forest that were no better than they should be. She did not allow the gossiping to touch her.

She was far too happy. As long as she could ignore the looming future, Sabrine reveled in more joy than she'd ever known.

For the first time since her parents' death, she had friends who were not fellow warriors. She had someone to call her own, a mate who belonged to her—even if temporarily—in a way he did not belong to anyone else in the clan. It had been so long since she had such a connection, she had forgotten the deep contentment it brought.

And that contentment was coupled with indescribable pleasure in her relationship with Barr.

For the first time since she had completed her initial training, Sabrine's days and nights were not filled with patrolling the skies and watching for any enemies encroaching on the deep forest where the Éan made their homes.

She'd forgotten what it was like to sit with a family for the evening meal, but that was what it felt like to share Barr's table with Verica and Earc. Even Padraig and the priest had become dear to her, often trying to draw her into their indecipherable conversations on topics that sounded like the spiritual beliefs among her people, but just different enough that she spent more time smiling and nodding than understanding.

They never grew impatient with her though, nor did any of the others mock her ignorance. Well, not since Wirp made another one of his zealously disapproving lectures at Barr in regard to sharing his bedchamber with her.

Barr had banned Wirp from the keep during mealtimes,

until such time he felt he could keep a civil tongue in his head. She had the feeling the old man had avoided a challenge only because of his age. And perhaps Barr truly was not as war hungry as the Faol of old and hoped to live by example.

Sabrine was happy to note that far from a stormy coupling, Verica's clear delight in her mating did not diminish as the days wore on. In fact, her contentment grew deeper each day, striking a poignant chord in Sabrine's heart even as she rejoiced for her new friend.

Perhaps the other woman's dual Chrechte nature made it possible for her to mate with a Faol and find joy that might last a lifetime.

Not that Barr accepted *their* mating could not last. On the contrary, the stubborn man made her affirm she was his each and every time they coupled. He plied her body with more pleasure than she would ever know again while insisting she recognize their mating at the most basic level.

Even had she wanted to resist, she had no choice but to comply. Their ability to mindspeak had only grown so that even when she was in the forest training the women and he was back at the keep training the men, she could hear him quite clearly in her head.

He delighted in teasing her with sexy whispers of what he planned for them when she returned from training the women. Or he would ask where she was when she was busy searching for the sacred stone. His tone always implied he knew she was up to something, but he was so obviously not worried. His naïve trust scared her.

She would not hurt him, or the clan that had come to mean so much to her, but others were not so safe. He seemed aware of that fact, but persisted in believing the best of her, when in fact, he should be more suspicious.

She'd grown more and more accustomed to the wolf growl in his voice and felt less revulsion when she thought of his Chrechte animal nature with each passing day. But she still could not stomach the thought of him shifting in front of her.

And he knew it.

She knew that her continued revulsion bothered him, but he never said anything more than to randomly remind her that his wolf was part of him, part of the man she was true mate to. She never denied it and he did not push for more. For her part, she was content never to discuss the matter in depth. She had no desire to spoil even a moment of the time they had left together.

She *had to* find the *Clach Gealach Gra* soon, and when she did, she'd have to go. Even if her wing was not healed.

The longer she stayed with the Donegal clan, the harder it was going to be to leave. And she would not risk not returning in time for her brother's ceremony.

Nevertheless, she felt almost equally compelled to train the Donegal women in the ways of fighting. They had been working on turning a curtsy into a move that hiked up the long skirts of a female plaid and made it possible for a woman to run faster, or kick an opponent with enough power to have effect.

She stepped back after adjusting a woman's stance for better leverage to flip her opponent. Before she could test the woman's new stance, a hand came around her waist from behind.

Though she knew the feel of that arm, Sabrine did not think about it, she simply reacted, sliding through the hold to roll on the ground. She came up with a kick intended to do damage in a man's most vulnerable parts.

Barr leapt back with not an inch to spare as her foot brushed the front of his plaid. "Well done," he said out loud. *Careful, My One, you will do damage to a part of my body yours enjoys very much,* he teased inside her head.

His complacent amusement sparked her annoyance. He did not believe she could do him damage when she had been defending her people from the Faol since her fifteenth summer.

She did not allow her eyes to narrow or her heart to accelerate. She kept her breathing normal, pretending to drop her fighting stance.

She curtsied. "Laird."

The other women around her followed her example, though the scent of shock at his appearance was like burning sulfur around them. Sharp and acrid.

Barr smiled, white teeth baring with a hint of his wolf despite his full human form. "Ladies."

And Sabrine struck. Hiking her skirts, she spun and leapt, landing a kick right on his sternum. She'd put her whole body and momentum behind it and his guard was down.

Barr was a giant among men, but he was not impervious and he went down, surprise and mild pain crossing his face. He recovered quickly though. Going with the momentum, he flipped over backward and came smoothly to his feet.

His stance on the ready, a ridiculous grin creased his face. "That was sneaky."

"How good of you to notice." She allowed her skirts to drop and brushed her hands as if dusting them off.

"I dinna think the others will expose their bare legs to defend themselves though."

"You would be surprised at what a woman will do when her child is at risk." Her own mother had sent Sabrine running for the haven of their people, while she, a trained healer, not warrior, had joined her mate to fight the Faol that stalked them.

Barr nodded, his eyes filled with an understanding that could be naught but her imagination.

"She attacked the laird," someone whispered.

Her frustration mounting, Sabrine frowned. These women needed to realize that even if it was their laird putting them at risk, they must fight back. The clanswomen were so different than the females among the Éan, and yet Sabrine felt a growing kinship with them.

It worried her.

"I merely sought to show you that what you have learned thus far is not without its uses."

"'Twas not a real attack," Barr said dismissively.

Preparing to take umbrage, Sabrine opened her mouth to speak, but Earc, who had managed to arrive in the clearing with as little forewarning as Barr, halted her. "Aye, if she'd meant to hurt him, our laird would be bleeding." The two wolves had masked their scent and moved in such silence, she had not known they were near until Barr had put his hand on her waist. Not for the first time, she was thankful the Faol that still hunted the Éan did not have her mate's prowess. "Our mysterious woman of the forest was merely proving a point."

She got the distinct impression that Earc knew the point had been directed more toward Barr than the women.

Barr's nod of agreement went a long way toward appeasing her ruffled feathers. The gentle brush of his hand down the back of her head and nape finished it.

Her raven preened under the much-craved attention, and it was all Sabrine could do not to let it show in her manner. From the very beginning, Barr had seemed to instinctively know what her raven needed, even as he fulfilled her every human desire as well.

The other women in the clearing were still staring at them in horrified silence (whether at their laird's public familiarity or Sabrine's strike at him was a matter for debate) when Verica asked, "Is aught wrong?"

"Nay." Barr looked around at each of the women, making eye contact in that special way that told each one he truly saw her as only an alpha could do. "We thought we would come and help you train for a wee bit today."

"You are going to train us?" Verica asked, her eyes rounder than the full moon.

"Nay. I am going to *help* Sabrine."

Earc said, "I also."

"We cannot train with men," one of the human clans-women said in purely outraged tones.

"How can you know you are able to defend yourselves against men, unless you practice with them?" Sabrine countered, once again frustrated by the clanswomen's overdeveloped sense of propriety.

"It is not seemly," another said, her scent turning sour with disapproval in less than a heartbeat.

"What are you? English?" Barr demanded, letting disgust lace his deep warrior's voice. "We are of the Highland clans. We submit to the king on our own choosing and we dinna follow the ways of the *Sassenach*."

The other women stood taller, giving the two who had spoken frowns. About ten of the women from the clan had wanted to learn how to defend themselves as it was. Not even all the Chrechte women had been willing, but Sorcha was there, her daughter Brigit and Verica. Aodh's wife, the new housekeeper for Barr, had wanted to learn to fight as well.

"Do you wish to be able to protect yourselves and your children?" Earc asked.

"It is not our place to protect ourselves. It is for the warriors of our clan to do." The first woman who had spoken said this.

Sabrine made no effort to hide her disgust. "And when there is no warrior near at hand to do so? What then?"

The other woman did not reply. She was here, so clearly she was open to learning. She had been a good student thus far. What was the matter with her now?

"Barr is not here to test us or catch us out as Rowland might have done," Verica said in a voice both soothing and laced with an old sadness. "He wants his whole clan to be safe and strong."

"'Tis right, that." Barr crossed his arms and nodded.

"You are all valuable and should not fear for your safety, no matter the circumstance."

"We live amidst a warring people; all must fear for their lives at some time or another," Sorcha said, but her eyes were filled with hope.

The more she'd learned to fight, the more peaceful she had grown. Still, she had the right of it now. There was much in their world that threatened their safety. Which was a reason to learn to fight, not to give up.

Barr shrugged.

Sabrine nearly rolled her eyes. The man was just too complacent in his own rightness. "Even in war, a woman should know she is not without her own resources to defend herself."

Verica nodded vehemently.

Earc smiled at her before turning a more serious expression to the other women. "We will help you gain confidence in your ability to fight not only an opponent of a size with you but one who is bigger as well."

"No offense." Sorcha curtsied. "But you and our laird are bigger than most men; could we not do this learning with smaller men from our clan?"

Barr's lips tilted, but the smile did not break forth before his expression turned deadly serious. "Earc and I are the most experienced and well-trained warriors in the clan. There is no chance you will accidentally come to harm training with us."

The man offered the best to his clan, be they men or women. Sabrine's love grew so that she could no longer deny its existence in that moment. She would love him until she breathed her last breath, and no matter the pain that might cause her, she could not regret it.

If he were Éan, he would be her ideal mate. If she did not have responsibilities to her people that made it impossible for her to stay among the Donegals, she would gladly spend her life as his true bonded. Faol or not.

He looked at her and winked as if he were reading her mind. He did that often and she wondered just as frequently if he was indeed doing just that, but the Faol did not have the additional gifts of the Éan. It was not possible.

Though sometimes, she could not help thinking, and mayhap hoping even more so, that things that should be impossible were not . . . with Barr.

Chapter 16

~~~~

The efforts to teach the women to defend themselves against bigger and stronger opponents went well. True to his word, Barr knew exactly how to push the women to the limits of their ability without allowing them to hurt themselves on his or Earc's strength. A true opponent, bent on doing them harm, would not be so considerate, but these women were not warriors.

In a dangerous situation, their more primitive instincts would come to the forefront and help them fight off any attacker. She hoped.

She called a halt to the training and sent the women back to the keep when the sun had moved another hour across the sky.

After the other women, Earc and Verica had left the forest, Barr turned to Sabrine. "You're a fierce fighter, even with a wounded arm."

"As a protector of my people, I do not have the luxury of allowing injury to stop me from doing my duty." Besides, her injury healed more each day. She hoped to be able to fly again soon. "The pain is almost gone anyway."

"Tell me more about your people."

It was not the first time he had asked. Though usually, he waited until after she was exhausted and relaxed from their lovemaking. Still, she had managed to deflect the questions with tidbits that could not hurt her people to reveal.

She opened her mouth to do it again, but he put his hand up. His eyes were dark with some unnamable emotion. "Dinna."

"What?" But she knew.

And he was aware of it. "Answer my question with truth."

"I always answer your questions with truth." Even when it was one he did not want to hear.

"Small truths. *Tell me about the Éan.*"

"I cannot."

"You can."

She shook her head. He was her mate, but he was Faol. She could not break her people's secrecy.

His countenance turned dark. "You yet do not trust me."

"It is not my place to trust you on my people's behalf."

"If not you, then who? This separation of the races must end."

Shock stole her breath. He thought the Éan could join the Faol? Live among the clans? Impossible. "The separation began with the Faol."

"And we, the Faol, will end it."

"You have gone mad. It can never happen."

"Only because you refuse to trust. According to our legends, all Chrechte once lived together as one People."

She knew that quite well. "We have been at war twice again the years since the Faol joined the clans."

"Aye. It is time for the war to end."

"One man cannot accomplish this."

"With your help, I can."

What he sought was not only impossible, it was impossibly dangerous. "Has Earc told you Verica's story?"

"Verica has shared her past with me. *But I am not her father.* He trusted the wrong Chrechte."

"You are right. He trusted *himself* to protect his family, but all his strength was not enough against the cunning of those intent on the Éan's destruction. Even now they would destroy our people from within."

"What do you mean?"

Realizing what she had almost revealed about the sacred stone and the Éan's need for it to beget the next generation, she sealed her lips tight and blocked his thoughts with all her Chrechte discipline.

"Damn it, Sabrine, you must give me your trust."

"On my own behalf, I might, but I cannot risk my people."

"I will not hurt them."

"You might not mean to."

"But you believe I will."

"Yes." The word came out in a whisper, but he heard it.

His frown was fierce, but worse was the look of pain in his eyes. "You will never accept my wolf."

She could not make words come. She shook her head, not to say he was right, but because she did not know what to say.

She realized he'd taken it wrong when his entire body went rigid with a stoicism that hid every nuance of emotion. A wall heavier than any she could have constructed came down between them.

She put her hand out to touch him. "Barr—"

He jerked away, for the first time looking at her with the disgust she had always dreaded. Only she knew it was not because of her raven; it was due to her cowardice.

"You are my true mate." He had never made the claim with anything less than contentment, but his words held no joy now.

"I have not denied it."

"Not since we began mindspeak."

His reminder she had tried to deny their bond hurt, though she could not deny the truth of it. She nodded, her throat going too dry to speak.

"You plan to leave me, to return to your people."

Again, she could do nothing but nod.

"You will steal my hope of children, my one hope of a companion and family."

She could not gainsay him. Neither she nor he would be physically capable of sexual intimacy with another so long as both lived.

Pain moved through her in a way it had not since her parents' death. "I am sorry."

"You are a coward."

She felt like a coward, but it was not all about her fear. "I have committed my life to the protection of my people."

"I have offered to share that burden."

"You cannot."

"You will not allow me to."

"Please, Barr . . ."

"Please what? Please do not bring into the light your plans to betray me, to betray our bond?"

"I cannot be your mate."

"You are my mate."

She turned away, unable to stand the look in his eyes any longer. "I cannot be your wife."

Only silence greeted that pronouncement.

Only the slightest shift of air gave her any warning before his big body slammed into hers, taking her to the ground as an arrow whizzed through the air where she had been standing. Barr was shifting into his wolf form even as they landed against the grass-covered earth.

Another arrow landed in the dirt beside them and Barr rolled them using his wolf's body before leaping to his feet. He turned and barked, as if telling her to run, and then he started running himself in the direction the arrows had come from.

Another deadly missile barely missed his canine heart as he leapt in the air and then continued in a dead run.

She twisted and rolled as an arrow hit the dirt where she had been. She rushed to the tree line with a crouching run, zigzagging from side to side in the opposite direction. Without the ability to fly, shifting would do her no good.

Until she was in the trees. There it would be easier to hide in her raven's body than her human one. She climbed the nearest tree, using her injured arm despite the pain it caused. Once she was amidst the branches, she shifted into her raven form, her clothing falling away to land on the boughs below.

She hopped from one limb to the other until she was high in the tree, then she moved to the edge and surveyed the forest with her bird-keen eyesight.

She could see the streak of blond fur rushing through the forest, but saw no sign of the would-be assassin.

Are you safe? he demanded in her head, breaking past the barriers she had put between them as if they were made of nothing more than mist.

I am high in a tree. I can see you.

Can you see our attacker?

No.

Can you see anything?

I can see much of the forest, but I see no man, nor a wolf besides yourself.

There is no scent trail to give him away. There should be a scent. The frustration he felt came across the bond, bombarding her already beleaguered heart.

You can mask your Faol scent.

Aye, but Rowland did not train his wolves that well.

Clearly he did. Or at least one of them.

A vicious curse sounded in her head, but she did not respond. This was the very reason her people could not come out of hiding. Why she could not leave them to fend for themselves.

Even if she could? She would not be safe in the Donegal clan. That was obvious.

You damn well would be. Those arrows were meant for me.

Maybe. He was not universally liked, particularly after allowing Earc to challenge Rowland.

The humans in the clan had believed it was a warrior's challenge and had been even more disapproving than the Chrechte over the fight between the much younger Earc and their former laird. No matter how poor a leader he had been, he was a clan member.

Still, she did not believe the arrows had been meant for Barr alone. Her feelings must have given her thoughts away, because Barr cursed again.

I would never be safe amidst your clan.

You damn well would be.

Like I am right now?

Just like it. His wolf's growl was so deep, she could barely understand the mindspeak.

You will not always be there to throw me to the ground to avoid an arrow.

I will.

How could she argue with such intransigence?

They both knew the arrows were clearly meant for both of them; whether because she was so obviously Barr's mate or because someone had discovered her Éan nature, she could not be sure. And ultimately, it did not matter.

Staying among the Donegals would be the height of stupidity and she was no fool. No matter what her heart wanted.

Stay in the tree.

While you do what?

Try to find a scent or sign to track.

She hadn't been in her raven form since the day they

met. It felt good—better than good, it felt wonderful—so she agreed.

Having no desire to dwell on the conversation they had been engaged in before the attack, Sabrine used the time to hop amidst the branches, surveying the forest from all vantage points. She saw nothing out of the ordinary.

Her gaze was drawn again and again to the sky, her longing to fly an ache in her breast. She tested her wing, expanding and contracting it, but she could tell it would not hold for flight. A lone eagle flew in the distance, too far from the land of her people to be Éan, but seeing the noble bird caused another ache.

That of homesickness. She wanted to be among her people again, even if it was only the warriors in her group charged with protecting the others.

She wanted to see her brother before his coming of age ceremony. She wanted to hug him in a way she had not since they were separated by her warrior training.

She had lost so much, first her parents and then, by her own volition, the rest of her family as she left them to join warriors who had never managed to take the place of the others.

Now, she was giving Barr up and her heart screamed against the injustice. A true mate bond should never be abandoned. But she felt no more choice than she had the day she'd taken her vow as protector of the Éan.

Everything inside her contracted with an emotional agony she'd hoped never to feel again.

Since making her connection with Barr, she missed her family with a painful nostalgia she had thought long buried.

Memories she'd tried so hard to push so deep they would never see light again rose to the surface, choking her with old emotion that mixed with the new. Her mother teaching her the healing chants even as she sang Sabrine into sleep at night. Her father holding her brother high in the air to introduce the future prince among their people when the baby boy was born. Her brother's first steps, not to their mother, but to Sabrine.

She had been his favorite and she had abandoned him.

The inescapable torture that knowledge brought to her soul knocked the breath from her bird's body. She nearly fell off the branch, but she managed to stay perched as more memories choked her.

Her mother's stories of the time before the Faol turned on their brethren, the Éan. The sound of her mother's laughter, her father's voice as he spoke the Chrechte words of ritual in his role as king of their people.

The look on her aunt's face when Sabrine insisted on joining the warriors for training, denouncing her role as princess. Leaving her family to deal with their grief as she managed her own the only way she knew how to.

Wetness from her eyes rolled onto her feathers, but she ignored it.

Princesses did not cry. Warriors did not show weakness.

The sound of a wolf scratching at the bottom of the tree she was in yanked her attention from the past to the present with a harsh jerk.

The wolf's pelt was a reddish brown she did not recognize; fear's metallic taste filled her mouth. She could not fly and she had no weapons with which to defend herself. She went absolutely still as the wolf's head came up and sniffed the air.

He snarled and barked. Though she knew he could not see her through the foliage, she did not doubt those sounds were directed at her.

He turned and loped away, then spun on his paws and took a running leap at the tree, landing high up the trunk. His claws dug into the bark and he began to climb.

Sabrine's heart stilled in her chest. She knew some of her enemy had taught themselves to climb in their wolf form to better get at the Éan. She had been warned by the older warriors, but she had yet to meet one herself.

She did the only thing she could: she herself climbed higher by hopping from branch to branch, hoping she could reach a height where the wolf's bigger body could not follow.

Without warning, a giant blond wolf came flying, his leaping body so high in the air he was able to knock the reddish brown wolf from the tree. The reddish brown wolf crashed clumsily to the ground, but the blond wolf landed smoothly on all fours. The other wolf turned and bared his fangs.

The blond wolf leapt. He clamped his jaws on the other wolf's neck and picked it up, an adult carrying a cub, but there the similarity ended. He sent the smaller wolf hurtling toward another tree.

The reddish brown wolf hit the tree with a thud. He yelped, landed and did not move again.

The blond wolf shimmered and then Barr's double stood there naked at the bottom of the tree. His scent was like Barr's but just off enough she could not mistake it.

"Come down, mate of my brother. It is time we met."

She was so shocked, she shifted without thought and then for the first time in memory, she fell off the branch she'd been perched on. She fell, but her reflexes took over and she grabbed the next branch, landing with a jar to her shoulders. She cried out in pain as her injured arm was strained, but she clung to the branch with her good hand and carefully felt with her feet for purchase on a limb below her. She found it and managed to make her way to the trunk of the tree where she took a seat on a sturdy branch, high enough up that the wolf could not touch her.

In an inexplicable, to her, bout of modesty, she turned her naked body to minimize his view of her.

After all, they were both Chrechte and shifters often removed their clothes communally before taking their other forms.

"Who are you?" she asked to cover her confusion with herself.

"You cannot tell?"

"My guess is Niall, brother to Barr."

"That would be me. My face isn't as pretty as his, but we're identical otherwise." He turned a scarred cheek toward her.

"No, you're not identical."

"That is what Guaire says."

"Is Guaire your mate?" she asked, though the way Niall said the other man's name left no doubt as to their relationship.

It was the same tone Barr used to say her name, or had done, before their harsh and painful words in the clearing.

"*Aye*. He is my true bond." He sounded so like Barr when her mate was pleased with something that despite everything, Sabrine found herself smiling.

"Who is the Faol over there?" she asked, indicating the still form.

"I was hoping you would tell me."

That made no sense. "Why did you attack him if you do not know him?"

"He was intent on prey. All I could smell was my brother's mate."

"But you do not know me."

"I know you are family."

Her heart contracted at the claim. If only that could be true. "I am Éan," she blurted out.

"I had that figured when you shifted from raven to human." His sardonic tone made her smile again.

Though it was quickly followed by a frown. "You saw?"

"My face is flawed, not my eyesight."

"I'd say your face looks pleasing enough to keep your mate on his toes around others."

His head thrown back, Niall laughed loudly at that.

Men. They could be so vain.

"Do you need help down?" he asked.

"No."

He nodded, the laughter gone as quickly as it had come. Without another word, he turned away. She had been naked around her brethren before shifting many times, but the Donegal clan must be wearing off on her because once again her modesty was relieved he didn't watch her make her way out of the tree. Sabrine fetched her clothing on her way down and donned it quickly once she'd reached the ground.

As she adjusted her final pleat, the wolf at the base of the other tree stirred. Niall had not killed him then.

She had been far more interested in meeting Barr's brother than the fate of the other wolf. It shimmered into human form as it came to consciousness.

She sucked in a sharp breath.

"You know this tree-climbing bitch's son?" Niall asked.

"He is Wirp, grandfather to Muin." She wished she was surprised, but she wasn't.

The old man glared at them from the ground. "You know damn well who I am, whelp."

Niall had the man on his feet and dangling over the ground between one breath and the next. "Who are you daring to call whelp?"

Wirp's brows drew together in confusion as fear became a rancid odor around him. "You are not the laird."

"Nay, I am his brother, the mean one." Niall's snarl would have done any wolf proud.

"They don't get meaner," Wirp spat.

"Well now, if you think so highly of him, what the hell were you doing trying to climb a tree and get to his mate?"

"I don't think highly of him," the old man sputtered.

Foolishly, Sabrine thought. Considering his circumstances.

Niall's scowl was every bit as intimidating as Barr's. "You insult my brother?" he asked in a tone both quiet and controlled that still managed to convey Wirp's imminent death at the wrong answer.

"He mated a raven." Each word dripped with venomous loathing.

Niall turned his head and gave Sabrine a smile of sublime delight. "He did at that."

"She's an abomination!"

Even knowing they were spoken by a prejudiced old man who should mean nothing to her, the words pricked at Sabrine's heart like the tip of a newly sharpened dagger.

"What is the matter with you?" Niall sounded truly perplexed. "My brother has managed to discover a member of the old race and draw her to himself. 'Tis a miracle our laird Talorc of the Sinclairs will thank him profusely for."

As if Barr had a thing to do with her falling out of the sky and infiltrating his clan. Men! Still, she liked Niall's interpretation better than Wirp's.

"She's carrion eater, not worthy to be called Chrechte."

"She's Éan, magical and powerful with Chrechte gifts a wolf will never know."

"You know more about my people than your brother," she could not help observing.

"I listened more closely to the stories than he growing up. And I believed them. Somewhere out there are Chrechte that share natures with the big cats."

She knew the stories he spoke of. Ancient tradition said that back before the Chrechte settled in caves, when they roamed the earth like the animal herds, there were more races of shifters and they all lived together, submitting to leaders much like the Éan's Council of Three. But those stories were so old, she had never given them credence.

The fact she was just such an unlooked-for legend to Barr made her rethink the truth of the oldest stories.

But those were thoughts for a different day.

"You hold no dislike for the Éan?" she asked, having to be certain.

"I am Chrechte."

"So is that hate-filled old goat." She jerked her head toward Wirp.

He dismissed Wirp with another wolf-worthy snarl. "Chrechte respect all life. We have learned the great cost of not doing so."

"I think some of the Faol have," she admitted. "But some still hate the Éan for their differences."

"Jealous more like."

"Me? Jealous of that abomination?" Wirp yelped, spittle flying.

Niall grew very still and looked down at Wirp. "Do. Not. Call. Her. That. Again." He punctuated each word with a small shake of the man dangling in his grip. "Ever."

"She has no place in our clan."

She might agree with him, but she didn't have to admit it to this horrible dog. "That is not for you to say."

"You are wrong. I will protect my clan from your kind, whatever it takes." The light of murder burned bright in his faded eyes.

She let death show in her own gaze. "You are welcome to try, old man. You'll not find me as easy a kill as others."

Fury at her challenge suffused him and he lost control, his wolf's scent filling the air around them for the first time. Memory washed over her for the second time in an hour, this one the most painful she had yet endured.

"You!" Quick as a snake, she grabbed the dagger from Niall's belt. "Drop him, let my parents' murderer face me."

Niall looked down at her with shock. "The females among the Éan certainly are different."

She didn't bother to reply, dropping into a fighting stance, rage turning the edges of her vision red.

"What the hell is going on here?" Barr's demand cracked like thunder.

"I believe your mate wishes to kill this old man. It's a fair want to my way of thinking. He was intent on killing her when I came upon them."

She looked at Barr, the anguish of earlier replaced with this new-old pain. "He killed my parents."

"You are certain?"

She looked back at the now-hatred-filled visage of the older Faol. "Yes."

"No doubts?"

"I smelled his scent on their bodies. I'll never forget it. He's kept it masked, or I would have known earlier."

Barr turned to Wirp. "You stand accused of murder. What say you?"

"It is not murder to rid the world of an abomination."

"You do not deny the charge of killing?"

"She looks just like her mother. It is how I knew she was raven from the moment I saw her." Wirp's implied admission and lack of any remorse cut at Sabrine's soul.

How could he think killing her gentle mother and the fair and giving ruler her father had been a good thing?

"They never caused you harm."

"Their existence caused offense; that is harm enough."

"That is admission enough." Barr's cold tones sent a shiver through even her.

But the old Chrechte did not appear affected. "If you are looking for a confession, I will gladly claim the kills. Her father was king of his people. His death was a great blow to them, but not enough . . . not nearly enough, for here his daughter stands." The fury and repugnance in his face and voice made Sabrine want to shake.

But she would not let this disgusting murderer see her weak.

"You are guilty." Once again, Barr's voice carried the weight and chill of final judgment.

Wirp shrugged. "Accuse me before the clan then."

Suddenly, Niall released him.

Barr stepped forward. "I am laird. I need no one else to find you guilty."

Wirp's eyes filled with understanding and fear came too

late as Barr grabbed the older man by the head, twisting and yanking at the same time. The snap of breaking bone sounded and the light of life died from Wirp's eyes that quickly.

Barr allowed the body to fall.

She stared at him in shock. "You killed him."

"Chrechte justice is swift. He admitted to killing two others of our kind; he showed no remorse. I had only one course of action open to me."

"Will you hide it as a hunting accident?"

"I am not Rowland. The clan may well petition the king for a new laird, but I will not pretend to be less than I am. I am leader of this people and justice is my responsibility."

"I wanted to kill him." Only as she said the words, she realized that no matter how much she might wish she had, killing in anything other than defense did not come naturally to a raven. *"I could not do it."* The words came out a whisper.

The knowledge broke something inside her and she fell to her knees, all strength gone.

Chapter 17

━━━◆━━━

A harsh keening sound accosted her ears, but she could not cover them. Could not protect herself from the broken sound so filled with pain.

The grief of her parents' death welled up from deep in her soul and mixed with her sense of failure, shattering her heart.

She had abandoned her brother when he needed her most, believing she was doing what was best for him. Now, she had no choice but to abandon her mate. No true Chrechte would abandon the mate gifted them by grace.

You are no failure. He spoke in her head as his arms came around her. *You may be defender, but you are not killer.*

You killed him. Even in her head, her voice was harsh from strain.

He admitted to murder.

If he had denied it?

I would have brought him before a tribunal of Chrechte elders.

From the Donegal clan?

Nay. There are too many there with twisted thinking yet. At least he acknowledged that. *I would have taken him to the Sinclairs for Talorc to judge and mete justice.*

Out loud, he whispered shushing noises as he rubbed her back and held her close. The awful wailing grew louder and she realized it came from her the same moment the heat of the tears rolling down her face penetrated. "I am crying." She hiccupped.

"I noticed."

"I do not cry."

"Today, you do."

Remembering the raven's tears in the tree, she could do naught but agree. "Yes."

He did not rush her or try to get her to stand. He simply held her, comforting her in the years-old grief as she cried with agonizing constrictions in her chest.

All the while, she was aware, she did not deserve this warrior's care. She had thought to leave him in loneliness and still he comforted her.

𝕹iall carried the dead body back to the keep. Barr held Sabrine's hand firmly while they walked. He had wanted to carry her, but she had refused.

He had been unable to hold his anger at her in the face of her emotional distress. She believed she had to leave him, but now that her enemy had been identified, she would come to realize she could stay.

She had no choice. She might not yet realize it, but his beautiful raven-natured mate carried his child.

She could not leave him. She would not.

They stopped in the courtyard, clanspeople streaming out to see what had happened.

"Was it a hunting accident then?" Muin asked, his expression stoic.

"Nay." Barr intended to say more, but Niall cut him off.

"I found this man attacking my brother's mate."

Several gasps sounded. The word *mate* being whispered vehemently revealed that the shock could well be due more to the public claiming than the fact Wirp had been stopped in an attempt to hurt Sabrine.

Muin's face crumpled, but he did not do as Barr expected. The younger man dropped to his knees before Sabrine. "I am so sorry."

"It is not your fault." His mate's voice was hollow, drained of emotion.

"You would not be the first woman he attacked." Muin's head dropped. "He went after my mother, but I stopped him. I thought he would not do it again." The shame in the young Chrechte's voice was heartbreaking, even to a hardened warrior like Barr.

This clan had a vein of wrongness running through it that had to be healed.

Exhaustion lining her face, Sabrine laid her hands on Muin's head. "You are not responsible for the evil of your grandfather."

"I should have told the laird."

Sabrine seemed incapable of responding to that. Others in the clan were not. Several negated his words with shakes of their heads, but one woman stepped forward.

She was of an age with Muin's mother, though mayhap a few years younger.

"Wirp took what he had no right to take from me. He was an evil man. I did tell our former laird, but Rowland told me it was my fault for being too alluring." The woman spat the words.

A moan of sorrow sounded from Muin.

Regardless of her own fragile state, Sabrine knelt down and hugged the young man, her head resting against his while her hand smoothed a soothing circle on his back. She would make a wonderful mother when the babe came.

"It was not your fault. Rowland did horrible things and let others get away with the same. Barr will heal this clan."

Her confidence in him gave him hope when her rejection of his wolf had all but robbed him of that commodity.

"With all your help, we will make this clan a place of safety and joy for all its members," Barr affirmed.

No shouts of approval came, but something far more telling, the fragrance of relief stole over the entire assembly until he felt as if he'd been sampling young Zachariah of the Sinclair's mead again.

It was time to make one thing clear. He would have no dishonesty between him and his clan as Rowland had so clearly excelled at doing. "I will not lie to you, by omission or otherwise. My brother did not kill Muin. It was my job as laird to mete justice and I did so."

This time the cheers did come, shocking him and echoing around him with deafening approval.

In the midst of this, Guaire stepped forward, looking much the contented man with a mate he had longed for all his life and not expected to have.

For all that he was human, Niall's true bonded had some very distinct traits of the wolf.

He put his hand out and Barr took it, then pulled the smaller man into a hug. "Guaire."

"Laird. Talorc sent me to train your seneschal. Though it would appear that may well be the least of your worries. Niall escorted me on the journey."

Ah, so that was the story Talorc had decided to use. Some human members of the clans were odd about same-sex matings. So, Niall and Guaire did not live openly as mates, but they were happy all the same. With their Chrechte brethren and even some of the humans, they could be as open as any other mated pair. In truth, two bachelors living out their years together was not so uncommon among the humans in the clans, either.

How convenient that I assigned a new seneschal to the

task mere days ago, Barr said to his brother with their mental bond.

Isn't it?

Niall must have repeated the words to Guaire because he smiled. "Good."

Some looked confused by the random response, but most were still reeling from the situation with Wirp.

"We will have a funeral pyre in the forest tonight." Barr did not look forward to yet another death vigil for a wolf with a twisted soul, but he could not dismiss his responsibility as alpha to his pack.

Several clansmen looked unhappy.

"Attendance is not required," he said.

Once again relief was a palpable presence among them. So Wirp had been even less beloved than Rowland.

Who else among the clan had fed the disease of violence and betrayal of the trust placed in them to protect the clan?

It was a question he had no answer for when his brother asked him just that the next day. They were leading a group of young Chrechte warriors on a hunt, much like he'd been doing the day he found Sabrine in the forest.

Earc remained at the keep, training the human soldiers, and Guaire had stayed behind to begin schooling Aodh in the ways of being a seneschal.

Barr and Niall fell back from the others, letting the younger men close in on the boar.

"They're not going to bag this kill making that kind of noise," Niall said quietly as he leaned against a tree.

"They'll learn." Or he'd have to do some head-banging.

"Aye."

"Sabrine says she will not stay."

Niall, never one for many words, just looked at Barr.

"She is here for some reason of her own that I have not yet discovered, but once she's accomplished her goal, she will be gone."

"You are sure of this?"

"Aye. I think she is looking for something." He did not think she had found it yet, but he could not be certain.

"She is your true mate."

Niall had not made it a question, but Barr answered anyway. "She is."

"Does she know this?"

"She tried to deny it at first, but she has accepted the truth now."

"And she would leave you?" Though his voice did not rise, Niall's fury at such a reality was there in the skin gone white around his scars.

"She believes she has no choice."

"She is wrong."

"I have told her."

Once again Niall went silent, as if contemplating a mate who refused to accept Barr's word as law. Finally, he sighed. "Guaire is not afraid of me."

"He never was." Barr had tried to tell his brother, but Niall had been so certain of his lack of appeal because of the scars, he had not believed.

"He does as he pleases." The frustration this caused Niall was a subtle tension in his voice.

"But he would never leave you."

"He almost did."

Barr remembered then that his brother had finally claimed his sacred mate when the other man had left the Sinclair holding, intent on going to live among the Balmoral.

"He would not do so now that you've claimed him."

"Nay."

They went silent again, the sound of an unsuccessful rush at the boar filtering through the trees. Barr would allow the younger ones some time to bumble on before stepping in to show them the way of the hunt . . . again. Perhaps they would even find success.

Though he was not hopeful.

"Guaire threatened to follow me here if I did not bring

him along." Niall sounded both mystified by and proud of his feisty mate.

"It was your idea to make the journey?"

"I sensed something was amiss."

Niall did not need to say more. Their bond had always been a particularly strong one, even for Chrechte brothers.

"Talorc let you go?"

"Without question. You are his friend."

"Is Abigail still giving him fits?"

"She likes to go walking in the forest."

Barr almost laughed. He could well imagine how that pastime would go over with his former laird. "Alone?"

"When she can get away with it."

"He's kept a guard assigned to her?"

"She's sneaky."

"Guaire is her helpmate, I bet."

"Aye." The growl in Niall's voice expressed far more than his single-word answer.

"She is not yet carrying then?"

True mates would always produce offspring, but when they came? That was up to Heaven's dictates.

"Actually, she is."

"I'm surprised he doesn't have her tied to his side."

"I told him before leaving."

"He didna realize?" Barr asked in disbelief.

"He was too close and the shift in her scent was slight."

"Probably a human child then."

"Aye."

"Talorc is happy?"

"He was babbling when I left."

"Babbling?" Talorc? That was something Barr would like to have seen.

"Oh, aye. I laughed."

"And that did not give him heart failure on top of the news of his wife's pregnancy?"

"I laugh more now."

Because of Guaire. "I'm glad."

Niall shrugged.

"You will tell them I share their happiness when you return."

"I will."

Barr nodded, his mood turning somber as quickly as it had lightened at the good news as his thoughts returned to his own mate.

Niall's thoughts followed his own. "Sabrine came to your clan with hidden motives then?"

"She did."

"Wirp's death was not her objective?"

"I do not believe so." She hadn't been searching for a person, she'd been looking for something.

Niall did not look convinced. "She could now be gone."

"Nay. She is training the women of the clan to fight." Or she had been when they left for their hunt.

She was probably done now and once again pretending to visit his clansmen while looking for whatever it was she was so intent on finding. She did not realize how those visits had endeared her to the hearts of his clan.

Everyone else had begun to accept her as his mate, everyone but her. Not that she denied the mating, but refusing to promise the future was the same as denying the importance of their bond.

"She cannot accept my wolf nature."

"Because of this feud?"

And they were back to the topic that had started their discussion. "Aye. She does not feel safe among the Donegals."

"Would she feel differently among the Sinclairs?"

"I do not think so." The truth that his true one was so distrustful of all of his kind had become an open wound on his soul.

"With time, she will learn to trust."

"And if I do not get that time?"

Niall's silence was answer enough, but then his brother

growled and pushed away from the tree. "Then you damn well make the time. You are a warrior, you do not give up."

For Niall, that was quite a speech. And it so closely resembled Barr's own thinking on the matter, he felt a smile break over his face. "If she can train our women to fight, I can teach her to trust."

Niall nodded, his own mouth curving in a tight smile. "She's an unusual female."

"Not among the Éan."

"Even among them, I am betting."

Perhaps his brother was right. "She is special."

"She is planning to abandon her true mate." Niall's scowl grew darker with each passing second. "That is not the kind of special I want for you."

"Watch it, you're starting to sound like an old woman, not a warrior."

"I am your brother before I am a soldier to my clan."

They clasped hands and hugged, then stepped back.

"She has not left yet," Barr reminded himself and his brother.

"Her arm is injured. She cannot fly."

Barr nodded, acknowledging Niall's intelligence. He too suspected that his mate would leave him as soon as her injury was healed enough for her to fly again.

"Does she realize she is pregnant?" Niall asked.

"I do not think so."

"Tell her."

"And if she still insists on leaving?"

Niall had no answer and neither did Barr.

If his mate knew she carried his child and still insisted on abandoning their mating, he was not sure even his warrior's strength would stand against that.

Sabrine could feel Barr's unhappiness and frustration across their link. She did not believe for one moment it was because the hunt for boar was not going well. Though she had no doubt the younger hunters were making more than their share of mistakes. Barr's patience for training hunters who should have learned these lessons many summers past was beyond anything she had seen among her own people. There was little tolerance for Chrechte who could not contribute to the people's welfare from an early age. Small children were cared for with great affection and attention, but childhood was left behind at an earlier age among the Éan than the clans.

With their very existence at risk, they had no choice.

So, as much as she might wish she could believe Barr's dark emotions were due to his untrained hunters, she knew they were not.

The burden of anguished guilt crushing her heart like a giant boulder only grew heavier.

She knew she was the reason Barr was unhappy. What she did not know was how to fix it.

No more than she knew where next to look for the *Clach Gealach Gra*. She had searched homes, getting to know their occupants in the way her mother had taught Sabrine as a young girl. She had searched the caves the Chrechte used for their rituals, but there were no hidden chambers as in the labyrinth of tunnels at the sacred springs. She had searched the forest, but no Éan power called to her, no matter how far she ventured forth from the main Donegal holding. She had searched the keep, but the only Éan power within emanated from Circin and Verica's chambers. As to be expected, because she was older and had a very powerful Chrechte gift, Verica's (and now Earc's) chamber had a stronger Éan presence. Yet no matter where she looked, she found no sign of the sacred stone.

She was close to enlisting Verica's help as time grew shorter with each passing day. Sharing the secrets of the Éan, even with the other raven shifter, did not sit well with

Sabrine. She'd spent too long protecting the mysteries of her people from outside eyes.

But she had to weigh the risk of revealing the secret against the risk of not finding the *Clach Gealach Gra* and what that would mean to the Éan. One was clearly of heftier import than the other.

Knowing so did not make the prospect of spilling secrets any more palatable though.

"What has you looking like the milk in your porridge has gone sour?" Verica's soft voice broke through Sabrine's reverie.

The other woman sat beside Sabrine on the long bench at the table in the great hall. Her faithful apprentice was nowhere in evidence, which was probably a sign. Now was the time.

"I am not eating porridge." In point of fact, she wasn't doing anything but staring at a table that had been washed most carefully by the new housekeeper. Well, that and wondering what to do next.

Verica smiled, an indulgent expression in her friendly blue gaze. "'Tis an expression."

"Oh." Naturally.

"Do they not say such among the Éan in the forest?"

Sabrine shrugged. "Perhaps. I spend little enough time in the village." And it had been so many years since she lived with anyone but warriors, she did not remember the nuances of living among the regular Éan.

"There is a village?"

Sabrine opened her mouth, intending to deflect the query, but then changed her mind. Verica needed to understand it was not simply a handful of warriors out in the forest that would be affected by the loss of the sacred stone. "Of sorts. Some live in the trees, some live in caves."

Not primitively as they had done in generations past, but much the same as the Chrechte now living among the clans lived in their huts. With cooking fires, food stored for winter, furs to sleep on and even simply designed tables and benches. Not that the hand carving in the wood of the furniture was simple, particularly for those of the royal lineage.

"And there are both ravens and eagles?"

Again, Sabrine made herself answer. Verica deserved to know about her people, even if she would never live among them. "There were hawks once as well; none have been seen since before my grandmother's time though."

"Is she still alive?"

"She is the oldest of the Éan." A spiritual leader, her grandmother had been disappointed when Sabrine chose to follow the path of the warrior. A strict adherent to Chrechte traditions and spiritual truths, Anya-Gra would be furious to know her granddaughter planned to abandon her true mate. Maybe even angrier than Barr. "She and I do not see the world through the same eyes." And that knowledge made something in her chest hurt as it always did when Sabrine thought of it.

"That is difficult." Verica's warm tone was filled with understanding and compassion. Would she feel the same when she knew Sabrine intended to leave the Donegals and their laird?

"Yes."

"Is that why you were looking so unhappy when I came in? You were thinking of your grandmother?"

"No." Now that Barr had sent the elder Chrechte to live with their families, rather than in the keep as they had done with Rowland, it was safer to discuss more things openly.

However, she wasn't taking any chances. Sabrine opened her senses, seeking anyone nearby enough to hear their conversation.

There was no one. Not even the tiny heartbeat of a rodent betrayed that small presence.

They could have had this conversation in mindspeak,

but Sabrine worried her control was slipping. She'd been giving too much away when she and Barr communicated through their mental link. She did not want to risk doing the same with Verica.

"Do you know about the coming of age ceremony for our people?" Sabrine asked.

Verica had told her there were no other Éan left in the clan. She and her brother were the last of the ravens since their mother's death. Presumably, their Faol nature made it possible for them to procreate without the coming of age ceremony and at least pass their wolf nature on to the next generation.

Verica nodded, an odd expression coming over her features almost as if she'd had a disturbing revelation. Certainly she had become far more agitated than the question warranted, unless she had not had the ceremony performed for her coming of age. But no, she must have because she had her special Éan gift, a powerful one of prescience no less.

Verica licked her lips, her hands wringing the pleats from her plaid. "My mother performed it for me and I did it for Circin."

"In the caves of the sacred springs?"

"Aye." Verica's eyes filled with an inexplicable tear and a sickly cast came over her features.

"The Faol have stolen the *Clach Gealach Gra*." Though perhaps the other woman already knew this and that explained her upset. "Without it, our people will die out as those who have not laid their hands on the *Clach Gealach Gra* during their coming of age ceremony will not be able to pass our Éan gifts on to the next generation, including the raven or eagle nature itself."

Legend had it that there had been a sacred stone for each of the bird families, the eagle, the raven and the hawk. But only one remained and with it gone, so was the hope of the Éan race.

"I didn't mean to . . ." Verica's words trailed off, her agitation growing and a profound sense of regret more than matching it. Then she grabbed Sabrine's hand. "Come, please. You must come with me."

Chapter 18

Jerking Sabrine to her feet with desperation-driven strength, Verica dragged her up the stairs and into the room the healer now shared with Earc. She rushed to the chest where she had kept her grandmother's weapons and flung open the lid.

Not usually stupid, or willfully blind, Sabrine felt things begin to fall into place. The Éan power she felt whenever she was in Verica's room, which she had attributed to Verica's powerful Éan gift and the ancient Éan magic clinging to the sword and dagger she'd cared for so carefully.

Before the other woman drew a doeskin bundle from the trunk, Sabrine knew what it held. The key to the Éan's continued existence.

The sense of betrayal she felt was staggering. "You stole our sacred stone?"

Verica was not only Éan herself, she was Sabrine's dearest friend, no matter how short the duration of their acquaintance. This woman had stolen the key to their people's future?

"Not on purpose!" Verica's face twisted with desperate emotion, tears standing out in her usually peace-filled eyes. "I thought I was protecting it."

"Did you know that without it, we could not pass our Éan gifts on to the next generation?" Sabrine asked, giving her friend a chance to claim innocence.

"My mother said something about that, but I don't see how that can be true."

Sabrine was momentarily struck dumb by her friend's words. "You would have destroyed our people *because you do not believe in our ways*?"

"No, it's not like that." Verica began to pace, her distress growing rather than calming with each step. "I didn't know there were any Éan left. Not until you came here."

"But I have been here for more than a sennight." Near half a month. "You never once mentioned your theft."

"I wasn't *stealing* it; I worried the Sinclairs would find the chamber of the Éan and take or destroy the stone. It was before I knew they were not like Rowland, hating all who descended from a bird's nature."

"But you told me nothing."

"Today . . . as soon as I realized what you were looking for, I brought you here for the stone."

It was true, but Sabrine was still caught up in her horror at one of her own kind nearly destroying their people, good intentions or no. She shook her head, her body rigid with mental distress.

Verica held the bundle out to her. Sabrine took it, the power surging around them as she connected to the stone, even through the doeskin, as only one of the royal line could do outside their sacred ceremonies.

"I know I should have said something right away, but I wasn't thinking of it."

"You weren't . . ." Sabrine's voice failed her.

"So much has happened in the time since you came."

It was true but no great comfort. "My youngest brother is due for his coming of age ceremony. It may well have happened."

She had refused to dwell on that possibility, unwilling to consider that she might not be successful in her quest.

Anya-Gra had said she would wait to perform the ceremony until the next full moon, though all knew if she waited any longer, he might as well not have it at all. Sabrine's brother was close to his final change into manhood.

And Chrechte magic did not always wait for the spiritual leader's schedule; sometimes a different moon called to the raven within a Chrechte's soul.

She herself had been called by the crescent moon, receiving a gift of unparalleled power for her generation during her ceremony.

"I'm sorry."

Before she had come to this clan, Sabrine would have waved off both the words and the anguish in her friend's voice. Her first and only priority would have been the *Clach Gealach Gra*.

She could not ignore Verica's clear distress though. The other woman was far too intelligent not to realize the full implications of her actions and be not only horrified by them but struck with a terrible sense of guilt.

Which she did not deserve. "Disaster has been averted. That is what matters."

Whether it had happened in time for her brother she would only discover upon returning to her clan.

The moisture in Verica's eyes spilled over and she did not look even remotely convinced.

Sabrine placed the wrapped bundle on the bed with great care and then turned to face Verica and, drawing on instincts she'd suppressed for years, put her arms out.

The other woman accepted the embrace even as she started to cry in earnest. "I did not mean to hurt anyone."

"I know. And no one has been hurt." She prayed to the giver of life that her words were true.

"Your arm was when you got shot out of the sky."

Sabrine awkwardly patted Verica's back, much more adept at fighting than comforting. "It worked in my favor. Barr brought me among his clan without questioning my motives."

Verica stepped back, wiping at her wet cheeks with the backs of her hands. "You planned to have Barr find you in the forest all along?"

"Yes. I knew it had to be this clan that had taken the stone. It disappeared before the Sinclairs had their first ceremony in the caves."

"I went for it as soon as I heard we had lost the disputed land to their clan." Verica sighed. "I did not tell Circin. He nearly got himself killed challenging the Sinclair for rights to the caves."

"Nay. Talorc would never have killed an untrained boy." Barr stood there, the door open behind him, an unreadable expression on his face. "I willna bother to ask what that is." He indicated the bundle on the bed. "You wouldna tell me; after all, I'm *Faol*." He said the word with all the revulsion Sabrine had ever shown for it.

He turned and walked out without another word.

Her heart aching, Sabrine stared after him. She wanted to chase him down and demand he listen to her explanations, but she did not know what they should or even could be.

"He doesn't know why you're here," Verica said with certainty.

"No."

"Go after him."

And do what? Beg for mercy when she had so clearly deceived and used him? He was a warrior, like her, not a spiritual leader. Forgiveness was not his first reaction to betrayal.

She would not have thought walking away was, either. He had not yelled at her, or accused her of it, or well . . . anything. He'd simply left and that hurt more than she'd thought it possibly could.

If there had ever been a chance he would love her, it had been destroyed. And looking back over her actions of the past sennights, she did not know what she could have done differently.

Her heart cried out for her to change the situation even now, but her warrior's mind, taught that betrayal was met with death, said there was no hope.

She said all that she could think to say. "Maybe this is for the best."

Leaving Barr angry with her should make the prospect less painful.

It didn't, but it would no doubt make it easier for him to let her go.

And as a warrior for her people, her chances of living out her years to old age were slim. He would not be without a mate forever.

Accepting the inevitability of her own death had been taught since the beginning of her training as a protector of her people. An Éan who accepted that dying for her people was a great honor and most likely inevitable did not hesitate to put her life at risk for those who relied on her for their safety.

Thoughts of that future had never hurt as much as they did in this moment.

"Don't be stupid." Verica was unimpressed without doubt. "My mother did not have time to teach me everything about the Éan, but she told me that a Chrechte's true mate is the most important gift our natures will ever impart to us. You cannot simply dismiss your responsibilities to Barr because they do not easily coincide with those you have toward the Éan of the forest."

The healer's intuitive wisdom was staggering, but

Sabrine could not give in to the allure of the words. "Not all Chrechte even find their true mate."

"Those that do should be even more grateful then, shouldn't we?"

"Earc is your life's mate then?"

"Aye, and do not think you are going to change the topic."

"What do you want me to say?" Sabrine sat hard on the bed, causing the *Clach Gealach Gra* to bounce.

"I do not want you to say a thing *to me*. It's Barr you need to talk to."

"Nothing I can say will make our reality any easier to accept."

"What reality? That you love each other?"

"We don't." He didn't love her, at any course, and she should be glad.

Why her heart insisted on bleeding, she did not know.

"What is going on here?" Verica asked, her tone truly perplexed.

"What do you mean? I came to find the *Clach Gealach Gra*. I have found it; now I must let the others know and return it to the Éan chamber in the caves at the sacred springs."

"So, get Barr to return it with you."

"I cannot tell him about our people."

"He is your sacred mate, you *have* to tell him."

"I will not betray my people."

"So, what? You plan to betray your mate? You're leaving and not coming back—that's why you're so upset and Barr is so angry, isn't it? *He knows*."

"He's always known. I have not lied to him." Deceived him, yes, but never actually lied.

"And he's hurt."

"Yes."

"So, don't leave."

"I have no choice."

Once again, Verica looked far from impressed. "Of course you have a choice. If you were dead, then you would not have a choice. As long as you draw breath, you can fight for your future."

"This from a woman who did not even know the proper way to draw a dirk when I met her?" Sabrine had been fighting when Verica was still being coddled as a child in her mother's household.

Verica crossed her arms and glared, not giving an inch. "There is more than one way to fight."

"Is that what your mother told you?"

"Aye."

"And it worked so well for her." It might be a cruel thing to say, but the truth could not be ignored.

"I think so. She had years with her sacred mate. They had children and she loved us both so much. She was happy; though it was wrong that happiness was cut short by Rowland's evil, she still had it."

"That evil still lives in this clan."

"Wirp is dead."

"He was not the only one."

"Why do you say that?"

"Do you think I am wrong?"

Verica's look said it all. No, she did not believe Sabrine was wrong. No doubt she would continue to hide her Éan nature.

"You know I am right." Though it gave her no pleasure to say so. "Yesterday, before Wirp attacked me, someone else shot at Barr and I with arrows."

"It was Wirp."

"No."

"You cannot be certain."

"I am. He could not have gotten past Barr to reach me in the forest."

"He was masking his scent."

"His Chrechte scent, yes, but his body odor? No, the

man was rank with hatred. And he wasn't moving stealthily. He would have left tracks if he had come from the direction of the arrows."

"Maybe Barr missed them."

"You think?"

"But . . ."

"I didn't see him; for him to have gotten to me, he had to be coming from the other direction."

Verica's eyes filled with fear. "Who would try to kill Barr?"

"Those arrows were meant for us both."

"But not necessarily because you are Éan."

"You think someone is so angry with Barr's leadership, they have tried to kill him?"

"I haven't noticed anyone but the elders with that kind of hatred and even most of them have settled into his way of doing things," Verica admitted. "No one grieved Rowland's or Wirp's death with strong emotion."

Sabrine agreed and that led to one conclusion for her. "While no one truly grieved their passing, that does not mean others did not share the two's unreasonable hatred of the Éan."

"You cannot abandon your mate because you're afraid." Verica's shock and disbelief were a palpable presence between them. "You are no coward."

Barr thought she was and mayhap he was right.

"I will not be the reason Barr is assassinated by one of his own clan members."

"Like my mother, you mean?"

"No. Rowland was power hungry. He used your mother's heritage as an excuse for his evil actions." But someone in this clan wanted Barr dead and she did not believe that person was driven by anything more than a deep and abiding hatred of their brethren with a bird heritage.

"You think it would be different with you and Barr?"

"Barr is bringing this clan to a better place; I cannot get in the way of that."

"You are part of *that.*"

For a brief moment, Sabrine admitted to herself that she wanted to be. So, so much. "I have made him hate me."

"You've made him angry. You are an intelligent woman; you can change that."

"I have never found appeasement one of my strengths," it was her turn to admit.

A mischievous smile shone on Verica's lovely face. "Lure him to bed and then tell him the truth."

"The truths are not mine to tell." Always, she ran up against that immovable wall.

"They are if you trust Barr not to betray *your* secrets."

Her heart was desperate to believe that, but her training fought with the desires of her woman's soul. "What if he tries to force a reconciliation between our people and leads our enemies to us?"

"You really think I would do that?"

Sabrine spun, not caring that he had once again come upon her completely undetected. This time, when she saw her mate, she allowed her deepest inner instincts to lead her. She rushed across the room and grabbed both his arms, as if she could hold him there.

"I am not going anywhere." He was not smiling, but something in his beautiful gray eyes said he knew the fear leaping in her chest.

"I don't want to, either, but I have no ch . . ." She stopped, unable to utter the claim again.

Were the words even true? Verica's earlier challenge demanded Sabrine rethink her defeated attitude.

She was no meek maiden to accept a path that would only lead to more pain for both of them. She was a warrior, like generations of the Éan before her. She was a princess, though she had renounced her claim to lead.

But most important, she was Chrechte and that meant she did not dismiss the gifts her nature bestowed, whatever they may be.

Barr's return had loosened her hold on the certainty there was no hope for their future. She did not know why, but his clear willingness to fight for their mating could be met with nothing less than her own warrior's determination.

Could it?

"Wirp was not the bowman," she said, not sure why those were the words that tumbled from her mouth first. Perhaps they were a test. To this point, Barr had repeatedly refused to acknowledge the very real danger some in his clan posed to her.

"Why do you believe this?"

She told him.

He nodded. "I came to the same conclusion."

"You did not say."

"I expected you to realize it as well."

"And maybe you did not want to give me another reason not to feel safe here."

He shrugged. "You do not trust me to protect you."

The concept that she should had never occurred to her. "I am my people's protector."

"As your mate, I am your protector."

"And I am duty bound to protect you."

"He won't thank you for leaving because you believe doing so will stop whoever tried to kill him yesterday," Verica said, showing not the slightest regret at revealing that confidence.

"You think your leaving will keep me safe?" he asked with the pure shock only a truly confident man would feel.

"It is a concern of mine, yes."

"What exactly?"

The door opened without a knock, Earc coming inside,

showing no surprise at finding his laird and Sabrine with his wife. Niall and Guaire followed closely on his heels.

The look Niall gave her left Sabrine in no doubt that Barr had shared her plans to leave with him. Guaire gave her a look that mixed compassion and censure so well, she thought he would have made a very good spiritual leader.

Earc was looking at all of them with an expression of amusement that never seemed far from his features. "Should I be concerned? This is the second time I have found my wife entertaining my friend in a bedchamber."

Verica smacked his arm. Hard. And blushed even harder.

Barr didn't laugh, but some of the tension in his body fell away. The thing he invited his friend to do was anatomically impossible and intensified the heat in Verica's cheeks.

It was Sabrine's turn to smack her mate. She did it right on the center of his chest. "Behave. You'll have your healer's cheeks catch fire and start smoking soon."

"I note you are not pink-cheeked." Niall said it with a question in his voice.

She had heard far worse among her fellow protector brethren, and not always from the males. "I am a warrior."

"Who was as innocent as any pampered daughter on our wedding night." Barr's satisfaction at that fact was far too complacent.

And Sabrine didn't know which part of that comment to take more umbrage at. "We're not married."

"We're mated. You spoke vows that night. So did I."

Niall was back to glaring. While she wasn't looking at him, she could feel the fury directed at her from Barr's brother.

He forgets I do not need a defender, Barr said to her across their mating link.

He hates me.

Since you plan to leave me, that should not matter. Oh, there was no small amount of anger in Barr's growling mental voice as well.

"I will come back." She said it out loud, wanting the others to hear her commitment as well.

She would not betray her Chrechte vows, no matter the personal risk to her for keeping them. Though, she did not know how to reconcile this with her former pledge to her people. She knew only that mating vows superseded all others, no matter what her warrior's training dictated.

It had taken her long enough to come to terms with that fact, but she would not let herself forget it again.

She couldn't; her love demanded she remember.

He stared at her, his eyes searching, and then seemed to realize those words were yet another vow. One she would not break.

"I will go with you." His were just as solemn of a promise.

From the corner of her vision, she saw Niall cross his arms and nod with certain agreement. Earc made an approving noise, but neither Guaire or Verica said anything.

Sabrine had no doubt that if she looked away from Barr long enough to assess their expressions, she would find agreement on them as well.

None of them understood.

"You can't."

"Are you certain of that?" One sardonic brow rose.

It should have irritated her, but all she felt was this awful wash of love go over her. No matter how annoying his obstinate refusal to comprehend their true differences, she found him entirely irresistible.

But she would not let him suffer under the illusion that he could accompany her. "Barr—"

"You are mine."

"Yes."

"I will go with you."

"My people would kill you."

"You'll protect me."

He thought he was teasing her, but he did not know how true those words had to be.

Of all the Éan, she was the only one who *could*. It was still a risk.

"I *am* going." There was no room for argument in his tone.

She could not agree, but she would not deny him either. "I have much to tell you."

"Finally."

"Do not betray my trust."

"You are my mate, a gift *I* will never dismiss."

Oh, he was just piling on the guilt and he looked like he knew it. "I'm sorry."

"For what exactly? Believing I have so little value you could just leave me? Mistrusting me? Refusing to accept my wolf? Threatening to take my child?"

Chapter 19

Barr almost felt badly for the way his mate's face drained of color and the utter shock that shone in her eyes, nearly swallowing the brown with the black of her pupils. But it was past time she came to terms with what being his mate meant. All of it.

Her inability to accept his wolf had caused all of this. While he might understand her difficulty, he was not the Faol that had killed her parents or any other Éan for that matter.

He was her true mate, the one male alive who could match her and protect her, and she should damn well realize that.

"I'm . . . You think I'm . . ."

"With child? Aye. My babe grows inside you." How she would react if that baby was born Faol and not human or Éan, he did not want to consider.

Her own deeply ingrained and formerly justified prejudices would have to be conquered by then. He refused to consider any other alternative.

"But I . . . My menses . . ."

He'd never seen her at a loss for words. It would be adorable, if it wasn't due to her upset over carrying his child.

"I am Faol, not Éan, but we have our gifts as well. Your scent has changed."

"No . . . It's not . . ."

"Aye. I noted it immediately." Niall's claim had her spinning to face Barr's brother.

"How could you tell the change in my scent? You'd never met me before."

"My brother's scent is mixed with yours."

"I thought you meant you could smell his scent on me."

"You carry his babe and by your scent it is wolf."

Barr had suspected, but his own feelings were too involved for him to claim certainty.

"You can't know that." She stumbled back, away from him . . . away from the news his brother had imparted. "The Faol's change does not happen until they are on the cusp of adulthood."

It was all Barr could do to stop himself from grabbing her and pulling her back to him. He had had his fill of his mate moving away from him, threatening to leave him and rejecting the very essence of his nature.

Niall shrugged. "Barr and I have always been able to tell things from scent that others could not."

Sabrine turned back to face Barr, her expression almost accusing. "When did you realize?"

"Three days past."

"And you said nothing."

He clamped his jaw, refusing to speak.

"Perhaps he wanted you to decide to stay without the knowledge you were pregnant with his child," Verica said softly, now wrapped safely in Earc's arms.

Barr scowled at her. She could keep her observations to herself.

But Sabrine's eyes had widened with understanding. "I'm sorry," she said again.

This time, he chose simply to nod an acknowledgment of her apology. It made no difference what prompted her regret.

She had promised to come back and he trusted her word. So, she had made her choice to stay without knowing she carried his child.

"I did not want to leave you."

"You were set to betray my brother and your mating bond. No Chrechte should be so callous to the gifts our natures bestow upon us." Niall's tone left little doubt that he was still angry over the insult Sabrine had dealt Barr.

Meeting his brother's eyes, Sabrine swallowed and nodded. "You are right."

"So, you are finished dismissing our mating as if it is of no account?" Barr pressed.

Sabrine's eyes filled with hurt. "I said I would come back."

So, she did not like having her word doubted. No more did he.

And he was not about to let her leave the clan without him. He would not have done so before she became pregnant, but now there was no chance.

Surely she was wise enough to realize that.

"I have your child in my womb? Truly?" The look of wonder in her gaze went far toward appeasing his anger.

"Aye." He frowned, unwilling to trust her apparent happiness considering her revulsion toward his wolf. "Do not discount my brother's words. It is likely our child will be Faol."

"And it will grow up believing no Chrechte an abomination." The smile that broke over her face was like the sun coming out after a storm.

It lit the room around them and made him ache to make love to her, but the time for revelations had come.

This time hers.

"You said you had much to tell me."

She nodded, her delight dimming. "I do."

"Then we should retire to my bedchamber."

"Verica and Circin deserve to know more about their people."

Shock went through him with lightning-bolt intensity.

But it was Earc who demanded of his mate, "Circin has a dual Chrechte nature as well?"

The look of chagrin that passed over Sabrine's features left no doubt she hadn't meant to reveal another's secrets.

Verica sighed and looked up at her mate. "I should have told you."

"But it is no easy thing to trust another with the secrets you do not consider yours alone, is it?" Sabrine asked. "I am sorry I revealed Circin's."

Verica shook her head. "No. It is all right. I trust those in this room, if for no other reason than my sacred bonded does."

The underlying message of Verica's words was not lost on Sabrine, who cast a sidelong glance at Barr with a disgruntled frown.

He gave her a look that demanded she answer the implications of the healer's statement. He took nothing for granted with his mate.

Sabrine took a deep breath and then turned to look at him and only him again. "I trust you and therefore, I trust those you hold in high esteem."

He could see how hard the words had been to utter and once again, the urge to join with her nearly overwhelmed him. She was finally truly his.

"Good."

She frowned, but her brown eyes twinkled with something other than annoyance. "You are arrogant."

"You have noticed this before."

"Sometimes it is more glaringly obvious than others."

"It's a family trait," Guaire said, with full-out laughter in his voice.

Niall growled, but his mated didn't so much as blink at the implied threat. He just gave Niall a smile that had Barr's fierce brother melting like the mist in the sun. Niall pulled Guaire into his arms and kissed him quite thoroughly before letting the redhead settle with his back to him. After all the years Niall had spent lonely and pining for a mate he thought feared him, Barr would never grow tired of seeing the evidence of his brother's new happiness. The look of contentment on the scarred face squeezed his own heart, though he would never admit it aloud.

You are happy for your brother. Sabrine's voice was soft with indulgence inside his head.

Aye. He has found contentment with Guaire.

I have never seen warriors so at peace. Her voice held puzzlement and a longing he did not understand.

She could be that at peace with him. Did she not realize this?

Verica is so happy, despite the risks of living here amidst potential enemies.

This clan is her family. And I will discover those who would kill for the sake of killing. 'Tis my duty as her laird.

You are so sure of yourself.

As are you.

A sense of surprise pulsed between them.

He almost laughed out loud. *You are every bit as confident a warrior as me.*

"As charming as Verica and Earc's chamber is, perhaps these revelations could be made in a spot more comfortable," Guaire said with a smile for Verica, interrupting Barr and Sabrine's quick mental exchange.

Barr had no doubt his brother's mate had known exactly what he was interrupting. The seneschal of his former laird was a highly intelligent man, if only a marginal warrior. Earc bristled and once again Barr nearly laughed; Guaire's charm had only grown with his confidence after mating with Niall. While Talorc showed no jealousy of the man's deep friendship with his mate and wife, other warriors were not so tolerant.

Turning toward the door, Barr said, "We will meet in the hall."

"What if Padraig or Father Thomas return from their calls on the clanspeople?" Verica asked.

"They are visiting the clansmen that live on the edges of the holding," Barr threw over his shoulder. "They will not return for a sennight at the soonest."

He had been concerned about the priest and Padraig traveling without escort, so he had sent two of the better-trained soldiers with the two men.

"Aodh is marking inventory in the mead and ale stores," Guaire added helpfully. "And his wife is overseeing preparations for the latemeal in the kitchens."

Earc fetched Circin and they all met in the hall around the table they shared during meals. Sabrine began by telling them about the Éan of the forest. Circin's eyes grew round as he realized not only did the others at the table know about his dual nature but that other ravens existed.

He asked question after question, all of which Sabrine answered with patience and a new openness that pleased Barr.

Barr's awe grew as his mate explained about the life of the Éan in the forest. The bird shifters continued to follow the ancient Chrechte ways and yet, somehow humans found their way into the village. As mates, as friends, as advisors.

"You don't allow them to leave if they stumble on your village?" Circin asked in stupefied curiosity.

"Our lands are far from any of the clans. Those who find us are seeking a legend. If they find it, they must forfeit their old lives."

"Or what?" Verica asked.

Sabrine gave Verica a look of stoic pragmatism. "You know Chrechte law for revealing our secrets."

"You kill them?" Verica's eyes widened. "But what if they promise not to tell?"

"We have not had to enforce the law in the last fifty years," Sabrine said.

Barr noted it was not an answer to Verica's question, but a sidestep. His mate was good at that particular tactic and seeing her use it on someone else increased his admiration, rather than his annoyance, as when she used it with him.

Looking unconvinced, Guaire asked, "No human has found the Éan in that time?"

"None have attempted to leave after doing so," Sabrine replied grimly.

Guaire nodded his understanding and Niall nodded his approval. The consequences might be harsh, but Barr too understood and approved the upholding of the ancient law.

There had been a time when the Faol lived separately from the humans as well, before MacAlpin's betrayal, when the law was enforced even more strictly among them. It was still punishable by death to reveal the secrets of the Faol to those who would do them harm.

"Is that part of your responsibilities as a warrior?" Verica pressed Sabrine. "To kill those who break the ancient laws?"

For the first time, Sabrine's emotionless countenance cracked and unhappiness showed through. "Ravens are not predators like the wolves. Killing in anything but defense is almost impossible for our natures to tolerate."

She sounded like she thought that was a failing. Barr reached out to her through their mating bond with his best attempt at soothing. *This is not a weakness in you,* he said, hearing the growl of his wolf in agreement.

He was a warrior, not a nursemaid, after all.

She looked at him, her eyes filled with gratitude. He met

her gaze, his own going heated. Her pupils dilated and the sense of sadness dissipated.

"Then how do you enforce the law?" Circin asked, breaking the connection.

Sabrine jerked and then appeared to give herself a mental shake.

Barr liked having such an effect on her.

She drew in a breath and let it out. He could feel her indecision before speaking. "Death sentences are carried out by the eagles. They have the predator nature of the Faol, but their numbers are small. It is why we have so little success in our war with the wolves."

Barr understood the frustration in his mate's tone. "Because you can never go on the offensive."

Sabrine nodded, the cost that limit to their nature had on her, and the other ravens, in her haunted eyes.

"Are there other Faol, besides those in this clan, that hunt the Éan?" Verica asked, sounding worried.

"Yes."

"Who?" Barr demanded.

"We are not familiar enough with the clans to name them."

"But they did not wear the Donegal colors," Earc guessed.

"No."

"Describe their plaids to me," Barr instructed.

Sabrine rolled her eyes at no doubt what she considered his arrogance again, but did as he asked. The colors she described were unfamiliar to Barr. He thought the priest would know who they belonged to though. He would ask Father Thomas when he and Padraig returned.

"You said your parents were killed by Faol hunting the Éan?" Barr asked.

"Yes."

"Have any Éan been killed in this secret war recently?"

"Three Éan have disappeared in the last year. The year before, an equal number and two additional deaths we know to be the result of wolf attacks."

The numbers were small, but then the remaining Éan were not a large population and the loss of one pack member could devastate, Barr knew full well.

The indiscriminate killing had to stop.

The questions continued and Sabrine continued to answer them with an honesty that he would have enjoyed earlier, but he was glad she had finally decided to trust him and those he held in confidence. When she explained about the Éan's sacred stone, he understood fully her desperation to get it back for her people. The continued existence of her people hung in the balance. As her mate, he was equally determined to see it tip in the Éan's favor.

One day, she would understand and accept that truth.

She still wasn't leaving Donegal land without him by her side, but he agreed that the return of the *Clach Gealach Gra* to the Éan was of the utmost importance and urgency.

He wanted to talk to this Council of Three she'd spoken about as well. It was time for the secret war to end. The Faol still waging it only succeeded with breaking the newest law of the Chrechte, that of only waging war on behalf of their human clan, because they were doing so under the cover of the Éan's secrecy. He intended to explain that to the Council of Three. Besides, no one fought a wolf as well as another wolf. None could sue for peace with as much effect, either.

Of course a wolf suing for peace rarely included diplomatic parlay.

Aodh's wife came with the evening meal and by necessity, their discussion turned to more innocuous subjects.

Sabrine waited until she and Barr were alone in his bedchamber that night to again broach the subject of returning to her people alone. He simply did not understand the risk he took by accompanying her.

"No." Barr stripped his plaid and weapons off, going

through his nightly ritual with the weapons, placing them in easy reach.

"Be reasonable. You cannot leave your clan right now, or your pack. They need your leadership."

"Niall has agreed to stay and assist Earc in leading the clan and continuing to train the soldiers. Guaire will do his best to teach Aodh the ways of a proper seneschal as well." Barr's tone said the plans were set and not going to change.

She did not remember even a hint of such conversation at the latemeal. "When did you discuss this?"

"At the evening meal."

She must not be thinking clearly as suddenly she realized Barr and his brother had done so with mindspeak. Barr had closed himself off from her again and she had assumed it was because he was still angry she had been prepared to leave him.

Perhaps it had simply been the result of him holding another mindspeak conversation. "How far away can you and Niall connect with your minds?"

She was curious about these different gifts of the Faol that she had known nothing about.

He dropped the bar on the door and then climbed into the bed for the first time without making sure she was naked and there before him. "Farther than most and not as far as you and I."

Rather than ask what she really wanted to, which was what he was doing in bed without her, she said, "I did not know the Faol had such differing gifts."

"There is much about the packs you do not know, but then you aren't interested, are you?" He didn't sound particularly upset by that claim, but then he didn't sound particularly anything, his voice as emotionless as the expression on his face.

"What do you mean? Of course I'm curious about you. You're my mate."

Barr merely shrugged and turned over, facing the opposite

wall. "We leave for the sacred springs before light in the morning."

"Why so early?"

"I do not want to be followed."

She would feel more comfortable traveling undetected by his clan as well. "Thank you."

She would still ask Verica if she would allow Sabrine to borrow her grandmother's sword and dagger. Traveling without weapons was an anathema to Sabrine. It had been hard enough leaving her own behind in the forest to come into the clan under the guise of defenseless human. And they were still high in a tree on the way back to the Éan's lands deep in the forest.

Without her ability to fly, they might as well have been in a wolf's stronghold.

Barr did not bother to reply to her gratitude and she made no effort to prolong conversation. Not when it was so clear he was uninterested in talking with her.

She removed her clothing quietly, wondering if she should offer to sleep elsewhere. But that was stupid. He was her mate, and further, he was pack alpha. If he did not want her in his bed, he was more than capable of making his desires known.

Verbally. He was no child to sulk and get his way. No doubt he had his reasons for his silence, but at no time had he ever implied by so much as a look that he did not want her in his bed as his mate.

As mother of his yet-to-be-born child, he was even less likely to reject her place in his life.

Part of her could not help wondering if he wanted her only because she was his sacred mate and pregnant with his child. The love she felt for him was clearly not returned.

But then what did she know of emotion and love? She had lived as a warrior, among warriors, many of whom had taken mates for the sake of continuing the Éan race rather than any strong emotional connection.

How was she to know how a male Chrechte acted when he was in love with his mate? Except, she'd seen Earc with Verica and Niall and Guaire with one another. The affection they held for their mates was more than apparent.

Unsure how to deal with a Barr who did not react with instant arousal when they were alone, and annoyed by her own insecurities, Sabrine determinedly climbed into bed with him.

He made no move to turn and take her in his arms. Nevertheless, she reached out to touch his back, simply laying her hand against his shoulder blade behind his heart.

He surged up and over so quickly she let out a very unwarrior-like yelp of surprise.

He looked down at her, his features golden in the firelight but cast partially in shadow. She could not read his expression, but the feel of his hardness against her thigh told her things were not so different than every other night. With no words, he lowered his head and claimed her mouth in a heated kiss.

Relief flooded her and she responded with all the feminine longing in her heart.

Their lovemaking was powerful and overwhelming, his body possessing hers with an intense hunger she reveled in. It was only as she drifted off to sleep, held tightly in his arms, that she realized he had not done his usual verbal claim staking.

He had not prompted her to acknowledge that she was his even once.

Sabrine stared at the horse Barr had prepared for her to ride. It was a lovely white mare and appeared to have a quiet disposition. Not that it mattered.

"I do not ride."

Barr stopped what he was doing with his horse, a huge brown stallion that frankly scared Sabrine spitless. Not that she would admit to the weakness. He turned to face her, but looking as if he was trying to decide if she was merely being difficult or serious (which she was), he did not speak.

Guaire, who had come with Niall to see them off, was not so reticent. "Why not?"

"I do not have a horse." In fact, there were less than a handful of horses living in her people's lands, and those owned by some of the humans that lived among the Éan.

"Have you ever ridden one?" Niall asked, unable to hide the shock he felt.

Though she could tell he tried.

She felt her cheeks heat, though she didn't think she should be embarrassed—after all, her people had their reasons for not keeping the great beasts—and shook her head firmly.

"You will ride with me then." Barr immediately started moving the things he had tied behind the saddle on the white mare to his giant brute of a horse.

"I . . . uh . . . I'm not sure that's a good idea."

He faced her again, his strong jaw set. "I will not risk you falling off and injuring yourself further because it is the first time you have ridden."

"I could shift and ride the horse in my raven form. She could keep her seat with her claws."

"How is it that you can shift at all?" Guaire asked. "I thought Chrechte females could not shift when they are pregnant."

"Once the third moon of our pregnancy has passed, we lose the ability to shift until the first full moon after giving birth."

"The Faol cannot shift into their wolf form from conception," Niall added for his clearly curious mate.

"You are too vulnerable as a raven with your wounded wing," Barr said, ignoring the discussion of shifting.

"It is almost healed." She would be able to fly again soon.

"Almost will not keep you safe."

She had never had anyone so concerned for her well-being since her parents' deaths. Once she'd renounced her status as future leader of her people in favor of joining the protecting warriors, her entire life had been seen as forfeit to the safety of others.

"Your horse is big."

"Like me."

This was true. But Barr's size did not scare her. "I do not make it a practice to be so far from the ground unless I am flying."

"I will make sure you do not fall."

"I have no intention of falling." Though she was not quite sure how, precisely, she was supposed to avoid doing so.

"Then you have nothing to fear."

"I did not say I was afraid."

He merely looked at her. He was wolf; of course he had scented her concern about riding one of these great beasts. "I have never actually wished to ride."

"We are not walking. The journey would take three times as long."

She had no argument. Time was not on her side. But still she hesitated.

Barr jumped up onto his horse, making the huge animal seem even bigger. Then Niall's hands were on her waist and she was being tossed upward. Barr caught her, swinging her around to land, straddling the horse behind him.

It was a good thing she was not one of the modest clanswomen because her skirts were rucked up to reveal a great deal of her leg. Guaire stepped forward and adjusted them without a word, getting awfully close to the powerful back legs of the beast. She could not help admiring his courage.

She gave him a taut smile as her own was tested. "Thank you."

He nodded.

"Hold on tight," Barr instructed as the horse began to move.

She could only do so with her healthy arm; she hoped that would be enough. He kept the horse to a quiet, steady walk until they were in the forest and then they were galloping and a completely unintentional scream snaked out of her throat. She bit it off almost immediately but was mortified all the same.

Warriors did not cry out in fright. Ever.

Nevertheless, she tightened her hold on her mate until he grunted. Her other hand held his belt in a deathlike grip and she pressed her body against his, following his movement more easily than that of the swift-moving behemoth beneath her.

Chapter 20

$\sim$

They rode hard until long after the sun rose in the sky. Shortly before midday, he stopped near a stream where they dismounted in silence. Her legs were weak as water and she had to hold on to Barr for several moments before she could walk. He did not rush her, but she felt the need to resist clinging.

Things had changed between them and she did not understand this feeling of vulnerability that plagued her. Love was not a comfortable emotion and she did not understand why others thought it so wonderful. Perhaps when you were certain of its return, the overwhelming feelings brought joy rather than distress.

Neither spoke while they ate food Barr pulled from the pack on the horse. She was busy trying to determine if they had been followed, unwilling to be surprised by the arrival of an enemy like she had been with Wirp in the forest.

She did not know why Barr kept his own counsel. It

could have been for the same reason, or it could have been that he had nothing to say to her.

She realized she did not want to know if the latter was the case and, even when she was fairly certain no danger lurked around them, did not initiate conversation.

The burbling water over stone was the only sound to break the silence around them. Even the animals were quiet, but that was often the case when predators were present. And as controlled as he was, Barr was one hundred percent predator.

Suddenly Barr stood, his gaze intent as he carefully surveyed the surrounding area. "You have weapons?"

"Yes." Verica had not hesitated when Sabrine had gone knocking on her door in the wee hours to ask to borrow the sword and dagger before leaving the keep that morning.

"Good."

Without another word or any warning, Barr shifted to his wolf. Sabrine reached out, wanting to touch this Faol that was also her mate, her sense of revulsion completely absent and now replaced by affectionate awe. Barr seemed oblivious to her desire, though. The magnificent creature leapt the stream, running into the forest. All that remained where he had been were his plaid and weapons.

Battling disappointment she doubted he would understand or even believe she could feel, Sabrine jumped to her feet, her senses alert to any sign of danger.

Something had triggered her mate's instincts, but she could not tell what. She did not think it would be a nearby danger, or he would not have left her alone. Despite his clear respect for her fighting skills, the man was too protective to leave her unguarded against imminent threat.

She gathered his things and took them to the horse, which had stopped munching on grass by the stream and now stood without noise but its own quiet breathing.

She patted the horse. "Can you please sit down?"

She didn't know how to get the large animal to lower

itself, but she did not want to sit on the ground under its belly. That just seemed unsafe. Still, she had to be near for her gift to protect them both and knew that she would not be able to remain standing if Barr was gone very long.

She wished she had the gift of communing with animals, but she didn't, and hers would be useless if she could not get this great beast to cooperate.

Proving his master had chosen well, and that he was more intelligent than he looked, the horse lowered his body to the ground. His legs folded under him, he looked quite settled. And calm.

She hoped that looks were not deceptive in this instance.

Gingerly, not wanting to startle the big animal, she moved to sit beside him. When he did not show any antipathy to that, she carefully settled against him, letting her body rest against his much bigger one.

Closing her eyes, she concentrated on sending for the image of empty forest as if she and the horse were not there. Once she felt the image settle around her and the large beast completely, she opened her eyes and searched the area for evidence of a threat.

The quiet of the forest took on more sinister connotations as not even a birdsong could be heard. Nothing moved among the trees. No rustle of sound to indicate even a rabbit lurked in the under foliage. Yet, her senses picked up no scents that might indicate danger.

She did not let the lack of overt signs deter her from maintaining the shield to her presence and that of the great beast Barr held in such esteem though. Each minute she had to project the image around them drained her strength further, but she could do naught else until her mate's return.

If she had only herself to protect, she would have taken the *Clach Gealach Gra* and climbed a tree. Blending into branches would have been much easier than building the image of an empty spot by the stream around her and the horse.

But she could not risk the big beast. He belonged to her mate and therefore had great value to her. Thankfully, the horse did its part, maintaining a silence she would not have thought the animal capable of doing.

She lost track of the time Barr had been gone as she grew weaker and increasingly weary. She slipped into an almost trance as her raven maintained the shielding image.

Only the sound of her mate shouting in her head brought her out of it, taking her from that nether place where her gift manifested itself. The image dropped as she released the shield, knowing Barr was near enough to protect her; the stoic horse, whom she now considered bloody brilliant; and the sacred stone.

Suddenly he was there, right in front of her, pulling her into his strong arms. "Where were you? What was that? What is the matter?" he demanded, each question coming out in quick succession, so unlike her unflappable mate.

She tried to speak, but no words came forth. She cleared her throat and licked her lips and then croaked, "Needed to protect the stone and the horse."

Barr groaned.

"He's a smart horse, I think." Her throat convulsed and she had to stop speaking while she tried to swallow moisture that was not there. "Thirsty."

Barr released her, but before she had a chance to complain even inside her head, he was back with the water skin. She drank, the liquid reviving her a little.

She took some gasping breaths before drinking more, then resting against his hard chest. "Like this," she said softly.

A strange choking noise came from his throat. "You were not here when I returned. I thought you had ridden the horse somewhere safer, but there were no tracks."

"I cannot ride a horse."

"You will learn."

She just thought she might. "*You* will teach me."

"Aye. No other."

"I like your horse. He stayed silent."

"I'm sure he likes you, too." The indulgence in her mate's tone was a great improvement over the coldness of the day before.

He didn't like secrets. That had become very clear to her.

"I can put up a shield that none can see through and even mask the scents behind it, but I cannot hide sound."

"What kind of magic is this?" he asked with no little awe.

It brought a weak smile to her face. "It is the gift bestowed on me by the *Clach Gealach Gra* on my coming of age."

"'Tis amazing."

"But tiring when used on such a grand scale. Your horse is not small." And she had needed to hold the shielding image all around them—she looked at the sky—for nearly an hour this time.

"You could have taken the stone and hidden in a tree."

"But whatever predator caused you to go seeking in your wolf's form might well have come after the horse."

"I do not know what I sought, but I found nothing. No signs or scents to track."

"Why did you leave?"

"My wolf warned of danger."

"A Faol's instincts are true."

"Aye."

"We should move on."

"Aye."

This time she rode settled on his lap and napped against him, trusting her safety completely to his strength. It was an entirely new experience for her, as she recovered from her efforts to protect herself and his horse beside the stream.

She was not surprised when they did not stop to eat and rest again as the hours wore on. Barr continued to push through, encouraging her to eat the apple he pulled from the horse's pack. Taking one for himself as well.

No doubt they would travel as far as possible this day.

However, eventually, they stopped near a small, clear loch fed by a stream from the north.

"We will make camp here," he told her as she stretched, trying to get her walking legs again after the longer ride.

The summer days were at their longest and she protested. "But it will not be dark for hours yet."

"It is a more defensible position." He indicated a small cave entrance not far away.

"You believe we are being followed?"

"My wolf says yes."

She nodded, not doubting his Faol nature. There was a reason they made such formidable enemies.

"So, why the sacred springs?" he asked as they shared another cold repast, each sitting against the base of a tree and facing the other.

She would rather be sitting against him, but he was once again unapproachable. "What do you mean?"

"Why not take the stone directly to your people? Traveling to the sacred springs for your Chrechte rituals must carry great risk of discovery."

"We travel in our bird forms. Despite Muin's zealous adherence to his grandfather's teaching, few simply shoot birds from the sky as a matter of course. Especially those among the clans to the farthest north."

"Still, it is a risk."

"Yes. There is ancient Chrechte power in the caves, though such a place is worth some days' travel."

"You do not have caves like them in your part of the forest?" he asked.

"None that resonate with millennia of Chrechte rituals and matings." Her grandmother claimed no other place would so benefit their people when the sacred rites were performed.

"The old Chrechte ways are very important to the Éan, aren't they?"

"Yes." As their numbers diminished under the attack of

their Chrechte brethren, their ancient ways were what kept them going.

Barr ate for some moments in silence and then asked, "What happens once you return the stone?"

"I return to my people and tell them I was successful on my quest."

"We go to the Éan together."

"Yes." Part of her actually looked forward to him meeting her grandmother, though she was worried how the others would respond to him because of his wolf nature.

"Anya-Gra prophesied as a young girl that the wolves would join the fight to save the Éan." Her grandmother had told Sabrine about the prophesy when she came of age. "I did not believe her."

"I have no difficulty believing *that*." His sarcasm was not lost on her.

She frowned. "You blame me for my cynicism? How could I see the wolves as our salvation when they were the greatest enemies we faced?"

She was not the only Éan skeptical of such an event, either, though she did not mention that truth to her mate. No doubt he had it figured out already.

"Your greatest enemy is unreasoning hatred, not the wolves themselves."

"Perhaps it is easier to make such a distinction when you are not the one considered an abomination," she replied with some acerbity.

Though, as she said the words, she wondered if he had meant the Éan's hatred as well as that of the wolves still trying to kill them.

Barr sighed. "Aye, no doubt." He stood.

"Where are you going?" Was he about to disappear again?

"I'm going to put our things in the cave."

She got up to follow him. "I did not mean to offend."

"I am not offended." He took the pack from the horse's back and slapped its flank.

His brown coat gleaming in the late evening sun, the horse ambled toward the water for a drink.

"Are you not?"

He stopped and turned to face her, his expression far from one of offense. What shadowed his gray gaze was much worse. It was pain.

She put her hand out, needing to touch him. "I . . ."

He stepped back from her. "I am wolf."

"I know." Hurt confusion claimed her as this was one thing over which there had never been any doubt.

"You despise my wolf."

"I don't."

"Dinna lie to me."

"I'm not." Determinedly, she stepped forward, putting her hand against his heart. "Your wolf is as much a part of what makes you so fierce and wonderful as any other aspect of your nature."

And she had learned to love the beast as she did the man who had introduced her to softer emotions more powerful than duty or even honor.

He did not respond, simply looking down at her with unreadable eyes.

"Shift." She would prove herself to her mate. "Bring forth your wolf."

"The last time you saw him, you could barely stay in the same room."

"I was wrong. You have shown me that not all wolves are my enemy. Surely you realize this." Their gazes locked, and she saw doubt in his. She pleaded, "Please. Let me show you."

The air shimmered around them and then he fell away to be replaced by the wolf. A huge, magnificent and powerful wolf, just like the man. With jaws big enough to snap her limbs, he inspired awe rather than fear in her.

She put her hand out, touching his head. "You are beautiful."

I am wolf, he said in her head.

She almost laughed, but the moment was too profound. "I am aware. You are my mate."

I am. There was something in his voice, something besides his natural arrogance and warrior's indifference.

That something had her dropping to her knees and putting her arms around his neck. "You are."

She buried her face in the soft blond fur of his ruff. A spark of atavistic fear touched her heart, but she banished it. This wolf was hers, her mate, her protector, definitely not her enemy.

She showed him a raven's affection, rubbing her head against his. A deep rumbling noise sounded from his chest. It was not a growl; his scent indicated it was a noise of pleasure, so she did it again. This time he pressed back, rubbing his head against her and then his big wolf's body pressed forward, seeking further attention.

Mark you with my scent. The voice in her head was more growl than man's voice.

"How?" she asked out loud, loving the soft and rich thickness of his wolf's pelt against her face.

An image formed in her head of his wolf, rubbing its fur smelling so clearly of him against her clothes, against her body, sharing that scent so that it was well and truly mixed with hers.

It was all about possession and mating. And yet there were no sexual overtones to the need.

"This is a Faol ritual, isn't it?" she asked.

The positive response in her head was all growl and no actual words.

She laughed softly. "Do what you need to."

He tugged at her plaid and she removed it. He seemed content for her to leave her shift on as he rubbed his head and body against her sides and legs, leaving behind the distinct scent that he usually masked.

He nuzzled the small of her back with his snout and she

laughed, ticklish though she had not known it. He yipped and she laughed again, their solemn ritual degenerating into a game of wrestling that had her laughing as she had not done in years.

He had her pinned to the ground, his wolf's tongue lolling from his grinning mouth above her. The fresh scents of the forest mixed with his unique fragrance and she breathed in deeply, discovering how much she really liked it.

She could not speak the words of love burning in her chest, but she could tell him that there was no part of him she could or would ever despise again.

"Barr, acting laird of the Donegal clan, pack alpha and my mate, I accept you, and every part of who you are, irrevocably as not only my mate but the other half of my soul." The love was there, if he wanted to see it, but she would not press it on him when his feelings were not in the same place.

The air shimmered and a man now pinned her, a large man who blocked out the waning light and overwhelmed her every sense with his presence. Furthermore, a man whose arousal grew against her hip with insistent rapidity.

"Thank you." And then his mouth claimed hers gently and with a wealth of tenderness that brought moisture to her eyes.

She closed them, unwilling to allow him to see her weakness, and returned the kiss with every bit of emotion clamoring for release from her heart. She could feel his wolf's presence in a way she had not before.

Had he been holding back? Had she blinded herself? She would not let it matter; what did was that, finally, their mating was truly that of the Chrechte and not merely two human bodies coming together.

Their lovemaking was slow and tender, ending in a mutually shared pinnacle that made her world fade to nothing but his body above hers. She could see naught but him; she could feel nothing but the way their bodies still joined;

she could hear nothing but the sound of his heart and his breathing.

Until the sound of an eagle's call shattered the joy-filled silence between them.

She turned her head in time to see the bird swoop from the sky, talons extended. It was clearly going for the pack Barr had removed from the horse and dropped when she had sought to make peace with him.

Barr rolled aside, shifting as he did, his wolf's body leaping for the bird, while she dove for the pack—for the *Clach Gealach Gra*, which she must protect at any cost.

She threw herself on top, curling herself around it as the eagle changed course, flying out of Barr's reach. Her mate shifted back to human form and grabbed for his dagger.

He pivoted and went to throw it.

Do not kill him, she screamed into her mate's head.

He didn't bother to reply, sending the dagger into the air. It snagged the eagle's wing and the bird tried to right itself, but could not. It spun and lost the air from under its wings, tumbling toward the earth with nothing to break its fall.

Except Barr was there, waiting, his arms extended. The eagle landed against him with a thud, its talons digging into his chest, even as it fought for its freedom.

She was on her feet and running, throwing her arms around the flapping wings, pinning them to the bird's body as Barr grabbed its talons with hands careful not to wound. Once again, she was struck anew by the honor and deep commitment to life of her mate.

In an instant, the eagle was a man. His elbow came back, striking her in the chest and knocking the air out of her.

In the past, she would not have let go. But in the past, she had not had Barr. Nor had she carried his babe. She did now, though, and she had no choice but to release the fighting man before he could do damage to her and the child she carried.

Jumping back, she scurried out of the way so Barr could subdue the eagle shifter without worrying about her. Despite the blood from the wounds in his chest making him and his opponent slick, he did it quickly.

When Barr had the eagle shifter immobilized, so she could see the man's face, Sabrine could barely breathe for her shock.

He was clearly Éan, but she had never seen him before. "Who are you?"

Barr smacked the man's head and said, "I'll introduce you."

"You?" she asked in shock.

"Aye, this is the *human*, Lais." He stressed the word *human* and drew it out with clear mocking intent. "Cousin to our Brigit; I've been training him to fight. He still has a lot to learn."

Lais glared at Barr.

"Though his strength with a bow has been lauded to me by his relatives." The significance of this statement was not lost on Sabrine.

"It was you. But why?" Why would a bird shifter try to kill Barr, a wolf who so clearly stood for what was good and honorable among the Faol? And her, one of his own people?

The very idea went through her heart like a poison-tipped spear. Knees going weak, she stumbled back a little, almost tripping on the bag with the *Clach Gealach Gra*.

He would have taken it and done what? Kept it for himself? To what purpose?

Her throat so tight she could not speak, she simply stared at the young man who would destroy his own people.

"Sweeting . . ." Barr spoke softly as if to an easily startled animal.

She let her gaze shift to him. The warmth and compassion she saw in his eyes were very near her undoing.

She had spent her entire life knowing she and all her brethren were hated by the Faol, but to be so despised by one of their own? That was a gaping, bleeding wound in her soul.

"My precious warrior princess—"

"I'm not."

"What?" he asked, oh so gently.

"A princess. I renounced my claim to the throne."

Barr's eyes widened.

"You're nothing but a murdering raven." Bone-deep loathing infused every word out of Lais's mouth.

She would not look at him. This kind of hatred was too hard to take. "Ravens cannot murder, unless their nature has become so twisted, their bird no longer has the power to influence emotions and thought."

"Liar."

The sound of a blow being struck sounded. Lais oophed and fell to the ground with a thump.

Barr's hand landed on her shoulder. "Sabrine, my own, please put your shift on."

The mundane request almost made her laugh, but she was afraid if she started, she would not stop until it ended in hysterical tears.

"Your possessiveness is showing. We are Chrechte."

"I *am* possessive." He did not sound sorry at all.

And she did not mind. She would much rather think about her mate's unreasonable dislike of nakedness. He'd been quick to cover her in front of Muin that first day in the forest, too.

She looked around and found her shift, pulling it on quickly. Though it made no sense to her, she felt better with this small barrier between her and the eagle shifter.

She was Chrechte, but maybe more human than she had ever realized.

She looked at Barr. "Better?"

"Aye." He smiled, though his eyes still reflected that tender concern.

She made herself turn and face Lais. "Ravens do not murder. I have never killed except in protection of my people."

"Ravens killed my father, the last eagle shifter."

Chapter 21

Something snapped inside Sabrine and she stormed over to the puling hatchling. She was so tired of the deceptions, so sickened by Rowland's legacy in a clan made up of truly, mostly good people and the Chrechte intent on protecting them. "*You idiot.* First, your father was not the last eagle shifter, though if you'd succeeded in stealing the *Clach Gealach Gra*, a generation from now would see the end of the entire Éan race."

"Good. The ravens deserve to die. They've been tormenting the other Chrechte for hundreds of years."

"Where did you hear such stupidity?" As if she didn't know. "And I didn't just say ravens. You would have succeeded in ending the eagle shifters, of whom there are not many, but who do still exist in freedom in the forest. You who should fight for your people's existence would have done what the hateful among the Faol had failed to do, though they have tried for more than two centuries."

"The Faol tried to protect my father." But the youth's voice faltered with lack of conviction.

Barr demanded, "What wolf tried to protect him and failed?"

"Rowland." Lais's shoulders drooped, his gaze dropping as if he knew already how unutterably foolish he had been to trust the former laird.

Barr snorted derisively. "The same man who raped your aunt was your father's would-be savior? The same man who nearly destroyed the clan with his selfishness? You hid your nature from him, didn't you?"

The boy nodded, his sadness and confusion even more evident.

"You sensed it was not safe to tell him of your nature."

"It made no difference. I cannot pass it on."

"You missed your coming of age ceremony?" Sabrine asked in pained tones.

Lais nodded. "My father told me about it, about how wonderful it would be, what gifts it might bestow, the ones I would lose if I did not follow the old Chrechte ways; he died before my time came."

A great deal of Sabrine's anger drained away. "So, you thought to make other shifters pay for your loss?"

"No. I . . . the ravens . . ."

"Would have helped your father, had we known about him. We would have made certain you had your coming of age ceremony and received all your gifts from the *Clach Gealach Gra.*"

"You aren't stupid in training; how is it you still believe Rowland told you the truth of your father's death?"

"Why would he lie?"

Sabrine answered when Barr seemed stuck for words. "Because in his own twisted way, he had a sense of justice. If you were not a shifter, a true Éan, he did not want to kill you."

"But he . . ."

"Betrayed you and your family in every way possible." Barr had plenty of words to say now.

The boy's head bowed and though his tears were silent, she could smell them. And she could not stand his pain, but before she could comfort him, Barr was there on one knee.

He laid a hand on the young Chrechte's shoulder. "You were deceived, like many before you."

"But my da. He was all I had . . ." The words trailed off in a pain-filled whisper.

Barr did not say anything, but he remained as he was, allowing the other man to grieve.

Sabrine finished dressing and then took the pack with the sacred stone into the cave. Emotionally drained and more exhausted than she could ever remember being, she laid out the bedroll.

Lais could sleep in Barr's plaid.

But first she would have to see to both his and Barr's wounds.

Neither man argued when she insisted on washing the blood away with sand and water from the small loch. Perhaps they noted her tiredness, or mayhap it was the snappish tone she used to order them both to the water. A more feminine woman, one like Verica, would no doubt take a softer tone and gentle approach.

You are as feminine as any woman and perfect as you are, Barr said in her mind as she carefully washed the blood and dirt from the wounds on his chest.

He and Lais would have to soak in the sacred springs when they reached them the next night, but for now this would have to do.

Thank you, she replied in mindspeak, too tired to talk even.

Barr was silent and Lais was subdued as she finished her ministrations.

Finally, she forced words from her mouth. "I am no healer like Verica, but this should help." She examined the eagle shifter's arm, now that it was clean of blood and dirt.

"You are lucky. Barr's dagger caused a flesh wound, but you could fly if you had to."

"I . . . I am sorry. It is not enough and I deserve my fate, but I am glad I did not kill you with my arrows." Lais bravely met her gaze.

She sighed. "Me, too."

"While I am not impressed by your accuracy, I am pleased in this instance that you missed entirely. If you had harmed my mate, I would have no choice but to kill you." Barr did not sound tired in the least.

"You mean you are not going to . . . to . . ." Lais looked lost for words, though she could guess what he meant.

So did Barr. "And waste my mate's efforts at tending your wounds? I wouldna dare."

Sabrine smiled for the first time in what felt like days.

Barr winked at her and she shook her head. Arrogant, *charming* man.

"You said there are more eagle shifters?" Lais asked tentatively.

"There are. If Barr approves it, I can ask them to take you to train."

"But I'm not a full Éan. I can never be one."

"Because you have no secondary gift? Nonsense. I am sorry the only children you can ever beget will be entirely human, but I assure you humans have been very happy with such for as long as our races have walked the earth."

"I am a poor warrior."

"You can be taught," Barr said grudgingly, clearly not ready to completely dismiss Lais's actions, no matter the confused beliefs that prompted them.

"Would you allow me to go to the Éan?" Lais asked his laird, cautious hope lacing his quiet voice.

"If I am convinced it is in your best interests, aye."

That seemed to stun Lais. "You would care?"

"Naturally. You are a member of my clan."

"But I tried to kill you."

"Did you? I have seen you hunt; I have heard the stories from your proud family. You are better than my other Chrechte warriors. And your accuracy with the bow is even better than Connor's. It makes me wonder why Rowland did not enlist your aid in his challenge with Earc."

"He tried."

"You refused."

Lais drew himself up. "I am no murderer." A stricken look came over his face. "I tried to be."

"Nay. If you had tried, you would have done at least some damage. The truth is, you are no murderer, but Rowland was."

"Do you really think he was the one who killed my father?"

"He or one who had his approval to do the deed."

Lais swallowed and nodded. "I hated the ravens because it was easier than hating him."

"Safer, too."

"I'm ashamed to say it, but yes."

Barr would undo Rowland's legacy of hatred and deceit strand by strand and Sabrine could not help loving him even more for it. *You are the most amazing man and Chrechte I have ever had the honor to know,* she sent to him via their sacred bond.

Barr's sudden, dazzling smile must have confused Lais because he started babbling apologies again, for trying to hurt them.

"If you had been really trying, you would have hit one of us the day you shot your bow."

Lais shook his head. "I *tried*."

"Nay. If you'd had a killing shot in mind, even my wolf's instincts could not have saved us from at least a grazing of one of those arrows."

A look of dawning understanding and wonder came over Lais's features, but then he sighed and went all stoic. "I do not deserve your mercy."

Men. A woman knew when to take a gift when it was offered, especially when that gift meant keeping her life.

"I do not agree." Barr's tone said that his opinion was the one that counted.

Sabrine did not fool herself into believing it was because he was acting laird, either. The man was simply too certain of his own opinions.

And right now? She really did not think he had cause to doubt himself.

The next day, Lais shifted to his eagle and rode on Barr's shoulder. A smaller man could not have managed, but Barr was no average warrior and had no problem riding every bit as swiftly with the large bird of prey perched on one shoulder and his mate in his lap. He had insisted on holding her, as if he could physically protect her from harm with his body.

And no doubt, he could.

The giant beast of a horse seemed not to notice the additional burden, either, and they reached the caves at the sacred springs an hour after night had fallen.

Barr was relieved when his mate showed no hesitation in leading him and Lais to the secret chamber of the Éan deep in the labyrinth of caves beyond the sacred springs.

The sound of chanting reached his wolf's hearing before his mate's steps faltered in realization they were not alone. But she did not stop.

She quickened her steps, clearly intent on reaching the cave before the ritual was complete. She was running by the time they reached the giant cavern lit by several torches with a stone dais in the center and two pools fed by the underground springs on either side of it.

An old woman, who bore a striking resemblance to Sabrine, wore a cloak of raven feathers and spoke ancient Chrechte over a boy on the cusp of maturity. It must be Anya-Gra, Sabrine's grandmother and the one who had prophesied the help of the Faol in the Éan's fight for survival.

Two large men came forward, barring their way with weapons drawn. Sabrine ignored them, rushing between them, narrowly missing their reaching hands with a smooth twist of her body. To join her, Barr could see he would have to draw his own sword and he was not ready to do that.

He crossed his arms and gave each warrior a look that told them he neither feared nor intended to cause trouble.

Dismissing them, he watched as Sabrine ran to the still-chanting priestess and practically threw the *Clach Gealach Gra* into her hands. A strange blue light pulsed around them as both hands rested on the stone.

Then Sabrine stepped back and bowed her head.

"Sabrine-Gra Gealach, raven princess, return your hands to the *Clach Gealach Gra*."

His mate's confusion reached him across their link.

Have courage, sweeting. Do as your priestess requires.

She is my grandmother.

Even more reason to obey. His wolf was laughing and so was he, though he was careful to keep it to their mindlink.

You are arrogant.

And you are indeed a princess; now act like it.

This time she did not deny it. She returned her hands to the now-white-glowing crystal. Blue light once again began to emanate from the sacred stone.

"Taran-Gra Gealach, lay your hands on the crystal."

The youth—this had to be Sabrine's brother, whom she had sacrificed so much for—did as he was told, showing only slight hesitation as his fingertips brushed his sister's.

The light flared purple and a strange hum filled the

cavern, the air pulsing with Chrechte power as Barr had never known it.

The boy shimmered, red flaring around him and then he was no longer a boy, but a raven. He let out a harsh caw, his head tilted back, his wings expanded and then the light shone around him again and the raven disappeared to be replaced by one of the ancient ones. Gasps sounded around the cavern, but Barr was too taken aback to make even that noise.

A dragon, its scales so dark a scarlet they were almost black, drew its head back and trumpeted in victory before breathing a stream of fire toward the ceiling.

Everyone in the cavern fell back in mingled awe and fear, their scents giving away their feelings even if their actions had not. Except Sabrine. His warrior princess reached out to actually *touch* the magical creature.

The dragon dropped his head and butted Sabrine with his snout. She laughed out loud. "My brother, you will be the king that saves our people."

"With his allies, the Faol who have learned to respect all life and live among the humans as their protectors." The old woman's voice resonated in the cavern, going through Barr like a second, more powerful heartbeat inside his body. "Taran-Gra Gealach will lead the Éan to a new day for our people."

As quickly as he had taken on the form of a raven and then a dragon the youth was once again in the form of a human. He dropped to his knees and bowed, giving thanks in ancient Chrechte to the Creator of all things. Then he stepped into the pool on the right of the dais, submerging entirely and then standing with a triumphant shout.

His coming of age rite of passage was complete.

"There is a broken one among us," the priestess intoned in that power-pulsing voice. "An eagle whose soul carries the guilt and pain of false beliefs that have torn at his heart."

Lais looked in panic at Barr.

"Do not fear. This is a good place and she cares for all

Éan." He knew he spoke the truth, though he'd never met Anya-Gra or even known of her existence before this trip.

Lais nodded and turned, stepping forward as if mesmerized.

The guards had fallen back like all the others when Taran had taken his dragon form. But they stepped forward now, as if to prevent Lais from approaching the priestess. And then, they moved aside as if under direct command, though Barr had heard no word spoken.

"Place your hands on the *Clach Gealach Gra*, young Lais."

"How do you know me?" he asked with awestruck tones.

The old woman smiled, compassion showing in eyes the same color as her granddaughter's and filled with an ancient wisdom Barr could not but admire. "The Creator knows all and I do his bidding."

Without speaking again to Lais, she instructed both her grandchildren to lay hands on the crystal as well. "Ravens will heal the heart that has spent too long reviling them."

Lais let out a sob but did as he had been told.

At first the color around them was almost black, but as time wore on it got lighter and lighter until all that remained was a pale yellow. The color of the sun.

"My hands are hot," Lais said in trepidation mixed with hope.

"Mate of my granddaughter, come here," Anya-Gra demanded imperiously.

Barr did not even consider disobeying. He stopped less than a foot from the tableau around the stone.

"Eagle, put your hands on the wounds you inflicted."

Lais turned and did exactly that, laying his palms over the worst of the gashes his claws had rent in Barr's chest the day before. Tingling heat raced along each of the wounds until all that remained was the heat from Lais's hands.

Barr looked down and felt no surprise that his chest showed not so much as a healing scar. Since meeting

Sabrine, he had come to accept that legend held truth and the power of the Chrechte was in more than their enhanced strength and senses gifted from their animal natures.

Lais was not so quick to accept. "I . . . but I thought . . ."

"The power in the cavern is stronger than it has been in all my years as spiritual leader of the Éan. In this circumstance, miracles happen." Anya-Gra waved her hand and water from the pool to the right of the dais surged up, drenching them both.

Lais stepped back, looking up at Barr with hope. "I feel cleansed of my guilt."

"Accept the gift."

Lais nodded and turned to face the priestess. "Thank you, mother of our people."

Anya-Gra smiled. "Though you are eagle, with instincts of war, you are healer and must trust and use your gift."

"I will."

Allowing his wolf to shine in his eyes, Barr looked at his mate and reached his hand out for her. She took it with no hesitation. Miracles happened.

"I love you," she said in the ancient language of their people.

He pulled her into the circle of his arms, letting the others fall away as if they were not there. "I love you with all that I am."

"Faol and man."

"Wolf and man."

She smiled, her beauty glowing so brightly that their souls mingled. "I love all that you are." She said it loud enough for every Chrechte in the cavern to hear.

The sounds of shock nearly matched those that he'd heard when Taran had taken on the form of a dragon.

But Barr could not make himself care. He would deal with her people's doubts and prejudices later. For now, it was enough she had released hers and embraced their mating with both her heart and her mind.

Their lips met and the air crackled like it did after a lightning storm. He did not know how long they kissed to seal their vows of love, but when their lips parted the others were in a circle around them, quietly speaking the ancient chants of a Chrechte mating.

That was no doubt Anya-Gra's doing. He would thank her later.

He had never known such a sense of peace as he spoke his vows in entirety and received hers in return. The priestess spoke the final blessing on their true mating, a sound like the clap of thunder shaking the very ground they stood on.

She ushered the others out of the cavern, leaving him to mate with Sabrine in the original way of their people. When they reached orgasm together, the blue light shone around them again and Barr felt it go through him like a warm wind.

"I will love you until the day I die," he spoke his personal promise against her lips.

Her eyes shone with fierce joy. "I feared you could not return my love."

"I feared you would never accept my wolf."

"I love him; I love you."

"I am your ideal mate, even if I am Faol."

Sabrine stared up at her husband. They would still need to be married in the way of men, but their vows had been spoken and would never be broken.

Of equal interest to her was her husband's claim. "You *can* read my mind."

His smile revealed nothing but the deep and abiding love in his heart for his warrior wife. "Can I?"

"Do not tease."

"You sometimes send thoughts I know you do not mean to."

"That is not possible."

"You trust me enough not to hold your control so tight, and you always have. It gave me hope when you flinched from my wolf in revulsion."

"But . . ."

"You are mine."

She had no desire to deny it. "Oh, yes, just as you are mine."

"Aye, your husband who can hear your thoughts." From his teasing tone, she could not tell if he meant the words or not.

"That is not possible."

"This from a woman whose brother shifted into a dragon?"

She had not been sure at first he had actually shifted into their ancient ancestor. "I can project the dragon, but not shift into it."

"You are my fierce warrior princess. You need no dragon form to be strong."

She loved the pride she heard in Barr's voice. Her strength pleased him when she knew many men, Faol and human alike, raised in the clans would not feel so happy about it. "My brother will be king."

"Because you stepped aside."

"I did not want to be queen. I thought I could do more to protect my people as a warrior."

"You have. You would never have left your lands as a queen and we would not have met."

"And my mate will bring the wolves prophesied to help us fight those who would destroy us." Perhaps her husband's arrogance was justified. She almost smiled.

"Finally, you comprehend."

"It was hard to trust."

"In your head, but your heart believed me from the first."

"I think you are right."

"I know I am."

"Arrogant."

His laughter echoed in the cavern and in her heart, which had spent too long devoid of joy. She had not only found her sacred mate, she had found a new path to life not bound by duty and death.

A miracle indeed.